Kate Storey started her career teaching English and Drama, and when she had her family, combined all three to write novels about family drama. Originally from Yorkshire, she now lives in a London suburb with her husband and two teenage daughters, so expects there's plenty more drama to come.

Also by Kate Storey

The Memory Library
The Forgotten Book Club

Praise for Kate Storey

'A moving, warm and comforting read.'
Jennie Godfrey, *Sunday Times* bestselling author of *The List of Suspicious Things*

'Beautiful and emotional.'
Sue Moorcroft, *Sunday Times* bestselling author of *One Summer in Italy*

'Kate Storey has done it again – vivid, lively characters and a heartwarming plot that never crosses the line into saccharine.'
Laura Pearson, author of *The Last List of Mabel Beaumont*

'A lovely story that celebrates books, family and kindness. Touching and beautiful.'
Hazel Prior, author of Richard & Judy Book Club pick *Away with the Penguins*

'Tender and moving, *The Forgotten Book Club* is one to treasure. A beautiful story of love, loneliness and the endless power of friendship. Community gold at its best.'
Phaedra Patrick, author of *The Library of Lost and Found*

'A wonderful cast of characters who found their way into my heart straight away.'
Celia Anderson, author of *USA Today* bestseller *59 Memory Lane*

'A gorgeous novel that pairs my (and many people's) perennial love for books about books with themes of family – and just how complex they can be.'

Platinum

'An utterly gorgeous page turner about the power of books, family and forgiveness.'

Eva Glyn, author of *The Dubrovnik Book Club*

'A beautiful, poignant tale of family, friendship and the power of books. I was completely swept away.'

Annie Lyons, author of *The Air Raid Book Club*

'Books about books are always the best but add in an emotional plot and a heartwarming ending and this is a must read! A gorgeous story full of community, love and the power of books.'

Annabel French, author of *A Wedding at the Chateau*

The Last Page Café

KATE STOREY

avon.

Published by AVON
A division of HarperCollins*Publishers* Ltd
1 London Bridge Street
London SE1 9GF

www.harpercollins.co.uk

HarperCollins*Publishers*
Macken House, 39/40 Mayor Street Upper
Dublin 1, D01 C9W8, Ireland

A Paperback Original 2026
3

First published in Great Britain by HarperCollins*Publishers* 2026

A catalogue record for this book is available from the British Library.

ISBN: 978-0-00-873641-5

Set in Sabon LT Std by HarperCollins*Publishers* India

Printed and bound in the UK using 100%
Renewable Electricity at CPI Group (UK) Ltd

In loving memory of Joe Timoney

Prologue

Erin thanked the last customers of the day and followed them to the door. They smiled and nodded in reply, but their eyes were already on the heath and the church beyond. Erin didn't blame them. She knew that, to most of the tourists visiting Blackheath, she was essentially part of the furniture of The Bookmark Café, grey in comparison to the Technicolor world outside. Beyond the safe walls of her little domain, adventures awaited – for other people, at least. She was more comfortable in familiar surroundings, where life was predictable and there were no unwelcome surprises.

She spun the sign, which had been hanging on the door since her mother opened The Bookmark almost forty years ago. The side that said *open* now faced into the room. That always amused Erin; when the café was closed to other people, it was open to her. It felt fitting, since this room was her sanctuary.

Allowing her eyes to travel across the café, as she always did at the end of a long day on her feet, she assessed how long it would take her to clear up before she could relax. Now she was in her mid-fifties, her legs ached more than they did a decade ago when she took over the café. She hadn't changed the decor in all that time. Why would she? Her mother had wonderful, if a little bohemian, taste. A hotch-potch collection of prints they'd picked up over the years hung randomly on the white-painted exposed brickwork. Each picture had a coffee theme, and Erin could remember where and when they'd come across each one. Her favourite, a woman relaxing on a striped beanbag, holding a mug, a book obscuring her face, hung over the fireplace.

She let her gaze drop to the six brown leather armchairs around the low pewter-topped tables. The seats were saggy, the leather faded and marked, but she liked to think that gave them character. The plump cushions in various sizes added a pop of colour, as did what she called 'Kiddies Corner', where a collection of plastic toys were scattered on a wipe-clean laminate square. She wanted the café to be a home from home for her regulars, and few homes were perfect. She preferred to see the café's imperfections as similar to the lines on an ageing face, each had a story behind it. And stories were Erin's favourite thing, just like her mother before her.

Those old leather chairs were always the most popular seats in the café, not least because of the paperbacks she placed on the low tables in the centre at the start of each shift. She chose books from the wall of shelves at the far side of the café to suit her mood, often watching the faces of the people who picked them up, and stayed for longer than the time it took to finish their drinks. She liked to imagine them feeling the same things she did when she first read the pages. Sometimes she'd ask how they were finding it, allowing for a precious moment of connection in both their days.

The café had been a little quieter recently. Passing trade had fallen off since Victoria decided to retire, closing the gift shop next door. The shop had been a treasure trove, packed with greetings cards, old-fashioned board games, trinkets, and brightly coloured cushions and homeware. It was where much of the decor of The Bookmark had come from, since Erin's mother had found it hard to resist the odd piece of glassware, or quirky candlestick. Victoria lived in a mews house a few doors along from her old shop, so at least she was still around, even if the road was noticeably less busy since the place closed.

A mewling sound made Erin turn and look down through the glass in the door. Tybalt, Victoria's grey tabby cat, stared up at her with imploring amber eyes, then tapped an impatient paw against the doorframe. Erin laughed and let him in, watching as he stalked towards the armchairs and bounced into one with an agility that belied his heavy frame. 'Evening,' she said. 'Good day?' The cat ignored her and began to lick along the length of his fluffy tail. As soon as she sat down, she knew he would jump onto her lap, curl into a ball, and she would feel the vibration of his contented purr on her thighs through her jeans.

She could hardly wait, but first she had to finish clearing up. She closed the door again then pushed her bottom against it to propel her forwards, and used the momentum to scoop up the two empty china cups from the table the customers had left and take them through to the kitchen at the back. Once in there, she used what her son, Jack, called her 'Tetris skills' to fit every last piece of crockery into the dishwasher. Whenever anyone saw her stack the mismatched fine china, one of The Bookmark's trademarks, into the industrial-sized behemoth of a dishwasher, they were aghast at her recklessness. Little did they know she was probably the least reckless person in Blackheath. Scrub that, she was probably the most risk-averse person in the whole of the country. If her mother hadn't demonstrated that the beautifully decorated china could withstand the rigours of the machine, Erin would still be sluicing out every piece by hand, terrified it might break. Because no matter how careful you were, cherished things could break and sometimes they could never be repaired. She knew that better than anyone.

To the soundtrack of the machine's slosh and hum, she washed her hands and dried them on a tea towel with the café's bookmark logo, then tucked the towel into a tote bearing the same logo to take home to wash. The merchandise was Jack's idea. After his first year studying film and media, he'd come home with all kinds of ideas about how they could 'maximise the business's potential'. She smiled at the thought of her son's energy and enthusiasm. He would be home soon, ready to start the next phase of his life, whatever that might be.

The uncertainty made her thoughts race, so she did what she always did when she needed to be distracted. She went back into the main room and crossed to the white bookshelves which covered the whole of the wall opposite the door. She pushed the rolling ladder aside and crouched low to the shelf slightly obscured by the counter which, by day, held cakes and pastries under large glass domes. She wasn't proud of the way she stashed away the books she'd earmarked to read herself. The ethos of The Bookmark was to allow anyone to read anything they chose from the shelves. But on more than one occasion, she had been looking forward to starting a particular book, but when her break time arrived, it was nowhere to be found. Scanning the tables, she'd inevitably spy someone else turning the pages.

At the very end of the lowest row, her eyes found the red spine with three dark figures silhouetted against a yellow sunset at the base. She pulled it from the shelf and took it over to the armchair in the corner nearest the books. She'd heard nothing but good things about Kristin Hannah's *The Women*. She already knew it was a story of friendship and courage set against the brutal backdrop of the Vietnam War, but Erin needed to know more than that.

She used to allow stories to unfold in the traditional way, from beginning to end. But then her own story had taken a turn so unexpected and so devastating that she no longer trusted endings to reveal themselves on their own.

To keep her sanity, she'd decided the unknown was to be avoided at all costs – even in a world of make-believe. To make sure she was always prepared for what was in store, she'd developed a foolproof strategy. In a habit she'd started when her life fell apart, she turned to the very last page of the book and read that, before deciding it was worth starting at the beginning.

Chapter One

The next afternoon, the café was quiet following the post-school rush, so Erin treated herself to another couple of pages of *The Women*, only brought back into the real world by the sound of a gentle cough. When she looked up, Susan was standing near the door, her lips pinched, hands clasped in front of her.

'Sorry, I was miles away,' said Erin smiling and turning down the corner of her page before placing the book on the pitted pewter tabletop.

Susan shook her head. 'I don't know how you can do that.' She nodded to the book. 'It's sacrilege.'

Erin laughed. That wasn't the only thing she and Susan disagreed on. The older woman found Erin's habit of reading the last page of a novel first ludicrous and she was never afraid to say so. Not that that stopped her coming along to the weekly book group, the premise of which was that, if the last page was satisfying, then the rest of the book must be worth reading. 'Really? You never mentioned it.' She grinned as Susan raised her eyes to the high ceiling. 'Why are you standing over there? You look like a vampire waiting to be asked in.'

'Charming,' said Susan, taking a tentative step into the room, bringing the scent of roses and something sweeter with her. Susan was always the best smelling person in any room. She didn't have a signature scent, but seemed to find an array of perfumes which suited her perfectly. 'You and Tybalt looked so peaceful, I didn't want to disturb you.'

Erin lifted the cat from where he was nestled in her lap and stood. He mewled crossly as she placed him gently on the floor. She made her way to the kitchen, speaking over her shoulder, 'I was in a field hospital in the middle of a war zone. I probably should have looked more traumatised than peaceful. Reading is weird, isn't it, the way you can just dip in and out of thousands of other lives?'

'Weird and wonderful,' said Susan.

'I'll drink to that,' said Erin. She lifted a cup with an intricate blue and silver pattern around the rim. 'Earl grey?'

'Please,' said Susan, finally committing to her entrance and joining Erin as she pressed the hot water button on the machine and boiling water hissed into the cup. Susan leaned on the door frame, running a hand over her neat silver bob to smooth any hair that dared to step out of line. None had. They probably weren't brave enough. Erin put the cup on its matching saucer and handed it to Susan, breathing in the floral-scented steam. 'That's on the house.'

'Oh, for goodness' sake. That's no way to run a business,' said Susan. 'You're as bad as your mother.'

'I'll take that as a compliment,' said Erin. And it was. She ignored the small voice inside Erin's head telling her she wasn't worthy of the praise. Her mother, Mary, had been an extraordinary woman, full of colour and zest for life. Erin was pale and dull in comparison. Susan dropped three pound coins onto the counter next to the till with a loud exhale. 'Thank you.'

'When the others get here, don't start with the free drinks nonsense. You're running a business, not a charity. It's kind enough to host us week after week, without handing out freebies on top.' Susan had been a regular of the café before she became a cherished friend. Her brusque manner had terrified Erin when she was in her early twenties, working in the café alongside her mother while she decided what to do with her life after her English degree. But that was decades ago, and she'd long-since learned that underneath her strident exterior, Susan was a caring, thoughtful soul.

Susan looked over at Kiddies Corner where Jenga blocks were scattered amongst giant Lego. 'I take it you've had a baby group in today?'

'They come most days,' said Erin, thinking she probably should have tidied up the toys before book group. In truth, she'd stopped seeing the mess in the corner. Babies and toddlers should be messy, and she didn't want their parents to feel like they had to put everything back in the box in the corner before they left. She was sure they had enough clearing up to do at home. 'I think word's got around that I don't freak out at a bit of mashed banana. I get a few different groups coming in during the week.'

Susan raised an eyebrow. 'As long as the parents are eating and drinking. Make sure they're not just using this as a crèche.'

'Yes, miss.' Erin saluted, despite the fact she would do nothing of the sort. She would have loved somewhere like this when Jack was small. The frazzled parents could take as long as they liked over their well-deserved latte. 'You're as bad as Jack for telling me off.'

Susan's lined cheeks rounded in a smile. 'When's he back? Bet you can't wait, can you?'

A little surge of excitement lifted Erin's shoulders. 'I'm picking him up tomorrow. Can't believe he'll be home for good. Where have the last three years gone?'

'And what's he planning—' Susan turned at the sound of the door opening.

'Joe, hello,' said Erin, grinning over at the man in the doorway. He might be thinner now, with wisps of grey hair where he'd once had a thick black mop, but to Erin, Joe O'Connor would always be a strong, reliable man. He'd been her parents' best friend and neighbour, and was now the closest thing to family Erin had, other than her son.

'How are you both?' Joe still spoke with a soft Donegal accent, despite having moved to South London with his late wife, Nuala, almost fifty years ago.

'Good, thanks. You?' Erin was glad to escape the conversation about Jack's future plans. As far as she knew, he didn't have any, and the uncertainty of that made acid swill in her stomach.

'Can't complain.' Joe came in and lowered himself into an armchair with a groaning breath. 'Well, I could, but who'd listen?' Tybalt jumped onto Joe's lap, purring audibly as the old man ran a hand over his marbled grey fur.

'I would.' Erin kissed the top of Joe's head, breathing in the familiar scent of the gel he used to flatten the remaining strands of hair to his head. She worried about Joe. He seemed to have aged decades since Nuala died five years ago. The memories of her parents and Nuala and Joe sitting here, talking and laughing, drinking strong coffee as an Ella Fitzgerald record played quietly on the record player in the corner, were still vivid in her mind. She could see her father's white-blonde head, his hair inherited from his Danish forefathers, thrown back as he guffawed at something Joe said; she could see her mother buzzing back and forth to the kitchen for drinks and slabs of Victoria sponge. Now Joe was the only one of the group still living, and Erin knew he was lonely. It was too sad.

The door opened again and Mercy trundled in, pulling her shopping trolley behind her. 'Good evening, my bookish friends.'

'Hello, hello. What's in the bag?' Erin already had her suspicions. Mercy was a recently retired librarian, and had brought along many of the books that sat on The Bookmark's shelves. They all benefitted when West Greenwich Library cleared out its old stock.

'Just a few books Jakub at the library gave to me. He always lets me have first dibs before anything goes off to charity or, heaven help us, recycling.' She made the sign of the cross over her ample chest.

'I really should pay him for those.' Erin pushed away the thought of her latest profit and loss spreadsheet. It was hard enough to buy the staples without offering money for books that weren't necessary, but it never seemed right to take them for free. Books were valuable to her, and she suspected the library needed funds almost as much as she did.

'Nonsense,' said Susan. 'It's a transfer from one free reading venue to another. You're not profiting. You're just rehousing them.'

Erin glanced at the shelves behind her. Her mother had instigated the *take a book, bring a book* policy, pinning up the laminated instructions for customers to borrow whatever they fancied, then either return it, or bring another to replace it.

As Mercy piled the contents of her trolley on the table for them to pick through, two more members of the book group, Riley and Hafsa, sauntered in. Erin glanced up from the dusty copy of *A Tale of Two Cities* she was holding in her hands and started at Riley's new hairstyle, or, more accurately, the lack of it. Her scalp was entirely bare. 'Blimey,' she said, trying to keep the shock from her face. 'That's a strong look.'

Riley ran her hand over her head and gave a lopsided smile. 'I know. Chegs got a bit carried away with the clippers.' Chegs was Riley's boyfriend, and in Erin's opinion, he got carried away a lot more often than he should. Not that she'd shared that view. Unlike Susan, she had a strict policy of only offering her opinions when she was asked for them. At twenty-four, Riley was the youngest member of the book group. Partly because she worked for Erin at The Bookmark, and partly because she was a sweet and slightly lost soul, Erin couldn't help but feel motherly towards her.

'You look like that Irish singer, you know the one, died not long ago, God rest her soul,' said Joe. 'Gave the Pope what for. What was her name?' He scrunched up his face and rubbed his fingers together, his skin making a papery sound. Tybalt raised his head and knocked it against Joe's hand, only settling back down when Joe resumed stroking along his spine.

'Sinéad O'Connor,' said Hafsa, sitting elegantly and rearranging her long cream skirt so it fell in graceful folds. Erin envied Hafsa's style. She'd presumed Hafsa always wore expensive clothes, but when she asked if she ever wore something off the peg, Hafsa laughed. She said her GP's salary didn't stretch to anything other than off the peg, not when she had three kids to support. 'This is from New Look,' she'd said, stroking the forest-green satin shirt, 'and this is Primark.' Erin stared at the pleated skirt in disbelief, until Hafsa twisted it around and showed her the label at the back as proof. It was the way she wore them that made her clothes appear like they were designed just for her. That, coupled with the fact she never minded when one of the group took her aside to show her a skin rash, or an inflamed set of tonsils, made her a popular member of the gang.

'Do you like it?' asked Erin, scrutinising Riley's face. Her huge blue-green eyes, slightly protruding ears, and perfectly round head reminded Erin of the bush babies she and her ex, Andrew, saw on the trip to Australia they'd taken back when she thought her story had a predictable ending.

Riley's shoulders lifted then fell. 'Not much I can do about it, is there? I asked him for a number four, but he thought this would look better.'

Erin's jaw tensed. She wanted to tell her that he had no right to decide what she did with her body. She'd never liked Chegs. She found him entitled and arrogant, and unworthy of the adoration her gentle, creative friend lavished on him.

'I'd smack him in the mouth,' said Susan. 'I mean, you look wonderful. You always look wonderful, but your hairstyle, your choice.'

Erin could have kissed her. She trod a difficult line as Riley's employer as well as her friend, so she was delighted that Susan spoke her mind. She shouldn't have been surprised. Susan always called a spade a shovel. Riley gave another resigned shrug, took her place on the same armchair she always did, and sifted through the books as Susan raised an eyebrow at Erin. Erin shrugged in reply. Riley hadn't asked for her thoughts, so she would continue to keep them to herself.

'Right then. Let's get started,' said Erin, when they all had steaming cups in front of them. 'I'm looking forward to hearing what you all thought of *Death at the Sign of the Rook*.' She was a massive Kate Atkinson fan herself, and loved the latest adventure of flawed ex-detective, Jackson Brodie. 'Come on then, who thought it lived up to the last page?'

Chapter Two

Erin scratched her top lip, hoping to cover the yawn that crept up on her as she tried to keep up with Susan's description of all the priceless paintings which had been plundered by the Nazis and never recovered. The subject came about because of Jackson Brodie's extensive investigation into missing art in *Death at the Sign of the Rook,* and it was one Susan seemed bizarrely knowledgeable about. This was one of the wonderful things about book group; they were such a diverse bunch of people, and they all had different experiences and wisdom to share.

Susan was going on a bit, though. Not that she'd ever let on, but Erin was pleased when Hafsa took advantage of a pause to tell an anecdote about the time she and her husband went to a murder-mystery evening at the Clarendon Hotel, across the heath, in relation to the murder-mystery event in the novel. 'It ended rather abruptly when the lead suspect, who was slurring his lines from the off, stumbled into the champagne fountain and brought it crashing to the ground,' she said. 'He just stared at it, swaying and blinking like this—' she moved her eyelids slowly over her soft brown eyes '—as if all the shattered glass and liquid came out of nowhere. We were all given a refund and a voucher for ten pounds off another murder mystery. Funnily enough, we never redeemed it.'

Undeterred, Susan took a pause in the discussion to regale them with a detailed description of Canaletto's missing *Piazza Santa Margherita,* only stopping at the sound of the door opening. A tall man who appeared to be in his mid-fifties, wearing a biker jacket covered in badges, stood in the doorway. 'Am I in the right place?' he said.

'That very much depends on what you're looking for,' said Susan, chin pulled back to her neck.

Erin suspected she was irritated at being interrupted, but that was no reason to be rude. 'Can I help you?' She met his eyes and felt the odd sensation of having met him before, despite not recognizing his face. His gaze lingered on hers, and she had to force herself to look away.

'Sorry, yeah, is this book club?' He shifted his weight onto his other foot, and raised his eyebrows, which were dark in comparison to his greying stubble and what was left of his closely cropped hair. 'The fella in the bookshop on the corner told me there was a book club here.'

'Come in, young man,' said Joe. 'You're in the right place, and you're very welcome.' That was typical of Joe. No one stayed a stranger for long with him around.

Erin smiled, but it was a little forced. It was a long

time since she'd felt an instant attraction to a man and it unnerved her. Physical attraction rarely led anywhere good, in her experience. Her attraction to her ex-husband had led her to overlook his flaws time and time again, and look how that had ended. On top of that, various people had come and gone from book group over the years, but it had been just the six of them for the best part of two years now, and the dynamic worked.

She'd stopped telling other people about the weekly meet-ups for fear of upsetting what she'd come to see as the perfect combination of characters: Susan's cynicism balanced out by Mercy's cheerful positivity, and Hafsa's scientific, analytical take on things, countered by Riley's creativity and thinking outside the box. It was a delicate ecosystem and she didn't want it messed with. Her insistence that the next book was always chosen by reading the last page had been challenged enough times by potential new members. She didn't want to have to explain, or more accurately, defend it, again.

'Yes, that's us, come in,' she said, standing. 'Can I get you a drink . . .?'

'Adam,' he said, striding forwards with his hand outstretched. 'Adam Darling. Good to meet you.'

Erin shook his hand. His grip was firm but not painfully so. Her mother always said you could tell a lot about a person by their handshake and could instantly take against someone with limp fingers, or a knuckle-grinding, power grab of a shake. 'I'm Erin,' she said, then introduced the others, before asking again if he'd like a drink.

'The prices are on the board,' said Susan bluntly, pointing at the chalkboard on the mantlepiece above the fireplace on the left-hand wall. 'Don't let her give you a freebie, even if she offers.'

'Wouldn't dream of it,' said Adam, amusement in his voice. 'A black coffee would be perfect. Decaf, if you've got it.'

She'd presumed as much. Caffeine in the evenings was a sign of recklessness in her opinion. 'Coming right up. Take a seat.'

'Thank you,' Adam said, when she handed over his drink a couple of minutes later.

The man was now sitting in the seat she'd left. There were six comfortable leather armchairs; the perfect number for the group as it stood ten minutes ago. She'd known he'd disrupt things, and now she had to sit uncomfortably. She dragged a wooden chair from a table and put it on the periphery of the group.

Adam leaped up. 'Sorry, I've taken your seat. Please, sit here.'

'You're all right, I'm fine here.'

'I insist.' He stood aside and held out his arm, gesturing for her to sit back in the armchair.

'Thanks,' said Erin, graciously accepting. Tybalt jumped from Joe's lap and crossed to Adam, bashing his head against his denim-clad shins.

'Hello fella,' Adam said, scratching under the cat's chin. 'What's your name?'

'Tybalt,' said Riley.

'Tibbles?'

'No, Tybalt, like in *Romeo and Juliet*,' said Susan. 'He spends most of his time in here, but he belongs to the woman who used to have the shop next door. When she got him, he was a fiery little creature, always picking fights with bigger cats, so she named him after a Shakespearian troublemaker.'

As if determined to make Susan a liar, Tybalt rolled onto his back and showed the white fur of his tummy. 'Yep, you seem like an absolute demon,' said Adam, grinning as he leaned down to ruffle the soft fur.

'He got old, fat, and lazy,' said Riley. 'The good life's made him soft.'

'Hard relate,' said Adam.

Erin laughed along with the others, despite thinking that none of those adjectives seemed to describe the man currently petting the cat. 'He still has his moments,' she said. 'Victoria's more than happy to be shot of him most of the time. I wouldn't be surprised if she secretly got the cat flap taken out of her door because he's still a bit of a pickle. His main hobby is tormenting any dog sitting quietly by a table in here. One day he'll get his comeuppance, won't you, Mr?' Tybalt ignored her. 'Now what did I miss when I was in the kitchen?'

'Adam's a journalist, but not the scuzzy type,' said Riley. 'He wouldn't go chasing Princess Diana through a tunnel or taking pictures of her mangled body in the car wreck.' She turned accusing eyes on him. 'Would you?'

He straightened up, his aptly named Adam's apple moving as he swallowed nervously. 'Erm, no, no, I would not do that.' Tybalt got to his feet and jumped back onto Joe's lap.

'You weren't even born when that happened, were you?' Erin said to Riley, confused and a little disturbed by her oddly graphic cultural reference.

'No, but my nan never stopped going on about it,' said Riley, seriously. 'She stopped buying the papers altogether after that. Gave journalists a bad name, that bunch of tossers.'

Adam shifted on the chair. 'I think it was more to do with the paparazzi . . .' He paused when Riley scowled at him. 'But I am absolutely not one of those kind of journalists. I'm an international reporter turned travel writer, actually.' He held out a conciliatory hand. 'Not the salacious, click-baity ones.'

So he said. Erin wasn't convinced. No one could deny that Princess Diana's death was a story, so what would stop him chasing it? 'Sounds adventurous,' said Erin. The last adventure she'd been on was that trip to Australia.

'Oh, how I envy you,' said Mercy, her voice full of yearning. She clasped her hands to her chest. 'I always dreamed of travelling the world, but I've never been away from these shores.'

'What stopped you?' Adam asked the question so easily, as if he didn't understand that not everyone could just jump on a plane to far flung countries on a whim.

Mercy let her hands drop. 'Life. Work. Time's winged chariot.'

The sadness in her voice made Erin view her old friend through fresh eyes. 'I didn't know you wanted to travel.'

Mercy gave a sad smile. 'It's always been at the back of my mind, but my parents left their home in Kenya to make a new life here, and it was hard for them, you know?' She peered around the group, and they nodded sympathetically. 'They made the commitment, and stood by their decision, but my mother never really felt at home here. I saw her keen for the country of her birth, for the friends and family she left behind. That made me nervous about leaving here, since it was my home country, where everything was familiar, I suppose.' She pursed her lips. 'That could be my excuse, though. I let the years slip through my fingers and now I'm an old lady.' She sighed. 'I think travel's a young person's game.'

Erin understood completely. Safety first. Why take the risk?

'It's not too late,' said Adam.

Erin eyed him suspiciously. It was all right for him to come in and make sweeping platitudes, but he had no idea about any of their circumstances. 'You make it sound simple,' she said.

'It is. You buy a ticket, then you go.' Adam held out his palms. 'Simple as that.'

Mercy chuckled. 'You almost convince me.'

'I suppose if travel is essential for your work, then it

is fairly simple. But what about family commitments, that sort of thing?' said Susan.

'Yeah, I suppose I'm lucky in that respect. I'm free as a bird,' said Adam. 'Nothing tying me to one place more than any other.'

'You're not local then? You won't be sticking around?' Erin fought a tinge of disappointment. Why had he interrupted the flow of book group if he wasn't going to be around long enough to read the next book?

'Not local, no. I'm originally from Brighton, and I've lived all over, but since I've decided to slow down a bit, work-wise, I've rented a place not far from here. It's been ideal so far, close to central London, but with all the open space on the heath and the park.'

'Welcome to the area,' said Joe. 'And welcome to The Last Page Book Group.'

'We're not your usual book group,' said Erin. Her voice sounded defensive, and she saw a question when she caught Joe's eye. She looked away. 'So, don't worry if it's not your bag.'

'Different how?' Adam's forehead creased.

Erin steadied her gaze, and resisted the urge to jut out her chin. 'We read a book a week, and we choose our next book by reading the last page first.'

Chapter Three

'That's absurd,' said Adam, his lip curling. 'You're joking, right?'

The word *absurd* cut her. Despite herself, she found she wanted this man's approval. She smiled demurely, even though he seemed to think he could come in and disrupt a perfectly happy collective. 'I'm not joking. We read the last page, and if it's a good one, then we know the story will be worth the hours we'll spend reading it.'

'But that's bonkers.' He laughed, and scanned the group, clearly expecting them all to laugh along with him.

Only Susan nodded. 'It is bonkers, but it's also true.'

Judas, thought Erin. That was the last time she offered her a cup of floral-scented hot water for free. She took a drink of her own English breakfast tea to prevent herself saying as much.

'But surely, the joy of reading a book is to see where the story goes?' There was pure disbelief in his voice.

'You say that as if it's the law,' said Erin, placing her cup back down on the pewter tabletop. She set her jaw, silently daring him to continue challenging her. She'd kept her book group going for a decade, defeating anyone who tried to change it. All right, the last part wasn't strictly true. Everyone who didn't like being asked to read the last page first quietly sloped off, without much of a fuss. Still, she was ready to defend her position to the death. She might be generally conflict averse, but the book group was her safe place, and she needed that to remain the case.

'Well . . .' His brow crinkled, as if he was thinking hard about his argument. 'That's how I feel about it.' There was a hesitation in his voice which suggested he wasn't as sure as he had been.

Erin ignored the change in tone. She had to be vigilant, especially since she suspected Susan would be quite happy to join in a mutiny. This man was a carefree travel writer with no roots. He could afford to just see where the words took him. Well, Erin wasn't. She had responsibilities, a son due home from university, bills to pay, and on top of all that, she had a business, her mother's precious legacy, to protect. Her book group was the one thing she could be sure of and that was crucial to her. 'Then maybe this isn't the book group for you.'

All eyes turned to him. He appeared flustered for a moment, then sat back and crossed his arms, the leather of his jacket squeaking as he did so. 'Nope,' he said. 'I've eaten sheep's eyes in the desert, and been chased by a polar bear in Alaska, so I'm not going to be put off a book club in South London because of a quirky reading habit.'

'If you'd been chased by a polar bear, it's highly unlikely you'd be here to tell us about it,' said Hafsa, with an arched eyebrow. 'You'd be little more than a red stain on the ice.'

Amusement made his grey eyes sparkle. 'All right, I might have exaggerated that. There was a polar bear, but it was more of an amble, than a chase, and I was filming from the back of a truck, so . . .' He made a clicking sound with his tongue. 'Am I going to be ejected from the group because of a little gentle embellishment, or can I stay and give this last page business a go?'

He wasn't giving up easily. 'What's your favourite book?' Erin said, as if that was going to make all the difference. It wasn't, but she needed him to prove himself if he was going to be allowed to continue to attend her much-loved Wednesday evenings with her friends. She crossed her own arms and waited for him to say something predictable, like Jack Kerouac's *On the Road*.

'Oh, is this the test? Okay, then.' Adam grinned, his eyes moving up to the left as he gave it some thought. '*The Glass Castle,* Jeannette Walls, I think. It's funny and sad and quirky. I love getting an insight like that into other people's lives, I suppose it's the journalist in me.'

Erin was pleasantly surprised. Her mother had bought her that memoir, and she'd been deeply moved by the unusual story of Walls' nomadic, impoverished childhood. Somehow, it made perfect sense that this man with the bright eyes would choose this beautiful book, and realizing that made her feel oddly vulnerable. Everything he did added to his attraction, damn him.

'What's yours?' Adam was looking directly at her, his expression warm and curious.

Her mind went blank. All she could think about was the way his mouth lifted at the edges, as though he was always on the verge of smiling. 'Oh, it's too hard to choose.' She gestured to the wall of books with the sliding ladder. 'I love so many, all for different reasons.'

'You made me pick, so it's only fair you do.' God, he was irksome. She made a mental note to tell the owner of the bookshop to never mention her book group to anyone ever again. Adam leaned forwards, resting his elbows on his knees. 'Go on, if you had a gun to your head, which would you choose?'

The idea of a gun's cold barrel at her temple did nothing to improve her clarity of thought. She turned to the shelves, scanning the spines for inspiration. Her eyes lighted on a dark blue book and relief washed through her. '*Hamnet*, Maggie O'Farrell.' In that moment, she felt the story, centred around Shakespeare's wife and son, was definitely her favourite book of all time, not least because it was one that didn't make her look like an uncultured fool in front of Adam. As soon as the thought occurred to her, she was cross with herself. First, because she didn't believe in snobbery where books were concerned – every book had merit if it was enjoyed by a reader – and secondly for wanting this man's approval. What was she, some pathetic schoolgirl, hanging out on the sidelines of the football pitch, hoping the striker would notice her?

'I haven't read that,' said Adam, sitting back again. Erin was glad to be relieved of his scrutiny. 'Should I?'

'You should,' said Susan. 'It's excellent. I enjoyed your choice too. Shall we all go around, saying our favourite books, by way of a proper introduction?' The others nodded. It was hard to say no to Susan since her questions always sounded more like instructions. 'You can tell a lot about a person by their choice of reading matter.'

'Why don't I get us fresh drinks while you all decide,' said Erin, keen to be on her own for a moment. It appeared that Adam was now initiated whether she liked it or not, and that left her unsettled. The book group had been a haven, a reliable gang of six, and now they'd been infiltrated and there was nothing she could do about it. Adam's presence made her uneasy. His biker jacket, his job, his lifestyle, and her attraction to him all represented risk. And Erin had spent the last two decades avoiding risk at all costs.

Chapter Four

As Erin walked home from The Bookmark in the half-light of the spring evening, her thoughts were a jumbled mass of contradictions. Adam Darling's eyes had lingered on her longer than anyone else as they all said their goodbyes at the end of book group. She was sorely out of practice at recognizing the signs, but that look seemed to indicate the attraction was mutual. Even so, she struggled to see his addition to the group as positive. Everyone else had welcomed him without any apparent misgivings, and he'd accepted the terms of the book group without further argument, but there was something unnerving her about the last couple of hours. Surely it couldn't just be that there weren't quite enough comfortable chairs? Whatever it was, she couldn't quite put her finger on it other than sensing a jittery feeling in the pit of her stomach.

Suddenly drained of energy, she pushed her weary legs to the end of Hare and Billet Road, then made the last effort up Dartmouth Grove to the approach of the two-bedroom flat she'd bought for her and Jack almost twenty years ago, in an Art Deco mansion block. She always thought mansion block was a grandiose term for the building which was originally constructed as a nurses' home, and then became, fittingly she thought, a home for single mothers. Admittedly, the facade and communal areas did look far better since the renovation, but back when she bought it, it was a shock to find herself there.

After she and Andrew married, they'd bought a small, terraced house in nearby Hither Green. She adored their home. After her fertility battle, and the failed rounds of IVF, finally having Jack felt like the fairytale ending at last. She'd decorated the nursery and anticipated their son growing out of his cot and into a toddler bed, then a single bed, all under that same roof, with his mummy and daddy and a life full of love. But where she saw a happy ending, Andrew found disappointment and dissatisfaction. He'd discovered a steady life with a wife and child wasn't what he wanted after all. He wanted a different story: a new, more exciting, more unpredictable one. One without two of the main characters, her and Jack, in it. He shattered her dreams of a happy-ever-after and left her to bring up their hard-won child on her own.

Already exhausted from becoming a new mother, Erin went through the next months shell-shocked. She couldn't afford to keep the house, and her parents had recently downsized from the semi-detached house she grew up in to a flat, so she had to find somewhere else to live, pack up the life she loved, and start again. The only consolation was that she found a place very close to her parents, so at least she had their support with Jack when losing the man she'd loved since she was a teenager, plus the life she'd always dreamed of, became too much to bear.

As she reached the front of the building, she remembered the awful first months after she and Jack moved into the boxy flat. The distress of that time would never leave her. The memories of the nightmare that came along with Jack's teenage years were still too fresh for her to bring to the forefront of her mind without feeling physical pain, so she didn't allow them to surface now. She pushed them away, looking forward to being inside with her feet up at last.

As she was about to turn into the communal driveway, she glanced up. Fingers of fear crept over her scalp when she noticed lights on in the window of her first-floor flat. The jittery feeling in her middle intensified. She'd turned the lights off when she left. She was sure she had. With fuel bills being what they were, she couldn't afford to leave a lamp on to welcome her home on dark evenings.

A shadow moved across the window. Her heart stalled. There was someone in her home. An intruder. She grabbed her phone from her bag with shaking fingers, glancing up to see the shadow move again, before dialling 999.

***

'Police. We're coming in.' The larger of the two police officers turned Erin's key in the lock of her flat, as she stood with her back against the wall near the top of the communal stairs, heart leaping in her chest. A patrol car with two uniformed constables had arrived eight minutes after she called. She'd followed them into the building, mouth dry as they checked they had the right flat, before asking for her keys. Now, the one at the front held a baton aloft as the other, a slighter man, had his hand poised over what Erin presumed was a pocket containing pepper spray.

In her head, she saw a masked intruder barelling out of her apartment, slamming the police aside as they launched themselves towards the stairs, a swag bag filled with all her most prized possessions bouncing on their shoulder as they escaped.

Her blood froze in her veins as she heard the door open. 'Put your hands in the air,' shouted the bigger officer. So there was someone in there. Acid burned up her throat.

'What the . . .' said a man's voice. Only it wasn't just a man's voice. It was a voice she recognized as well as her own. It was Jack's.

She leaped away from the wall, and rushed to where the police officers were standing. 'Jack!' It had briefly crossed her mind that it could be him, but she'd dismissed the thought because she was sure he would have called if his plans had changed.

'Mum? What's going on?' His hands were raised, his face ashen.

The officer's hand dropped to his side. 'This is your son?'

'Yes, I—'

'And you've given him permission to be in your property?' His voice was weary, and Erin couldn't blame him.

'I live here,' said Jack. 'Tell them, Mum.' Two red dots appeared in the middle of his cheeks, like they always did when he was frightened or embarrassed. She wanted to rush forwards and hold him.

'Yes, he does,' said Erin, her own cheeks flushing with heat. 'Sorry.'

'So, what, you forgot you had a fully grown member of the family living with you?' said the second officer, his irritation clear. He scrutinised Jack, making it clear he thought the young man was big enough and ugly enough to be noticed.

Erin searched the officer's face for signs he recognized Jack from that awful time when he was threatened with a Penalty Note for Disorder for possession of cannabis. That had been the pinnacle of a dreadful period, where Erin hardly recognized the boy she'd brought up singlehandedly. He'd begun to experiment with weed when he first started sixth form, and when she'd refused to allow him to smoke it in his room, he would stay out late, never telling her where he was going, who he was with, or when he'd be back.

Desperate and out of other options, Erin had begged Andrew for help. Much to her surprise, he'd stepped up, offering to share the burden of caring for their increasingly troublesome teenager. Jack started to stay at his father's flat in Lewisham at weekends, then during the week, until Erin hardly saw him. She'd accepted it as a necessary sacrifice. Jack's welfare was all she cared about, and if Andrew could manage him better than her and keep him on the straight and narrow, then that was all that mattered.

But it soon transpired that Andrew wasn't actually parenting Jack at all. Emails from school arrived, asking why Jack was absent, and when the call from the police station came, she discovered the truth; Andrew hadn't stopped Jack taking drugs, he'd joined him in some kind of messed up father–son bonding. When she picked up a tearful Jack from the police station, she'd discovered it was Andrew who'd sourced the cannabis their sixteen-year-old son was caught with.

Jack had refused to tell the police that and begged Erin not to share the information either. She agreed on the proviso that Jack moved back home. Thankfully, being picked up by the police seemed to be enough of a wake-up call for Jack to change his ways. He settled into his studies, and she hadn't seen any more evidence of drug taking, although she was always alert to the signs.

To her astonishment, Andrew didn't seem to think he'd done anything wrong. He took a new job in Hertfordshire soon afterwards and dropped out of Jack's life again, as if a child was something you could pick up and discard depending on your whims. Jack had been hurt by the way his father lost interest in him again, and it killed Erin to see him check his phone, hoping for a reply to a text he'd sent to his dad, and always being disappointed. Eventually he seemed to stop trying and accept that Andrew was absent again, and Erin hated her ex-husband even more than she had before.

To her immense relief, there was no hint of recognition on the face of the officer currently standing on their threshold. Of course there wasn't. Jack had been ticked off and sent on his way five years ago, he wasn't the boss of a notorious organised crime conglomerate. 'No, I wasn't expecting him. I'm meant to be picking him up from uni tomorrow,' said Erin. She turned to Jack, mortification and delight at seeing her son jostling for precedence. 'Why didn't you tell me you were coming home early?'

'I thought I had.' He took his phone from his pocket and opened Messages, then grimaced. 'It didn't send. Sorry. I did think it was weird you hadn't replied, but I knew you were at book club, so . . . sorry. My bad.'

'Huh,' said the first constable, tucking his baton into its holder on his belt. 'Next time, maybe give your mum a ring, eh?'

'Yeah, will do,' said Jack, shaking his head, a smile creeping onto his face. 'You never did like surprises, did you?'

'No I bloody well don't,' said Erin. There were few things she liked less. Despite that, she moved past the officers and took Jack in her arms. She gave him a fierce hug, then turned back to the police. 'I'm so, so sorry for wasting your time. Can I get you a cup of tea, or something, by way of an apology?'

'You're all right,' said the bigger man, his expression thawing as he viewed mother and son together. 'We'd best get off and catch some actual intruders.'

'Sorry again,' said Jack. 'That's not a mistake I'll make twice.'

'And if you're in the village, pop into The Bookmark, the café on Brigade Street, set back from Royal Parade. I own it, and there'll be coffee and cake on the house.'

'Might well take you up on that. Night then. Keep out of trouble.'

'We'll try. Thanks again. Bye.' Erin waited until the two men reached the stairs before shutting the door and playfully walloping Jack on the arm. 'You nearly gave me a conniption, you muppet.'

'Sorry.' He rubbed his arm, pretending to be hurt. 'I should have made sure you knew I was on my way.' He pulled her close and kissed the top of her head. 'A girl from my course was heading this way home. Her dad hired a van, so there was room for my stuff. It seemed like a no-brainer to accept a lift to save you coming up in the car to get me tomorrow. I got over-excited at the idea of seeing your face when you found me here when you got back from book club and forgot you hadn't messaged back.' He let her go and peered down at her face. 'I didn't think you'd call the feds.'

'The feds? What are you like? We're in London, not LA.' She narrowed her eyes. 'Although, it looks like I might have to call them again.'

His brow furrowed. 'Why?'

Erin lifted a finger to touch the soft dark hair above her son's top lip. 'To arrest you for a crime against good taste. What's that? It's not the seventies, you know.'

'Rude.' Jack smoothed down his moustache with his hand. 'I'll have you know this is the height of fashion.'

Erin laughed. 'The only man who ever suited a moustache is Tom Selleck.'

'Who?' said Jack.

'Urgh, never mind, you're too young to get it.' Erin glanced past Jack at the piles of black bin liners stacked in the narrow hallway. 'How much of that is washing?'

Jack grinned. 'Only about fifty per cent.'

Erin huffed, but in truth, she didn't care if the whole lot was a fetid pile of unwashed sheets. It might not have been the most relaxing of evenings, all told, but her lovely boy was home and that was the only thing that mattered.

Chapter Five

Erin felt like she'd won the lottery when she opened her bedroom curtains the next day to the beautiful late May sunshine. She'd taken the day off, leaving Riley to manage the café, so she could collect Jack from Birmingham. But he was already here, so there would be no stressful motorway driving and she had the whole glorious day ahead of her to spend with her son.

Her zeal didn't even diminish at the sight of the bags still *in situ* in the hall. They'd been too tired to tackle them yesterday, opting for a quick dinner and a re-watch of *The Royal Tenenbaums* instead. It was like old times, the two of them at either end of the sofa, a bowl of crisps between them, giggling at the same parts they always did. She wandered through to the kitchen, a scattering of spilled coffee granules telling her Jack had recently been in the vicinity. That didn't even annoy her, not yet anyway. Give it a week. As she wiped the counter clean, she dismissed the usual pang of regret that the surfaces of their galley kitchen didn't have room for a proper coffee machine, then lifted the kettle to check the weight, deemed there was enough water for a cup of instant, and flicked the switch.

'Morning,' Jack's deep voice shouted from the sitting room.

She smiled to herself as she walked through to greet him. Her chick was in the nest and all was well with the world. 'Good morning. Sleep well?' She lifted a coaster from the pile on the table and slid it under the mug he'd put straight onto the wood.

'Like a baby.'

'Huh,' she said. 'Not like you as a baby, then.' It was family lore that Jack had been a terrible sleeper. Even at ten months old, he still woke several times in the night, calling out for her if he lost his dummy. Erin resorted to leaving five of the things peppered around him on the mattress, but still, he'd cry until she came into his room and popped one back into his mouth. That time was foggy when she tried to recall it. She was in a pit of turmoil and grief when she should have been relishing her precious, if exhausting, time with her longed-for baby. Still, now he was home for good, they'd be making even more memories together.

'You're never going to forgive me for that, are you?'

'My eye bags won't,' she said. 'I looked like Claudia Schiffer before I had you.' That was a lie. She might have inherited her father's unusual combination of naturally blonde hair and dark eyes, but she knew her round face and soft features made her more girl-next-door pretty than beautiful.

'Is that right?' He shook his head gravely. 'I can only apologise for disrupting your international modelling career. Although—' he made a flourish '—I think we both agree I was worth the sacrifice, if you discount the minor teenage blip.'

'I suppose you're right,' she said, with an exaggerated sigh. 'And you need to forget about that blip. I have.' It was sad that he still felt the need to reference how difficult he'd been as a teenager. He'd made up for it a million times over since then simply by changing back into the thoughtful, funny boy she knew and adored.

'We need to talk about your cultural references, by the way,' Jack said. 'So far we've had Tom somebody or other I've never heard of, and a model from the nineties. You need to step out of the last century.'

'I liked the last century,' she said. That was true. Up until her thirties, her life had been exactly how she wanted it, most of the time, anyway. She had loving parents, a romantic relationship which had started in sixth form and lasted through university, despite everyone telling her it wouldn't, and she enjoyed her job as an events coordinator. The new millennium brought with it infertility, heartbreak, and the death of her father, then her mother and the myriad stresses of being a single parent. Was it any surprise she harked back to the past? 'When you've finished that coffee, let's make a start on those bags.'

An hour and a half later, the washing machine was spinning noisily at the end of the first load, and Jack's bedroom looked like a landfill site. Erin stood in the doorway with her hands on her hips. 'How did you fit it all in in your student digs? Your room wasn't much bigger than this.' Her flat was optimistically described as having two double bedrooms when she bought it, and when Jack was still small, the room felt perfectly adequate. But since he'd grown to over six feet tall and they'd put a double bed in there, it appeared to have shrunk to half its original size.

'It'll be fine when I've put everything away,' he said, sounding a lot less sure than his words indicated.

'Remember there's space in the drawers under the bed.'

Jack dragged the handle nearest him, and the drawer slid out to reveal an enormous pile of folders and colourful paper.

'What's that?' Erin stepped over a pile of bedding and peered in.

'All my old art stuff,' said Jack, lifting an A3 pencil sketch of an old, bearded man in ragged clothes, reading a newspaper.

Erin examined the drawing, a familiar pride blooming in her chest. 'I'd almost forgotten how good you are,' she said. 'That's incredible.'

'And you're not at all biased,' said Jack. 'He's got one leg twice as thick as the other, look.' He pointed, but Erin could only see the detail in the creases of his tattered trousers, and the delicately drawn, if slightly too long, fingers holding the paper.

'I think it's brilliant,' she said. 'You should take up drawing again. You always enjoyed it and you've got real talent.'

'I'll add it to the long list of things my mother thinks I could win awards for,' said Jack, folding the paper, as air whistled from his nose in quiet laughter.

Erin grabbed at the drawing. 'What are you doing? You'll crease it.'

'I can't keep everything, can I? There isn't enough space.'

'But . . .' Erin contemplated the drawer, a hollowness opening inside her. 'It's all your GCSE and A level stuff.'

'I know,' said Jack. 'But I've got all my degree stuff to put somewhere now.'

She thought of their old house, with its loft space where, if Andrew hadn't ruined everything, she would have been able to store their son's precious creations, instead of him feeling like he had to throw them away as if they meant nothing.

She could still see a younger Jack in her mind's eye, head bent close to the table, as he made careful marks on the paper with his 4B pencil, then smudging it to make shadows with his middle finger. She fondly recalled the grey smudged fingerprints appearing on the fridge door, and the white cupboard fronts, when he forgot to wash his hands. She might be seeing them through rose-tinted glasses, but those memories still mattered to her. The things her son had lovingly created with his skill and imagination mattered. 'Aw, don't chuck it out. We'll find somewhere.'

'We can't keep everything.' He picked up another piece and held it out. 'I mean, I don't even know what this was meant to be.'

Erin assessed the brightly painted triangles, trying and failing to work it out herself. 'It's an abstract.'

'Of what?'

'I don't know. You painted it.'

'An abstraction of talent, or talent abstracted,' he said, in a pretentious voice, viewing it from different angles. 'Seriously, this is not worth keeping.' He screwed it into a ball and threw it over his shoulder.

Erin watched it fall on top of an open bin bag. 'I don't think I can bear it,' she said. 'It might not mean much to you, but you've got your whole life ahead of you to make new memories. I'm more than halfway through mine, so I'm clinging on to the old ones.'

'I don't know which is worse,' he said, his expression turning serious. 'You harping back to the past, or me being terrified of the future.'

'Terrified?' Erin's shoulders tensed. She searched his face, scanning for signs of distress she'd missed. 'What do you mean?'

Jack swallowed. 'Forget it. I'm being melodramatic.'

'No, please. Tell me what you're frightened of.' The thought of her son being scared of the future made her heart ache.

'Well, things feel a bit . . . a bit big, overwhelming,

I suppose. It's all unknown, from now on, isn't it? When I went from school, to sixth form, to uni, it was predictable, you know? The biggest risk I ever took was leaving home and going to Birmingham, and even then, I was back here for the holidays. I always had a safety net. Now I'm heading into the real world and I've got to make real-life, grown-up decisions.' He tugged at the edge of his moustache, which made him seem oddly younger. 'I'm scared I'll make the wrong ones.'

'You won't,' she said, feeling helpless herself, because he was right; the real world was terrifying and unpredictable. 'You're bright, and you've got a good education. It will all work out fine, I promise.' That was a stupid thing to say. She couldn't promise, not when his future wasn't in her control. She hated not keeping to her word, and she hated not being able to predict or manage outcomes even more.

'I hope you're right. I do need to work out what to do with the rest of my life, though.' He picked his way to the small desk against the wall, which was piled with books and folders. He lifted a black notepad. 'I've been making notes of things I can do with a film and media degree.'

'That's good,' said Erin. 'I do love a list.' There was nothing more useful in events coordination than a trusty list. The only thing she liked more was the satisfaction that came with ticking things off. Sometimes, if she'd achieved something she hadn't been planning, she added it and struck it through immediately, just to get the little dopamine spike.

'Is it?' said Jack. He opened the notebook, showing her pages of handwriting. 'I've been scribbling down ideas, what I'm worried about, and what I need to do, but I haven't done anything about it. I told myself there was no point since I was moving home, but that was an excuse. All jobs are advertised online.'

That was worrying. Procrastination could be a sign he was suffering from anxiety, which was a step beyond worry. She should know. 'Well, you're home now. You can start looking, can't you? I'll help you.'

'Thanks, but graduate jobs in film and television are like hen's teeth.' Erin couldn't help but feel a pang of loss at her son's use of a phrase her mother used to say. His voice rose in pitch. 'I've got mates who've done five rounds of tests and interviews and still been turned down.'

'It's okay,' said Erin, putting a hand on his arm. 'Something will come up.' She wished she had something other than platitudes to offer.

'The perfect job isn't going to fall into my lap, though, is it? And I'm even frightened about what happens after I do find a job, I mean, is that it, you know, for the rest of my life? Will I start getting the train into work one day, then do the same thing, day in, day out until, one day, I wake up and find I'm sixty and my life has passed me by?'

'You're catastrophising,' said Erin, softly. 'The best thing to do when you're overthinking, is to do something practical to keep your mind occupied.' She only wished she was as adept at following this advice as she was at dishing it out.

'But what if—'

'We're going to save the what ifs for when we've got this mountain of stuff down to a hillock.' She rubbed his arm, then took the notebook out of his hands. 'This can all wait.' She scoped the room for a task that would keep him busy. 'Take all the artwork out of that drawer and put it on the floor in the sitting room. We can go through it together and decide what to keep and what to chuck out.' The notebook felt like a lead weight in her hand. It contained her son's worries, and his worries were hers.

'I hate not knowing what's ahead,' Jack said, lifting a pile of papers from the drawer.

'I know, love, I know.' Erin understood that feeling better than anyone. Had she passed down her fear of uncertainty to her son? He should be excited about the next chapter of his life, not fearful. She'd done that to him, and she didn't know how to make it right.

As she went through to the kitchen to make them both a fortifying cup of instant coffee, the letterbox flapped and a white envelope fell onto the hall carpet. She picked it up and opened it as the kettle boiled. Her heart began to beat more quickly as she read the first lines. It told her that the building which housed The Bookmark and the empty unit next door had been sold to a company called Galmouth Estates. The letter gave her notice that when her current lease was up in twelve weeks' time, the rental amount would be subject to change. She read the new figure in bold letters, then did the calculations in her head. It was eight thousand pounds each quarter higher than what she currently paid. That was thirty-two thousand pounds a year. Profits had been down since the gift shop closed. How could she possibly afford such a monumental increase? She couldn't.

Panic tightening her chest, she turned to the next page, where comparable rentals were listed, demonstrating that she'd been paying considerably below the market rental for years. Even if she tried to fight it, the evidence that she was only being asked to pay the going rate was there in black and white. With trembling fingers, she folded the papers up and shoved them back into the envelope, but she couldn't hide from what that figure in bold print meant for the future of her mother's café, or her only way of making a living. This was bad. This was very bad indeed.

Chapter Six

Now, whenever she opened The Bookmark, Erin couldn't help seeing the room through fresh eyes. She took in the cornucopia of prints, the painted brick fireplace, and the blue candlesticks with half melted candles on the mantlepiece, waxy bobbles dripping down their sides. She could remember exactly when her mother bought the Murano glass vase made up of multi-coloured squares that sat in the fireplace and caught the sun in the late afternoon, casting rainbow patterns across the grate. She loved every part of that room.

Now she was at risk of losing it, the memories attached to each item in her pretty, hotch-potch café seemed so precious that even the thought of it no longer being there every day at the turn of a key caused her heart to ache. When Tybalt slinked past her and bounced into his favourite armchair, tears sprang into her eyes. He'd already lost his cosy spot under the desk in Victoria's gift shop. Now he would probably lose his place here too, along with all the petting he got from the customers who adored him.

That thought made her press her hand to her chest.

What about her loyal customers? Where would they go if The Bookmark closed down? Where would the baby groups go? Nowhere else locally had a corner filled with wipe-clean toys. She knew many people came for the company in familiar surroundings more than the food and drink. And where else had a wall of books for customers to peruse? One dreadful thought tumbled over another. What about book group? They'd have to find a new venue. Everything would change, and if there was one thing Erin hated above all else, it was change.

During a restless night, Erin had thought hard about how to tell Jack and her friends about the rent increase. Jack was already dealing with enough change. If he knew that their income was at risk, then he might feel like he had to take any old job, rather than something he was passionate about. She didn't want to force his hand. She would keep it to herself for now.

It felt like a long day, and Zita was her last customer. As usual, Erin turned a blind eye when she tipped the sachets of sugar from the bowl in the middle of the table into her stained canvas bag. She'd been a regular of The Bookmark for as long as Erin could remember. She recalled once pointing out to her mother that Zita was sneaking the sugar into her bag. Mary had smiled and shaken her head. 'I know,' she'd said. 'She's a character, that one.'

'But she only buys one cup of coffee, then nurses it for two hours while she reads the books. And she takes more books than she brings in,' Erin said, indignantly.

'Why do you think that is?' Mary said.

'Because she's a cheapskate?'

Erin still winced when she remembered the disappointment in her mother's eyes. 'Or it could be that she's lonely, and she finds comfort here, reading and watching the world go by. We have plenty more books. It's not as if she ever comes during the breakfast or lunch rush, so we don't usually need the table.'

Stung, Erin countered with, 'Even if that's true, she shouldn't be stealing the sugar.'

'What's a little sugar? It's not worth losing a customer over.'

Over the years, Erin had grown oddly fond of Zita, who must now be in her eighties. She rarely spoke, other than to say a quiet thank you for the coffee Erin or Riley made, without her having to give her order. Erin had stopped trying to elicit conversation over a decade ago, and let the old lady read at the table nearest the door in peace. She often refilled the sugar bowl on her regular table shortly before Zita arrived at 4 p.m., in the full knowledge that it would be empty by the time she left.

Now, she was clearing away Zita's empty cup, trying not to become overwhelmed with worry about where the old lady would spend her afternoons if The Bookmark closed down. She still used the word *if* in her head, but really it felt more like a when. She shifted the chairs ready for the rest of the book group to arrive, biting down on the inside of her cheek to stop herself from crying at the unfairness of it all. People needed places like this. She needed it.

She went over to the old Pioneer turntable which had been her mother's pride and joy when she bought it back in the eighties. The LPs she kept at the cafe were stacked in the cupboard beneath, and she put her finger on one after the other, pulling them towards her, checking the sleeves. For her, choosing an album was like choosing a book. It had to be the right one for that moment in time. She let out a wobbly sigh when she saw Miles Davis' familiar face, lips pursed against a trumpet's silver mouthpiece on the cover of *Kind of Blue*. It was her mother's favourite, and it was perfect for calming the nerves Erin hadn't been able to shake since the letter arrived.

She slid the vinyl from the sleeve and breathed in the dusty, plasticky scent that always took her back in time. In recent years, she'd caved in and had The Bookmark wired with a modern sound system, but no amount of technology could replace the weight of a record in her hands, the lift and precise placement of the arm, and the distinctive crackle through the speakers before the first notes.

'Miles,' said a voice from the doorway. 'Good choice.' Joe wandered into the room, Tybalt rising to greet him as he walked towards the armchairs. Joe sat, with his usual noisy exhalation and Tybalt jumped onto his lap, staring up as Joe held his hands out in front of him, closed his eyes and moved his fingers, as if plucking invisible strings.

'Mum loved this one,' said Erin. 'Was it a regular on your set list?' She was eager to be distracted by one of her friend's tales of the time he was a double bassist, playing in various jazz clubs around London.

Joe opened his eyes and smiled. 'Of course. The bass notes move up and down the neck so beautifully, listen.' He closed his eyes again and Erin did the same, only opening them at the sound of the door opening. Her stomach gave an involuntary flip at the sight of Adam.

'Miles Davis,' he said, nodding as if he approved. He was wearing the biker jacket covered in badges again, and underneath Erin spotted a T-shirt with *Pixies* emblazoned above what looked like a black and white photograph of a topless Flamenco dancer. That seemed an odd choice to wear for a book group. What if someone was offended by nudity? He probably didn't care. He was probably the kind of man who wore what he wanted when he wanted regardless of who he might offend. It occurred to her that she was trying to find fault with him to counter her attraction. She didn't have the time or the energy to fancy anyone right now. She had enough disruption in her life.

'You're a jazz man?' said Joe, his blue eyes lighting up.

'Isn't everyone?' Adam approached them, the thick soles of his biker boots clonking on the parquet floor.

'Anyone with any sense,' said Joe.

'Joe's a double bassist,' said Erin, with pride. 'He's played with all kinds of famous musicians, haven't you?'

'Was a double bassist,' Joe corrected her. He held out his hands and rubbed at his thickened knuckles. 'Blasted arthritis put a stop to it a few years ago.'

'But you did,' said Erin. 'You had all those experiences.' She turned to Adam and found that he was watching her. A blush crept onto her cheeks. 'The stories this man can tell.'

Adam tickled Tybalt under his chin before pulling over an upright chair and sitting. Erin approved of the fact he didn't seat himself in one of the armchairs. 'I'd like to hear those.'

'Evening all.' Susan blustered in, smoothing down her hair. 'It's blowing a gale out there.' If it was, then her grey helmet didn't appear to have been touched by it. Riley followed after her, then Mercy, then Hafsa, who was wearing a coral-coloured jumpsuit, looking like she'd stepped off a catwalk, rather than from a GP surgery in Lewisham.

Riley peered at Adam's T-shirt. 'My grandad loved the Pixies.'

'Way to make me feel old,' he said. He glanced down at his chest, as if surprised to find the picture there. 'Ah, I didn't think about the graphic when I put this on this morning. Hope I'm not offending anyone.'

Joe leaned forwards and examined Adam's chest. 'Goodness,' he said. 'My late wife, Nuala, would have had something to say about that.'

'She'd have sent you home to change,' said Erin, silently acknowledging that her theory of him not giving a damn had been disproved. She recalled Nuala's fierce temperament, her views as fiery as her flame-red hair. She'd been a primary school teacher, and instilled feminism in her young charges decades before it became accepted. 'Anything that could be interpreted as exploiting women, and you'd know about it.'

Adam tugged the T-shirt out to examine the picture. 'She looks quite happy.'

Joe shook his head. 'Rooky error, son. You're seeing it through the male gaze. Think of the people behind that shoot. The man behind the camera, whoever decided the woman should be topless, all the unreconstructed men who are viewing her as just a body.' Erin glowed with pride. Adam might be oblivious to everyday sexism, but her seventy-five-year-old pal wasn't. She'd be eternally grateful to have been brought up around people as open-minded and thoughtful as her parents and their friends.

'Okay, I hear you, but . . . it's the Pixies. It's punk pop. I'd be very surprised if the women in the band weren't on board.' He turned to Riley. 'Help me out, here.'

Riley smiled. 'It's a nice shirt. I like it.'

'Anyway,' said Susan, slapping her hands on her thighs. 'Enough about breasts on chests. Let's decide on our next book. Who's got a suggestion?'

'I have,' said Riley. 'Chegs says I should read more classics.'

'Does he?' Erin crossed her arms, watching as Riley took a battered copy of *Great Expectations* out of her bag. 'Is he well read himself?' As far as Erin was aware,

Chegs worked in finance, not publishing. What a kind-hearted, empathetic spoken word performer like Riley was doing with a city trader was beyond her. She had the feeling Chegs was indulging his wayward side before ultimately settling down with a woman who wore her shirt collar up and a pastel jersey over her shoulders. Riley deserved better. Erin hoped she understood the subtext behind her questions, because her silent rule meant she couldn't offer advice or criticism without being asked.

'He says he is.' That did nothing to dispel Erin's suspicions. Neither did the frown that appeared on Riley's face, which suggested she was trying to think of a time she'd seen her smug twat of a boyfriend actually open a book. Or maybe that was Erin's imagination. 'Has anyone read this?' Riley showed the faded brown cover with figures in waistcoats and skull caps. Wasn't it about a woman who was jilted at the altar? The cover gave no indication of that.

'I read it years ago,' said Susan. 'I wouldn't mind a reread.'

'Let's hear the last page,' said Erin.

'Surely you don't need to hear the last page of *Great Expectations*?' said Adam. 'Everybody knows what it's about.'

Erin bristled. 'It's what we do.'

'But . . .' He raised his palms. 'It's Dickens. You either want to read it, or you don't.'

'He makes a fair point,' said Susan. 'Any idiot knows the premise.'

Erin scowled at her. It was bad enough that this man was coming in and upending things, without one of her own going rogue. 'We are called The Last Page Book Group for a reason,' she said. 'I'd rather follow protocol and keep things as they are, if that's okay with you?' She felt she had to add the question out of politeness.

'Protocol?' said Adam, with a tip of his head.

He wore a smile that could be described as flirtatious, but Erin wasn't going to concede her position just because he made her insides flutter. 'Yes. I thought you understood—'

'There's no harm in it, is there?' interrupted Hafsa, diplomatically.

'Is that true, though?' said Adam. 'Surely it interferes with your enjoyment of the book, if you already know the final outcome?'

'Not mine,' said Erin. 'It gives me a sense of calm. I like to know what's coming.'

'I just don't get it,' he said, scratching the stubble underneath his chin.

'We explained last week,' said Erin, her exasperation showing in her voice. 'I know it's not for everyone. If you want—'

'No, no, it's fine.' He raised his hand in a placatory gesture. 'It's good, actually. I'm always up for trying something new.' He directed the last comment at her, and Erin was sure she saw a hint of playfulness in his eyes that was as annoying as it was appealing. But as he sat back in his chair and crossed his legs, she reminded herself why it wasn't a good idea to develop feelings for this charming man. First off, she'd been taken in by good looks before. She wouldn't allow herself to make that mistake again. Plus, they were from completely different worlds. He was a travel writer and adventurer extraordinaire. She was a single mother with responsibilities, and a business that was three short months away from financial ruin.

He clearly had no idea what it was like when you had to know what was around the corner, or you were consumed by panic. She couldn't afford to be so gung-ho. There was no safe way of predicting the outcome of a relationship, so the best thing to do was avoid it altogether. She would put a spike in any feelings she had for him and preserve what she already knew made her feel safe: her solid, predictable book group. She took a breath before saying, 'Riley, will you please read out the last page?'

Chapter Seven

Riley flipped to the back of *Great Expectations*, but instead of beginning to read, she turned the pages, frowning.

'What's up?' said Joe.

'There's a long appendix at the back,' she said. 'But this bit's interesting. It says Dickens changed the ending.'

'Changed the ending?' Erin found the concept absurd. Things ended the way they ended. They weren't meant to be chopped about after the fact. Where was the certainty in that? 'What do you mean?'

Riley glanced up. 'Shall I read what it says?'

'Go on,' said Hafsa.

'It says, "Dickens, at the last moment, changed his original ending. His friend, Edward Bulwer-Lytton the novelist, pleaded with him to unite Pip with Estella."'

'Goodness,' said Susan. 'It would have been a very different ending if they really had gone their separate ways for good. I don't think I would have liked that at all.'

Riley continued, 'Dickens said, "I have put in as pretty a little piece of writing as I could, and have no doubt the story will be more acceptable through the alteration."' She blew out her cheeks. 'That's messing with my head a bit. This is such a well-known book, it's become bigger than the writer, do you know what I mean? I suppose I always thought all books come out fully formed, especially well-known ones like this. It feels like it was always meant to be this way and now we're hearing there were alternative endings. Mad. Obviously I know a bit about Dickens, I went to that Dickens museum in Kent with school, but I never really thought about him writing the words on the page, making the decisions about what happens to the characters. That's fucked with my tiny mind.'

'But surely you edit what you write for your performances? You don't resolutely stick to the first draft, do you?' said Susan.

'Yeah, I do. It would be a pile of shite if I didn't.' She wobbled her head. 'It might still be a pile of shite afterwards, to be fair, who am I to judge?'

'It's not,' said Erin. She might not like the way the conversation was going, but she wouldn't let her talented friend denigrate her own skills.

'Thanks.' Riley slapped her hands on her thighs. 'I never thought of someone like Dickens going through the process, you know? It's like imagining Shakespeare crossing out words and changing characters' names and things like that. Imagine if Cleopatra was called Sharon in the first draft.'

'Well, that was never going to happen, since Cleopatra

was the actual Queen of Egypt, not Sharon,' said Susan, haughtily.

'Whatever. You get my point, though.'

'Yep,' said Adam, looking a bit too pleased with himself in Erin's opinion. 'So, what I think we can take away from this is that reading the last page doesn't necessarily tell you the whole story.'

Erin resisted the urge to close her eyes and sigh. The last thing she needed was for him to think he was right about reading the last page first being a terrible idea. 'Back to *Great Expectations*. I'm just glad Dickens went with the ending that would be most satisfying for the reader.'

'That's worth a discussion in itself,' said Susan. 'Rewriting endings is a fascinating subject, don't you think? I wonder how many authors do that before the book goes to print.'

'I bet loads of them do,' said Mercy. 'It happens a lot when books get made into films, doesn't it? I can't tell you the shock I got when I watched *My Sister's Keeper.* The new ending changed the whole trajectory of the story. I sat there blinking, thinking I must've misremembered the book, before I looked it up and found out they'd intentionally changed it.'

'I like the idea that it's not set in stone,' said Susan. 'Imagine if life was like that, if we could write our own endings and change them, if we got one we didn't like?'

'What would you like your last page to be?' said Hafsa.

Susan narrowed her eyes. 'What an interesting question. I'd have to give it some thought.'

Riley bounced in her seat, her eyes bright. 'Top idea! Let's do it. Let's all write our own endings.'

'I'm not sure I want to commit my death to paper,' said Erin, grumpily. She wanted to get on with choosing a book. All this pontificating was ruining the usual rhythm of the group. 'It's too morbid for my tastes.'

'I don't mean how we die,' said Riley. 'I mean our happy ever after, kind of thing. You know, how you'd like the story of your life to turn out, or where you'd like your life to go if you were the author of it . . . which I suppose we all are, if you think about it.' She surveyed the group. 'Am I making sense?'

'Like, what would happen if all my dreams come true?' said Hafsa.

'Kind of,' said Riley. 'But not like a fairytale. More like what would you change in your real life to give you the most satisfying next chapters.'

'I know what mine would be,' said Mercy, her cheeks rounding as she grinned. 'I'd be on a Caribbean island, sipping a pina colada.' She held a finger aloft. 'No, wait. I'd be at a show on Broadway.' She gritted her teeth, 'Or in Greenland watching the Northern Lights. Gah. I don't know which to choose.' She chuckled and squished her cheeks between her palms.

'You could choose all of them,' said Joe. 'It's your story. Why limit yourself?'

'Ha. Good point. I have fanciful ideas for a woman who's never left the country, don't I?'

'I still find that hard to believe,' said Adam, his brow ridged.

'It's true. I got a passport when I retired, but I've never used it.'

Erin watched Adam's face for any sign of judgement, but he just appeared aghast. 'What would constitute a good ending for you?' She faced him, hoping she'd managed to keep the challenge out of her voice.

He raised his head and scratched under his chin. 'I don't know, really.' He turned to Riley. 'What about you?' He spoke quickly, and Erin got the distinct impression he didn't want to answer the question. Typical journalist, wanting to get everyone else to share their stories while keeping his own close to his chest.

'Mine's easy,' she said, dipping her chin coyly. 'I want to headline a big show.'

'A show?'

'Riley's a spoken word performer,' said Erin. 'She's very good.'

'She's big on TikTok,' said Joe, nodding. 'Whatever that means.'

'You know very well what that means,' said Riley, leaning over and tapping Joe on the knee as he chuckled. Tybalt opened his amber eyes and viewed them both with apparent disdain at being disturbed, before closing them again. 'Don't you pretend you're some old duffer who's behind the times.' She turned back to Adam.

'And I'm afraid big is an exaggeration. I've got a good following, but not enough to be booked for the kind of gigs I dream about.'

'A fellow writer. I'll look you up,' said Adam, appearing suitably impressed.

'What about you, Joe?' Hafsa said. 'What would you write?'

The smile dropped from his face. 'I'm not sure I should say.'

'You're not harbouring secret desires that would shock us to our core, are you?' said Adam, winking at Joe.

'Are you sure you don't work for the tabloids?' said Susan, eyeing Adam suspiciously.

'Promise,' said Adam. 'I'm just a nosey sod.'

Joe laughed, then his blue eyes misted. 'No, nothing that interesting. I'm worried about being disloyal to my Nuala, I suppose.'

'You could never be disloyal to her, Joe.' In her mind's eye, Erin saw Joe at Nuala's bedside when the cancer turned her into a fragile bird. She saw the love in his eyes and remembered the care he gave her until her last breath.

'I don't know,' he said. 'It feels wrong to say it, but I've recently been thinking how nice it would be to have some company in my dotage. Someone to share things with. No one could replace Nuala. She was a one-off. But the last five years have been long and sometimes the loneliness . . .' He trailed off, shifting the cat to one side so he could take a tissue from the pocket of his trousers and blow his nose.

Erin reached out and squeezed his shoulder. 'I think Nuala would want you to have company,' she said softly. 'She'd want what's best for you because she loved you. It's not disloyal, Joe.'

He put his hand over hers and smiled sadly. 'What about you, my girl? How does your story end?'

Erin tensed. She'd been hoping she would get away without anyone asking her. Now that the future of her café looked bleak, she didn't have the first clue how her life would turn out, and that scared her to death. 'I'll have to give that some thought,' she said briskly, then stood, needing to get away from the expectant gaze of her friends. 'Anyone for another drink?'

Chapter Eight

Erin hoped the group would have moved on from discussing the end of their own stories by the time she came back with the tray of hot drinks, but she was disappointed to find they were still in full flow. She distributed the steaming cups, catching Adam's eye as she put down the decaf black coffee he'd asked for. She fought against her body's reaction to the warmth in his gaze. If he thought he could win her around so easily, he was wrong.

Hafsa was speaking, 'I'm loath to say it, but I'm beginning to think my ending might be different to the one I always thought I wanted. I'm wondering if it was even my dream in the first place. My parents were doctors and it was always more of a "when you go into medicine" than an "if", and I didn't mind. I went along with it, and all the time I was growing up I imagined being a doctor would be really fulfilling. And it has been, for the most part. But it's changed beyond recognition in the time I've been a GP. I hardly ever see the same patient twice, and the workload is unmanageable. Sometimes it doesn't feel like I'm part of a caring profession anymore.

It's a numbers game, all about targets and quantifiable outcomes instead of individual care. I want to get back to believing I'm making a difference. I miss that feeling of doing something that makes people's lives better.'

She smoothed out a crease in the leg of her jumpsuit. 'I've never really admitted this, even to myself, but I'm not sure I want my story to end with a protagonist who's burned out and cynical, and that's the way I see it going if I carry on the way I am now.'

'I'm sorry you feel like that,' said Joe. 'I can only imagine what it took to get through all those years of training. I'm sure many, many people are incredibly grateful for the care you've given them.'

'Thanks, Joe.'

'Do you have any ideas for what your next pages might look like in an ideal world?' said Susan, her voice softer than usual.

'It's something I'd like to give some thought to,' said Hafsa. 'This exercise could be the push I need to think about making changes.'

Those words sent a shudder through Erin. She didn't like change. Change was never good in her experience. But at the same time, she didn't want to be the one to block a suggestion that Hafsa thought could be useful to her. To avoid the others noticing her unease, she went over to the record player and lifted the arm from the Miles Davis LP, and put it back in its sleeve. She took *A Love Supreme* by John Coltrane from the pile. She wanted something familiar and calming. She blew dust from the vinyl, then placed it on the turntable and lowered the arm. When she turned back to the group, Joe was smiling at her, and she knew he approved of her choice. 'Have we settled on *Great Expectations* for our next read, then?' she asked, seizing a brief gap in the conversation.

'I'm not sure about this one now,' said Riley, dropping the thick book on the table. 'If we're on the theme of reinvention, maybe we should choose a book based on that.'

'Good idea,' said Mercy. 'I'm going through my internal library system now.' She put her finger on her chin and tapped, her eyes trained on the print above the fireplace of the woman reading. The others sat in silence, watching as she hummed quietly. Being a librarian meant she'd worked with an inordinate amount of books, and coupled with her freakishly impressive memory, she could be relied upon to pick the perfect book for any occasion. The others didn't always agree with her choices, but they had to admit her recall was impressive.

After a minute, she nodded to herself. 'Okay, what about *Little Fires Everywhere* by Celeste Ng? It's a great story.'

'I loved that one,' said Riley.

'Me too,' said Susan. 'It's about letting go and moving forwards, so it fits, but since three of us have already read it, do you have any others in your memory bank?'

'Naturally, I do. *Small Pleasures* by Clare Chambers would be good.'

'Have you read that one?' asked Erin. Mercy smiled and raised her hands. Erin shook her head. 'You've read everything.'

'It's definitely worth a reread,' said Mercy. 'It's set in Southeast London, and I always like a local book.' She rolled her bottom lip over her teeth and focused on Erin. 'We should probably read the last page first, though. The ending is . . . it's emotional. It's based on a real-life event from the fifties.'

Riley stood and crossed to the wall of books, her hands in the back pockets of her low-slung baggy jeans as she perused the spines. 'Is there a copy here?' She turned back to the group. 'Someone search it up and show me the cover.' Tybalt hopped off Joe's knee and joined Riley, staring up at the wall of books as though attempting to help, before rubbing against Riley's shins then winding through her legs.

Adam took out his phone and tapped the screen. 'It's got big oranges with green stalks on a bluey green background.' He turned the screen out to the room, then Erin and Susan joined Riley in the search.

'Bingo,' said Erin, pulling the book out from the third shelf up. 'I can't believe I haven't noticed this before.'

They all returned to their seats, the cat choosing Adam's lap to sit on this time. Erin realized that she'd always considered Tybalt a good judge of character. Whenever he was in the café, if he wasn't busy tormenting visiting dogs, he gravitated towards the people she herself liked best. Now he'd chosen Adam and she couldn't help thinking that was an endorsement. She gave her head a shake. Was she seriously taking where a cat chose to sit as a reason to drop her guard? Ridiculous. 'Shall I read out the last page?'

'Just a sec,' said Susan. 'Can we clarify what we're doing about this writing exercise first?'

'Obviously, you do you, but I think I'll stick to the reading.' Erin sank back into her chair, disappointed the conversation had returned to this. 'We're a book group, not a writing group.' With a combination of guilt and relief at having spoken out against the initiative, she relaxed back in the sagging leather.

'I know. We could combine the two by picking books to go alongside what we're writing.' Hafsa clasped her hands together and turned her gaze on Mercy. 'You could find the perfect travel books that represent your dream to see the world.' She turned to Joe. 'There's loads of novels about love and companionship after loss, aren't there?'

'Are there?' said Joe. 'Righto.' He grinned. 'It's a long time since I've gone home with two sets of homework. Three if you include reading *Small Pleasures*. It's going to be a busy week.'

Erin stiffened. This wasn't the outcome she'd hoped for. 'I'm not sure I've got time for all this,' she said, swirling the last of her tea around in the bottom of her cup. 'Not with having this place to run, and now Jack's back . . .' She lifted the cup to her mouth and let the cold liquid roll onto her tongue. It wasn't fair to use Jack as an excuse.

Other than rarely wiping down the kitchen surfaces when he spilled things, he didn't create much extra work. Living away from home had made him more self-sufficient than Erin anticipated. If she was honest with herself, she quite missed him needing her in the way he did when he was younger. She'd been looking forward to having her boy home, but he was now a man, who had his own life, and was fully competent in the workings of the washing machine. He'd even asked her if she had anything that needed washing when he put a load on last night.

'I can do extra shifts if you need me,' said Riley, hopefully.

'Thanks,' said Erin, her stomach turning over at the thought of having to tell her one day soon that her job no longer existed. She resolved to share the news as soon as Jack was settled. 'But I'm not sure writing's my thing.'

'You won't know until you try, will you?' said Joe. 'If this old dog can give it a go, you can, surely?'

'Yes, go on,' said Hafsa. 'Learning new skills is good for the brain, and it will be more fun if we're all in it together.'

Unless she wanted to look like a curmudgeon, Erin had no choice but to agree. She put her cup down on the table, keeping her eyes on the intricate gold pattern on its rim. The gilt was fading. She should stop putting that set in the dishwasher or the pattern would be lost forever. Why did things have to change and spoil? Why couldn't everything just stay the same? 'Okay. I'll try, but I can't promise anything.'

'Yay,' said Riley, doing a little victory wiggle in her chair. 'Shall we all try to bring in our last chapters in a month's time? That should give us long enough, right? And what about bringing in a relevant novel whenever you find one, to keep it about the books? We could do that instead of choosing one we all read.'

Erin thought forward to a month's time and her skin pricked with fear.

'Works for me,' said Susan, patting her hair. 'I'm quite looking forward to the challenge.'

'Me too,' said Joe.

'Just for this month, though,' said Erin. 'We'll get back to normal at the start of July.'

'Deal,' said Riley. 'Cool.'

Erin tucked her hands under her thighs to stop herself squirming in her seat. She was even losing control of the book group which, up until last week, had been a stable and predictable part of her life. Things had changed when Adam arrived, and she blamed him for the disruption. She turned to glower at him, but when she looked his way, she was surprised to note that he was staring down at his hands, which were clenched tight in his lap. He appeared to be as uncomfortable with the plans as she was.

Chapter Nine

The unmistakable smell of frying onions and garlic greeted Erin when she arrived home that evening. She hung her bag and coat on the hook in the hall and went through to the kitchen, where Jack was stirring the contents of a large frying pan. 'Something smells good.'

'I'm making a veggie chilli,' Jack said. 'Thought you might like someone else to cook for you after feeding the masses all day.'

'Lovely.' Erin squeezed past Jack and opened the fridge. She grabbed a bottle of beer and held it aloft. Jack nodded, so she took two out, and shimmied past him again to the drawer with the bottle opener. The kitchen wasn't built for two adults to use simultaneously. Funny how big and empty the flat had seemed over the last three years, and now it felt tiny and cramped. 'Not that the masses have been flocking to the café in their droves. I wish they would.'

Jack took the bottle she offered and clinked the bottom of it against hers, before taking a swig. He put it down and glanced at her. 'Quiet day?'

'No more than usual. The regulars were . . . regular, at least.'

'Was Zita in?' He grinned.

'Yep. The sugar bowl was predictably empty when she shuffled off home. I'm surprised that woman has any teeth left. She'd be able to make six Victoria sponges a week with the amount of sugar she pinches from me.'

'Unless she's stealing it to sell it on,' said Jack, tipping a can of chopped tomatoes into the pan. 'Or maybe she uses it to feed her stable of champion racehorses.'

'Ha! I wouldn't put it past her.' Erin imagined the old lady holding out a handful of sugar to a whinnying thoroughbred. 'I should ask her for a cut of her winnings, or at least a good tip. Every little helps.'

Jack stopped stirring and turned to her. 'Are things not going well?'

Erin could have kicked herself. No matter how anxious she was about the future of the café, the last thing she wanted was to bring Jack to her worry party. 'Ignore me, I'm being a grouch. Book group was weird this evening.'

'Weird how?'

'Riley came up with this idea of us all writing our own last pages, the last chapter of our lives if we got the ending we wanted, or our next chapter, or something.' She couldn't exactly remember the criteria they'd settled on, but she did know that she was already being forced to focus on the future more than she would like.

'Deep,' said Jack, sprinkling chilli flakes over the simmering dish and folding them in.

'I know, right? I mean, who knows how their life is going to turn out?' The chilli hit the back of her nostrils and she coughed.

'But you can dream, can't you?'

'I suppose so.' Her dream was that everything would stay the same, but that was looking less and less likely. She took a drink, the cold, crisp liquid soothing the sting of the spice. 'What would your perfect last chapter be?'

'God, don't ask me,' said Jack. 'I'm stressed enough about what's coming in the next few weeks. If I look further ahead than that, I might go to bed and never get up again.'

'Oh, love, don't say that.' She wished she'd never brought up the stupid idea. 'You don't need to worry. Everything will work out.' She was a hypocrite and she knew it. Saying don't worry was about as useful as saying don't breathe, in her experience.

Jack looked about as convinced by her words as she was. 'I was hoping I could do some shifts at The Bookmark while I'm job hunting. That work for you?'

'Oh, right, yes, of course.' She couldn't say no without giving him a good reason, and he clearly didn't need another cause for worry. As soon as he secured something permanent, she'd tell him and everyone else what was going on. She might even have come up with a solution by then. The churning in her abdomen told her that was a fantasy, but if the café was going down anyway, what difference would Jack working there for the last weeks really make? She'd always worked at the café during her university holidays, and it had been a natural progression to take over when her mother became too frail to run the place ten years ago, but it was a thriving, profitable business back then. Jack had always preferred to work part-time in local pubs before, where there was more of a buzz. She'd presumed that was what he'd do to tide himself over now. Apparently not. 'You sure you don't want to work at The Crown again, or The Hare and Billet?'

'Don't you want me cramping your style?'

'Don't be daft. I thought you'd prefer to spend time with people your own age, that's all.'

'I'm catching Riley up,' he said. 'And I feel like working at the café would look better on my CV. Bar work is all right, but every student's done that. Unless I'm completely incompetent, I was hoping I could say I was the assistant manager of The Bookmark or something, if you ever trust me to run things on my own.'

'You've got it all worked out, haven't you?'

Jack shook his head. 'I haven't,' he said. 'I really, really haven't.'

Neither had she, but she didn't want to tell him that. She would let the new state of affairs sink in over the next few weeks, and try to come up with a plan for the future while Jack concentrated on finding himself a graduate position. She still had Riley to consider, though, so she gave herself a deadline. If Jack hadn't got a full-time job in four weeks and she hadn't managed to find a solution, she would share the grim news. If The Bookmark really did have to close, Riley and Jack would still have two months to find work elsewhere. As would she, she reminded herself, as terror mixed with grief threatened to swallow her whole.

***

The next morning Erin and Jack left the house together at six-thirty, and made their way down to Blackheath village. A mist hung over the heath to their left and there was a nip in the air, which Erin knew wouldn't last when the early June sunshine worked its magic. The weather was meant to be glorious for the rest of the week, and she hoped that would bring more tourists into the café.

'I've missed this view,' said Jack, scanning the vivid green ahead of him. The spire of All Saints Church reached majestically into the cloudless sky. Built from pale Kentish ragstone, Erin always thought it looked like the model of a perfect English church plonked in the middle of the heath. It could just be seen from the doorway of The Bookmark, and when there was a particularly pretty sunset, she would find herself drawn outside to marvel at the beautiful building against nature's spectacular backdrop.

'I'm not surprised,' she said. 'Bit different to Birmingham, isn't it?'

'Don't knock Birmingham,' said Jack. 'It might not be as pretty as this, but it's got its attractions.'

'Oh, yeah?' said Erin, glancing both ways before crossing Royal Parade and making her way past Buenos Aires Café, then turning right into Brigade Street. 'I thought you were a Londoner through and through.' In truth, that was one of the things she found reassuring; even though Jack went away to study, she always thought he would return, and when he did, he would stay.

'I am,' he said. There was a wistfulness in his voice that made her turn to look at him. 'But I might have to go where the work is.' He followed behind as she unlocked the door and clicked the fob on her keyring to turn off the beeping alarm. 'Beggars can't be choosers.'

'You'll find something in London,' said Erin. 'I'm sure you will.' She marched through to the kitchen, not wanting her son to see the worry on her face. Now the café was slipping from her grasp, she couldn't think about her son moving away again too, however much they both needed him to be in full-time work. It felt like she was losing everything she held dear, and it was all she could do not to drop to her knees and beg the universe not to make the changes she feared were coming her way.

Chapter Ten

'Morning.'

Erin turned from where she was leaning over to wipe down a low pewter-topped table, to see Adam standing in the middle of the room, a wide smile on his face. She blushed, convinced his grin was partly because he'd caught her with her rear end pointing skyward. She straightened up and tugged down her navy-blue polo shirt with The Bookmark's logo emblazoned on the breast pocket. 'Hi.'

'Okay if I sit anywhere?' He gestured out to the room, where only two of the tables were occupied.

'Yes, wherever you like, although I'd avoid Kiddies Corner. I'm expecting a few mums and babies to descend any minute. You here for breakfast?'

'Yep. I thought I'd work here this morning, if that's okay?' He raised his eyebrows.

'As long as you keep eating and drinking, the table's yours.' She felt bad setting out her terms, but he needed to know that if he was still there at lunchtime, she might need the space for paying customers, unless he was one himself. She'd never run the café like that, and hated doing it now.

That wasn't entirely true. She was happy when people like Zita or the baby groups hung out long after their drinks were finished, but a number of people had taken advantage of the space and free Wi-Fi over the years and that felt different. One woman started to regularly hold business meetings over Zoom, her voice loud and clipped, while other tinny voices came through her computer's speakers. Erin let it go on for a few weeks until other customers started to complain. She hated conflict, and her discomfort wasn't helped by the fact the woman didn't seem to see why her behaviour was a problem. She argued that other people were holding conversations, and hers were no different. She begrudgingly agreed to use headphones, but that only served to make her speak even more loudly. In the end, Erin resorted to switching the Wi-Fi off and pretending it was beyond her control the woman's meetings kept being interrupted. She stopped coming in after the connection proved unreliable.

'Understood,' he said, saluting.

'Black coffee?'

'No, I'll have an oat milk latte, please,' he said. 'I'm switching it up this morning.'

Typical, thought Erin. That man wasn't happy until he was trying something different. 'Coming right up. The breakfast menus are on the table.'

In her peripheral vision she saw Tybalt drop to his haunches and creep towards a fluffy Pomeranian who was snoozing by its owner's feet. Erin bounded forwards, just as the cat reached its extended claws towards the dog's tail. She scooped Tybalt up and deposited him on a free armchair, wagging her finger at him before making her way back to the kitchen. As she did so, she made a bet inside her head that Adam would go for a full English. She could already tell he was the type to ask for extra black pudding.

'Could you take the order from the man by the window?' she said to Jack, five minutes later.

Jack raised his eyes from the pan of beans he was pouring over buttery toast. 'Okay, but I thought you said I was on kitchen duties and you were front of house until I'd got the hang of things?'

She took the pan handle from him and nudged him out of the way with her hip. 'Yes, but that's Adam from book group, and I'm not in the mood to chat.'

Jack poked his head out of the kitchen and scanned the room. 'The fella with the biker jacket?'

Erin batted him on the arm. 'Don't make it obvious.'

'Don't you like him, then? He looks all right.'

Erin glanced towards where Adam was shrugging off his jacket, revealing another band T-shirt, The Police this time. His shoulders were broad and his biceps firmer than she'd expected. It occurred to her that she shouldn't have anticipated anything about his physique. She wasn't in the habit of noticing if a customer's arms were more muscular than average. This man was endlessly disruptive. 'He's fine, but I don't want to get into a conversation about that writing exercise.'

'Why not?'

'Could you just make him an oat milk latte and take his order, please?' She couldn't hide her exasperation.

'All right, keep your hair on.'

After a while, Erin peeked out from the kitchen to see what was holding Jack up. He was standing by Adam's chair, slouched back on one hip, as the two of them chatted. Jack clearly had no idea how important it was to keep moving in a busy café. Not that it was busy, at that point. She'd delivered the mushroom omelette and beans on toast for the only other people who'd ordered food in the last half an hour, and there were only two other occupied tables in the whole café. That wasn't the point, though. If Jack was going to work there regularly, he needed to speed up.

She decided to put two sausages in the frying pan in anticipation of Adam's order. The delicious smell made her stomach growl. It was hard to resist the high-calorie food she had to make sometimes. She bet Adam didn't have that problem. It was so unfair middle-aged women stored more fat than men of the same age. She was glad of another thing to hold against him. He had no idea how fortunate he was, with his high muscle density and fast metabolism. She was just about to add the bacon to the pan when Jack returned to the kitchen. 'You took your time,' she said.

'He's an interesting man,' said Jack. 'He's writing a piece on what's changed in the Lebanon in the thirty-five years since Terry Waite was released.' Erin vividly remembered her mother crying with relief when she heard the news that the humanitarian, who lived in Blackheath and worked at All Saints Church, had been freed after five years in detention. She'd taken Erin to witness the candle the church's reverend kept lit for the entire time, and they'd rejoiced at the sound of the church bells ringing in celebration at the gentle giant's release.

'Is he now?' Erin lay a rasher of bacon beside the sausages, pulling her hand back from the sizzling fat. 'Does he want black pudding with his fry-up?'

Jack's brow furrowed. 'He ordered avocado on toast.'

Erin turned to Jack. 'Did he?'

'Does he usually have a full English?'

'He hasn't been in for breakfast before, I assumed . . .' She trailed off, watching the bacon fat brown in the pan. She'd wasted good food – food she'd already paid for.

'Interesting,' said Jack, slowly. 'You thought that, because he's a taller than average middle-aged man he would want a fry-up.'

'No . . . well yes, but only because I've got years of experience of feeding middle-aged men.' She gazed forlornly at the contents of the pan. 'Do you want this?' At least if Jack ate it, the expense wouldn't be for nothing.

'Yes please,' Jack said with relish. 'Don't mind if I do. Why don't you finish making that, and I'll smash the avo for your man's actual order?'

Erin poked at the sausages, disgruntled about being wrong, and blaming Adam for it, as Jack took an avocado from the enormous fridge, then cut a thick slice of sourdough for toasting. 'I suppose the writing exercise will be simple for him,' she mused, 'since that's how he makes a living.'

'I asked him about that,' said Jack. He turned the labels of the spices in the rack to face him until he found the chilli flakes. 'He said he hadn't had a chance to think about it yet.'

Erin remembered the uncomfortable expression on Adam's face yesterday evening and wondered why he wouldn't relish the idea of writing his last pages. He was a writer by trade, and he embraced change and wasn't afraid of risk as far as she could tell. His motive for not wanting to write his own ending couldn't be anything like hers. She finished cooking the sausages and bacon at the same time Jack added a light drizzle of balsamic glaze to Adam's breakfast.

'Thanks,' Jack said, handing her the plate, and taking the sausages and bacon from her. She wanted to protest and ask him to take Adam's meal out to him, but he'd already bitten the end off a sausage and was chewing and waving a hand in front of his face, as if his mouth was on fire.

She tutted, slapped on a convivial expression, and delivered the plate to Adam, who greeted her with the same warm smile as before. 'That looks great, thank you.'

'You're welcome.' She swivelled to go back to the kitchen.

'Erin?'

'Yes.' She turned back.

'I hope this isn't an impertinent question, but how old are you?'

Erin tucked her chin into her neck, then realized that gave her a double chin and released it immediately. 'Why?'

'Sorry, it's just that I'm writing this piece about Terry Waite and wanted to talk to someone who remembered how people who lived around here felt when he was taken captive.'

'Oh, right.' Not such an odd question, then. 'I was . . .' She did the calculations in her head. 'About fifteen when he was taken, so around twenty when he came home.' Why didn't she tell him she was fifty-four? She wasn't ashamed of her age. Her mother had drummed it into her that ageing was a privilege not everyone got to enjoy.

'You're my woman, then. I take it you lived here around that time?'

'Blackheath born and bred.'

'Maybe I could take you for a coffee sometime, in return for picking your brains?' He glanced around the room. 'Although that might sound like a busman's holiday to you. A walk in Greenwich Park, maybe? Let's swap numbers. I'll message you when I know my schedule.'

Heat crept up her neck and the treachery of her own body made her furious. She wasn't a teenager. She should be able to talk to someone of the opposite sex without going red. 'Okay,' she said. She recited her phone number and he put it in his phone.

'I'll message you now, so you've got mine.'

Erin's phone buzzed in her pocket. 'Let me know when, and I'll make sure I'm not on shift.' Before he could answer, she turned and strode back to the kitchen.

'You look hot and bothered,' said Jack, dipping the last of the sausage into a dollop of ketchup, then shoving it in his mouth.

'It's warm in here,' said Erin.

'Is it?' He peeked past her at Adam. 'Were you two discussing your last pages?'

'No, he was asking me to help with the piece he's writing, actually.' She didn't know why she sounded so defensive. She had nothing to hide. 'We're going to go for a walk in the park to discuss it.'

'Are you now?' Jack grinned, the pulped sausage bulging in his cheek.

'I don't know what you're implying,' she said, 'but it's purely about his work.' Her face was irritatingly warm. 'And wipe that ketchup off your moustache before you go back out there.'

'Okay,' said Jack, his voice an octave higher than usual. He scrubbed at the hair above his lip with a piece of kitchen roll.

To Erin's relief, the café's door rattled open. 'Now stop being an idiot, finish that mouthful and go and earn your keep.'

'Whatever you say, boss,' said Jack, his lips still

twitching with a smile that told her she was protesting too much. 'Whatever you say.'

Only one table was occupied by 4 p.m., and the couple seated there were far too busy staring into each other's eyes over half-finished cups of tea to need two members of staff to serve them, so Erin told Jack he could go home early.

'Why don't you go?' said Jack. 'I can finish up.'

'No, it's fine. I'm breaking you in gently,' she said. 'Before the summer rush.' What was she doing, pretending she anticipated a massive surge in business? Having her head in the sand was one thing, but she shouldn't be blatantly lying to her son. They both looked across the empty room, and she wondered if Jack was thinking the same as her, that a summer rush was as likely as the couple at the table suddenly realizing they were ravenous and ordering everything on the menu. Maybe he could sense the café was nearing its end too. She hoped not. One of them riddled with worry was quite enough.

'Okay, if you're sure. See you at home.'

Erin took a seat in her favourite chair, but instead of picking up her book, she opened the search engine on her phone and typed in Adam's name. There were an astonishing number of results. He'd had bylines in every major British newspaper and several glossy magazines as well as more niche travel publications.

She turned her phone to show the cat, who seemed to have become a permanent fixture in the café since the gift shop closed. 'Look at how impressive our new friend is,' she said. Tybalt mewed as if he agreed with her, which made her smile. She tapped on a piece Adam had written for the *Guardian* about sustainability in the travel industry. 'Hot and socially conscious.' She gave Tybalt a firm stare. 'Don't tell anyone I said that first bit.' He responded by twisting and licking his bottom, which made Erin feel oddly judged. Turning back to her phone, she used her thumb and forefinger to enlarge the photo by Adam's name. She felt a trill of excitement that he'd asked her to help with a piece he was writing. The excitement was about the journalistic endeavour, she told herself, nothing to do with the handsome face of the man on the screen of her phone. Nothing at all.

Chapter Eleven

During the following week, Erin scrutinised the café's profit and loss spreadsheets, in a desperate attempt to see if she could avoid the inevitable and salvage her business. When she wasn't worrying about the finances or Jack, her mind always seemed to wander back to Adam. She anticipated him making a firm date for their walk in Greenwich Park, but even though he came in a couple of times for breakfast, he didn't repeat the suggestion.

As she scoured the wall of books for something to suit her mood at the start of her shift on Wednesday, she found herself wondering how long it could possibly take to write one article, and whether he'd found someone more qualified to help. That would be disappointing. He could at least have told her if that were the case. Why did he bother asking if he wasn't going to follow it up? She knew she shouldn't have allowed herself to be impressed by him. Just because he was a big-shot journalist, it didn't mean he was reliable or considerate.

Circe by Madeline Miller caught her eye. There was a woman who was not taking any more crap from men. She plucked it out and stared at the Grecian-style illustration of the mythical woman on the front cover, wishing she had the power to turn men into swine like *Circe* did. She indulged in a little fantasy of her ex-husband snuffling around a pen, pink and fat, read the last page, then dropped the book on the nearest table, hoping someone would pick it up and want a chat about it at some point during the day. Marching back to where Jack was cleaning the microwave in the kitchen, she decided that if Adam didn't mention the article at book group that evening, she would bring it up herself.

Riley was on shift that afternoon, and bowled in as the lunchtime rush ended, her eyes glistening with excitement. 'Ren's reposted my last video,' she said, her voice breathy. She ran a hand over her speckled scalp, where the hair had just started to grow back, as if she couldn't quite believe her own words.

'Who?' said Erin, at the same time Jack said, 'No way?'

'Show me,' said Jack, his expression almost as excited as Riley's. He pulled out a chair at the nearest empty table and Riley sat next to him, her phone in her shaking hand.

'I can't get my head around it. I mean, Ren? It's already gone viral.'

Erin stood behind the pair, keen to know what all the excitement was about. 'Who's Ren?'

'This guy.' Riley opened TikTok and clicked on a profile with a grid filled with images of a young man with a mop of dark hair, shaved at the sides, holding a guitar and leaning into a microphone. 'He's got over four million followers.'

'He's a singer, then?'

'Singer-songwriter, musician, rapper, producer, director. You name it, and he's killing it,' said Jack. 'I can't believe he's shared your post. This is epic. Come on, show me.'

Riley tapped the screen. A close-up of her beautiful face came into view. Her eyes were closed, and her lids shimmered with golden eyeshadow, below perfectly shaped brows. Her cheekbones shone with highlighter and her full lips were ruby red. As her eyes opened, the camera panned back and she began to speak, softly at first, then with more force. 'You like me, yeah, you like what you see? You want me, yeah, you think you want me?' Her hand, nails painted the same colour as her lips, rose up and Erin saw she was holding a handful of soil. 'This mask I wear, like a beauty queen, is your choice, not mine, how *you* want me to be seen.' She opened her palm and slid the soil across one cheek, then the other. 'What's behind this skin, you want painted, you prick? What's inside this mouth, you want wrapped round your—'

'Could you, erm, lower the volume a bit,' said Erin, aware customers were turning their heads. 'I mean, I like it, and I'm very glad this Ren character has shared it, but it might be a bit rich for the afternoon crowd.' She smiled apologetically at an elderly lady who was glowering over, while patting the Yorkshire terrier at her feet as if it was an ageing country vicar easily shocked by foul language. Erin had been forced to put Tybalt out after he kept tormenting the poor creature earlier, and she suspected this visit to The Bookmark might be the pair's last.

Riley paused it, her face freezing on screen in a snarl, and turned the volume down before pressing play again. Jack leaned in to hear, but Erin was content to watch the striking visuals, which showed Riley smearing the soil all over her face, then down her neck and over her clavicle.

'That's awesome,' said Jack, when the video came to an end.

'Wow,' said Erin. 'I get I'm probably not the target demographic, but that certainly got my attention.' She glanced back at the lady with the terrier, cross with herself for having been apologetic. Riley was a talented writer and performer who deserved to be heard and, from what she'd gleaned, the piece was about how what's under the skin is more important than surface beauty, and that was a message worth sharing.

'You are my audience,' said Riley. 'All women are.' She turned to Jack. 'And you, obvs. You're a feminist, right?'

'Course,' said Jack, without hesitation.

'Well, yes, I suppose I am your crowd, then,' said Erin, proud of her boy and her friend. 'Anything with a strong feminist message works for me.' She paused, then said, 'What does Chegs make of it?'

'Huh.' Riley put her phone down. 'Not much, actually. I offered to show it to him before I posted it, but he was always too busy, then when Ren shared it and it blew up, he watched it and got all sulky.'

'Why?' said Jack. His nose wrinkled above his moustache. 'It's brilliant.'

'He said people will think I'm talking about him.'

Are you? hovered at the tip of Erin's tongue. She wouldn't be surprised if Chegs was more interested in what Riley looked like than what was going on in her unique, creative brain. She was a strikingly beautiful woman, more so because she appeared to have no idea quite how stunning she was.

'I mean, way to make it all about him,' Riley continued. 'Anyone would think he didn't want me to succeed, the way he's acting. When the likes and shares started to tick up I got all excited and showed him, but he just warned me not to get too full of myself.'

'Do you think he's jealous of you getting the attention?' Erin was certain he was, but didn't feel like she could come straight out and say that.

'Oh, I hadn't thought of that.' Riley's lips drooped. 'He might feel a bit unnerved by it all, I suppose. Do you think he's worried I'll let it go to my head and change into someone else?'

Erin hadn't meant that at all. She wanted Riley to see her boyfriend didn't like not being on the top rung of the ladder, looking down on her for once.

'I'd better ring him and make sure he's okay before

I start my shift.' She lifted the phone and stood, talking into the speaker in soft tones as she went to stand outside.

'That backfired,' said Erin, making her way back to the kitchen.

'What do you mean?' Jack followed her and unhooked his hoodie from the back of the kitchen door, preparing to leave.

'From what I've seen of him, Chegs is a self-important . . . banker.' She leaned on the last word and was pleased when Jack nodded and laughed. She was tempted to tell him about the times Riley came into work with eyes red-rimmed from crying because of some insensitive thing Chegs had said or done. Erin always comforted her, keeping her counsel instead of saying what she really thought. She didn't want her friend to think she was judging, because then she might stop sharing her troubles with her. Riley didn't say much about her upbringing, but Erin gleaned that it was far from idyllic, and Erin had become a kind of substitute mum. It wasn't fair to give Jack any details. It wasn't her information to share. 'He doesn't deserve her. He should be proud of her, bigging her up, not trying to diminish her achievement or keep her humble.'

'Agreed,' said Jack. 'She can't see it, though?'

'No. She's too nice,' said Erin. 'She might be twenty-four, and have quite the potty mouth, but she's got this air of innocence about her. She has no idea how special she is.' She turned to her son and pinched his cheek. 'Bit like you.'

Jack softly batted her hand away. 'If you say so. Right, I'll get off. Those graduate jobs aren't going to find themselves.'

'Good luck,' said Erin, crossing her fingers. If Jack found the perfect job, that would be one worry off the list, at least.

'Thanks. I have a feeling I'm going to need it.'

Erin watched Jack say goodbye to Riley on his way out, wishing life was easier for them. It was hard to navigate the world when you had a tender young heart like those two. It was hard enough with fifty-four years of experience under your belt. Harder, perhaps, when responsibilities weighed heavy on your shoulders and you knew that happy ever afters were the things of fairytales.

Chapter Twelve

'Where's Tybalt?' said Joe, at book group that evening.

'He's probably sulking because I threw him out earlier when he wouldn't stop winding up a Yorkshire terrier,' said Erin.

'Do cats sulk?' said Riley.

'I doubt that little beggar does,' said Susan. 'If anything, he'll be punishing you for having the audacity to remove him from the premises. He'll probably expect a handwritten invitation in gilt lettering before he deems to come back.'

'Nah, he's not as choosy as you think,' said Erin. 'One shake of the cat biscuit tin, and he'll be here like a shot. Watch.'

They did as they were told, their eyes following Erin as she grabbed the ornate tin with *Fortnum & Mason* emblazoned above a picture of a carousel that she kept Tybalt's treats in. She opened the door and rattled the tin. Within seconds, he was at her feet, looking up expectantly. She dropped a couple of fish-shaped biscuits on the floor in front of him, closing the door as he gobbled them up, then wandered nonchalantly over to Joe.

'So easily bought,' said Riley, with an air of disappointment. 'You're not the cat I thought you were.'

When everyone was seated with a hot drink in front of them, Erin lifted her copy of *Small Pleasures*, which she'd enjoyed enormously, hoping to get straight on with the discussion. But before she could open her mouth, Susan said, 'How's everyone getting on with writing their last pages?'

Erin lay the book on the table, stood and went over to the record player and rifled through the sleeves. She didn't want to talk about writing. Her mind was full of wasps, every worry adding an extra sting, so right now she wanted the distraction of discussing books. She wanted to talk about what everyone thought of Jean Swinney's ending in *Small Pleasures*, not their own. Erin completely related to Jean's experience of living life on the sidelines, making do with the small things in life to lighten her load. If anything, the book's moving and unexpected ending – to anyone who hadn't already read the final pages before embarking on the start – had confirmed her feeling that change never ended well.

'I'm enjoying it,' said Joe. 'It's made me think about the past, as well as the future. When I thought about what I want going forwards, I couldn't help but consider what got me to where I am now.' He surveyed the group, his soft eyes watery. 'I dug out all the old photos of me and Nuala, and what I realized was, I only want to share my life with someone now because I know what it is to love and be loved.'

Tears gathered in Erin's eyes. She might not want to think about her next chapter, but if it was beneficial for Joe, then she was happy the group had decided to do it.

'I was going through our wedding pictures,' Joe went on. 'My God, Nuala was a fine-looking woman. I don't know what she saw in me. I looked like a loon in this blue velvet suit. My shirt collar was this big.' He tapped his fingers on his shoulders and chuckled.

Erin plucked out *I Put a Spell on You* by Nina Simone and switched on the turntable. It was Nuala's favourite, and when Joe heard the first notes, he turned to her with eyes full of love. 'I was lucky to have her,' he said.

'You were, and she was lucky to have you.' Erin squeezed his shoulder as she returned to her seat. She'd grown up in a home full of love, and witnessed the same in Joe and Nuala. Was it any surprise she'd anticipated similar in her future? Maybe that was why the shock was so great when Andrew exploded their family. She'd thought they were set for life, like the people she'd grown up with, loved, and admired.

'I've grieved for five years, and I'm an old, old man, so I don't know how much longer I've got left. I think Nuala would want me to make the most of whatever time is still ahead of me.'

'I'm sure she would, and you're not that old,' said Hafsa. 'I see plenty of patients who've got more than a decade on you and are still living their best lives. Seventy-five is the new sixty.'

'Is that so? Could you please tell that to my knees?'

He rubbed his leg beside the cat as the others laughed and nodded. He turned to Susan. 'Have you decided what's in store for you?'

Susan let out a sigh. 'I'm not sure, but I agree, it's already been an interesting exercise. Over the last year my time's been filled with helping the girls with their wedding. Then the house hunting with Bella and Sophia.' Her face lit up at the mention of her daughter and daughter-in-law. 'And did I tell you they're planning to start IVF soon? It might not be long until I'm a grandma.'

'How exciting,' said Hafsa.

'It is,' said Susan. Her face turned serious. 'But I know it can be a long road, and it's not my journey to take; it's theirs. While I was thinking about this writing exercise, I realized I've been caught up in their lives and their next steps, and I'm lucky because they don't seem to mind—'

'They adore you,' said Riley. 'Of course they don't mind. I saw them in The Crown a couple of weeks ago and they were talking about how grateful they are for everything you've done for them.'

'Ah, that's lovely,' said Susan, smoothing her hand over her hair as if the compliment made her uncomfortable. 'But it's probably about time I left them to it. Who wants their mother-in-law hanging around all the time? And there's a risk I could get too invested in becoming a grandma, and then that's all I will be. That would become my whole identity. I can see it happening. I know a few women who live for being asked to babysit once in a while, and I don't want to be a peripheral person, if you know what I mean, someone who's always waiting for an invitation to be allowed to take part in someone else's life. I've been a wife, a mother, and then I'd be a grandma. But who am I outside my relationship to other people? Thinking about my next steps has opened my eyes to the fact that I've lost sight of what I want to do with my own life. Stewart's still working long hours in London, Bella and Sophia plan to spend the whole summer in France when the schools they teach at break up. What about me?'

As Susan spoke, Erin thought about how lucky she was to be a business owner. That gave her purpose and an identity beyond her role as Jack's mother. A small voice told her she only had the business because her mother had passed it on, and it was her mother's legacy more than it was Erin's. Erin was the one who was about to lose it all. There were the wasp-thoughts again: sting, sting, sting.

'What about you, Riley?' asked Susan.

'I've already started.' She grinned. 'I'm TikTok famous.'

'Is that right?' said Mercy, nodding her approval. 'You go, girl.'

Riley snorted. 'I'm not really, but I have got a few thousand new followers, and my older stuff is getting shared loads. I'm a slightly bigger fish in a fucking enormous ocean. But at least I'm out there swimming.' She mimed front crawl with her slender arms.

'Nice work.' Mercy rubbed her nails on her shoulder, a proud expression on her face. 'I've been busy too.'

'Oh yeah?' said Riley. 'Spill.'

'I've been reading the internet,' she said.

'All of it?' said Adam, his eyes full of amusement.

'It feels like it,' Mercy chortled. 'I start looking into one destination I fancy, and I end up reading everything I can find about it, then deciding I definitely want to go there—' she lifted her hands '—then somewhere else catches my eye, and I get all excited about that. I'm like a schoolgirl again. It's like all this potential has opened up for me.'

The energy radiated from her and she appeared more like a giddy young woman than the kindly retired librarian Erin knew.

'I love this for you,' said Adam. 'The world is a big and beautiful place, you should see as much of it as you can.' He rubbed his fingers up and down the stubble on his chin. Erin found herself wondering how he always kept it the same length. It gave the impression of careless grooming, but the fact it never seemed longer or shorter meant that some effort was at play. She realized she was staring at him, and forced herself to concentrate on what he was saying instead of what he looked like. 'You know what, this is all interesting stuff. I know a few lifestyle journalists who might want to hear about this project.' Erin wondered if they'd take as long to write their articles as he was taking to write his. She was still planning to ask whether he'd found someone else to help with the piece about Terry Waite, but hadn't found the right moment yet.

'What about you, Hafsa?' said Mercy. 'Any ideas?'

Hafsa slumped. 'I haven't had time to think about it. Zahra's been having a tough time at school. Friendship issues.'

'Bless her,' said Erin. Hafsa's middle child, thirteen-year-old Zahra, had recently been diagnosed with autism, and while the diagnosis made sense of how she experienced the world, it didn't alleviate the symptoms or make other teenagers any kinder.

'Honestly, I think they need us more as teenagers than they did when they were babies,' Hafsa said. 'I'm spending half the night staying up chatting things through with her. At least when they were tiny I just needed to feed them, cuddle them, and change their bums. Now I have to try to manage anxiety and talk about climate change, or the Middle East, or . . . whatever bee she's got in her bonnet that day, until the early hours. If I say I'm tired and need to go to bed she either cries because she feels guilty for being a burden, or accuses me of not being interested. I never know which way it's going to go, and I'm walking on eggshells all the time.'

'That sounds tough,' said Erin. She'd worried herself sick about Jack when he was that age, and it had got far worse before it got better. Not that she was about to tell Hafsa that. She was still anxious about him now with all the changes in his life. Such was life as a parent.

'Add hormones in, and whoosh.' Hafsa made an

explosion with her hands. 'I've been reading up on ASD, autism spectrum disorder, since her diagnosis and I'm ashamed at how much I didn't know. I'm a GP, for goodness' sake. I should have been up on this stuff.'

'You can't possibly know everything about every condition. It's not possible,' soothed Joe.

'He's right, that's your mother's guilt talking,' said Erin. 'We all know you've always done the best for your children. That's all anyone can do.' Once again, she wished she could practise what she preached. Her guilt about making Jack anxious about the future churned in her head when she'd been awake in the early hours of that morning.

'Thanks,' said Hafsa. She let out a long breath, as if releasing some of the tension she was holding. 'And what about you, Erin? What's in your last pages?'

'Feeling Good' played through the speakers, but the track did not describe how Erin felt when she was asked the question. 'Oh, erm—' She was interrupted by a loud ringing sound.

Adam lifted his hips and extracted his phone from the front pocket of his jeans. He frowned at the screen, mouthed, 'Sorry,' then stood and held the device to his ear as he left the room.

Erin took the opportunity of the distraction to lift her book back up. 'So, what did we all make of this? I loved it. I can see why it was longlisted for the Women's Prize.'

All heads turned as Adam blustered back in. 'I'm sorry, I've got to get off.' He lifted his leather jacket from where it was draped over the back of a chair and shoved his arm through a sleeve, dropping his phone as he did so. It clattered onto the wooden floor and skittered under a table. 'Shit.' He knelt to retrieve his phone and checked the screen, his face red and flustered.

'You okay?' said Riley.

'Yeah,' he said, his creased brow and florid cheeks suggesting he was anything but. 'Sorry. I, erm . . . I'll see you all next time.' He gripped his phone as if his life depended on it and strode towards the door, leaving the group staring after him, as Nina Simone's voice sang 'You've Got to Learn' into the quiet room.

Chapter Thirteen

June was disappearing before her eyes, and Erin still hadn't thought of what to write in her last pages. Instead, she was still spending any free time she had looking over the café's finances, which only seemed to confirm to her that there was no viable way of cutting costs enough to make the business work at the new rent. It was almost three weeks since she'd got the letter from Galmouth and she still felt her jaw tighten and tears well up when she even thought about discussing what the future held. But it wasn't just her future at stake. It was Riley's and Jack's too, and Jack seemed no closer to finding a graduate job. In a week, she told herself firmly, she would sit everyone down and tell them the truth. Then she'd send in her notice to quit to Galmouth, even though the finality of that gnawed at her insides, leaving her stomach raw and acidic.

'How are you getting on with the writing?' said Jack, wiping his hands on a tea towel, and coming over to where she was sitting at a table near the window, her laptop open in front of her. A little girl banged Lego pieces together in Kiddies Corner, laughing with delight at the sound. Erin loved to watch the simple pleasures of small children in the café. Usually it reminded her to live in the moment and enjoy the little things, like having Jack back home. But even a crèche full of giggling babies would struggle to quell the anxiety she was fighting now.

She closed the lid, so Jack couldn't see that she was actually viewing an Excel spreadsheet, not working on the writing exercise like she'd told him. 'It's a work in progress.'

'Top secret, eh? You're making me nervous.' He flicked the tea towel onto his shoulder.

'Nervous?'

'Yeah. What if your plans are to sell up and move to Venezuela? What would I do then?'

Erin couldn't help but laugh. Surely Jack knew her better than that? 'I can talk myself out of a long weekend in Wales when I've overthought all the things that could go wrong, so I'm hardly likely to set off on an adventure to South America. I'll leave that kind of thing to Mercy and Adam.'

'Fair point,' said Jack, making her feel sad that he recognized the truth in what she said. She was a terrible example to him. He deserved better. 'How is Adam?' Jack lifted his chin and peered down his nose at her.

'Why are you looking at me like that?'

'Like what?' He kept raising his chin and smiling.

'Stop it.'

'I'm just asking if you've seen your friend recently. You're the one making a thing about it.'

Was Adam her friend? She wasn't sure. He'd run off in the middle of last week's book group and she hadn't heard a thing from him since. He never did arrange that walk in Greenwich Park. She'd become used to him working at The Bookmark most mornings, and he seemed keen to chat whenever she had a free moment. He laughed at her jokes and seemed genuinely interested in her book recommendations, which added a little light to her days. He always had breakfast and sometimes he stayed for lunch too, so he was good for business. That was the main thing she missed about him, she told herself. 'I'll inquire about his well-being at book group tonight,' she said. 'And tell him you were asking about him.'

'You do that,' Jack said. 'And seriously, what have you written so far? I'm intrigued.'

'I'll tell you when I've finished, and not before. Stop trying to interfere with my creative process,' she said, imperiously. 'Now get back to work.'

***

At book group that evening, Erin found herself glancing at the door every few minutes, but half an hour after the start, she accepted that Adam wasn't going to turn up. She realized that looking forward to seeing him had been the only light in a very dark day, and now that light had been extinguished, her mood dipped even lower.

She pushed Adam from her thoughts and focused on

the group. They'd all brought along a book related to their plans for their last pages. All except her, anyway.

Mercy held up a copy of *Wild* by Cheryl Strayed. 'This was eye-opening,' she said. 'If a twenty-six-year-old woman can walk from the Mojave Desert to Washington state on her own, then I think I can get on a plane.' Her distinctive chuckle followed her words.

'I've seen the film of that,' said Erin. 'She's an impressive woman, all right.'

Mercy tapped a nail on the cover. 'She's an inspiration.' She made excited fists in her lap and smiled shyly. 'I've been thinking I might write a travel blog from wherever I go. You don't work in a library as long as I did without getting fanciful ideas about writing something yourself one day.'

Her gaze danced between their faces and Erin could tell she was nervous about sharing her plans. 'I think that's wonderful,' she said. 'I'd love to read all about your experiences.'

'You don't think it's too much? Every Tom, Dick, and Harry has a blog or a podcast these days, don't they? Who's interested in my musings?'

'Me, for one,' said Erin.

'And me,' said Susan.

'We all are,' said Joe. 'I'd be delighted to read about your travels.' He pointed a crooked finger at Mercy. 'You'll soon give Adam a run for his money, I bet.' Deep lines crossed his brow. 'Where is our friendly neighbourhood journo, anyway?' He looked at Erin.

'No idea.' She worked hard to appear disinterested. 'He hasn't been in this week.'

Susan's mouth formed an 'o'. 'He was in a bit of a flap after the call he got last week, wasn't he? Has anyone seen or heard from him since?' They all shook their heads. 'Do you think we should be worried?'

'I've got his number,' Erin said. 'Shall I message him and check he's okay?' She was more comfortable enquiring about him on behalf of the group, than herself, and this was a good excuse to see what was going on with him.

'Deffo,' said Riley.

They all stayed quiet while Erin tapped out a text. 'I'll just say, hope you're okay,' she said.

'Tell him we're missing him at book group,' said Mercy, leaning forwards as if trying to see what Erin had typed.

Erin felt obliged to add what Mercy said, despite feeling like it was a bit much. She almost typed that Mercy said they were missing him, but managed to stop herself. She contemplated adding a kiss, like she usually would when messaging a friend, but decided against it. A kiss on the end might be misconstrued. She couldn't remember the last time she'd agonised like this over a message. She was losing the plot. She pressed send, put her phone face down on the table, then immediately looked up and said, 'What book have you brought, Hafsa?'

Hafsa lifted a book with a boy in a red coat staring

up at a starry sky on the cover. '*The Curious Incident of the Dog in the Night-Time*,' she said. 'I've been giving it a lot of thought since we last met, and I think I know what my last pages might be about.'

'Tell all,' said Susan, resting her elbows on her knees, and her chin on her hands.

'The more I talk to Zahra, the more I understand the kind of support she needs, and I'm beginning to realize quite how hard it is for institutions like schools and even the NHS to help kids like her because of the volume of people getting diagnosed these days.'

'Is autism on the rise, do you think?' asked Joe. 'Is that the problem?'

'I actually think it's awareness that's on the rise. I don't believe there are more neurodivergent people than there were say, twenty years ago, just that now we know more about how it presents, especially in women and girls. Because of this new understanding, more and more people are diagnosed, and that's a good thing because they will be able to get the support they need, but the problem is, the support isn't always there.'

'What's your plan, then?' asked Erin.

'I haven't exactly formulated one yet,' said Hafsa. 'But I'm beginning to think my medical background, plus being a parent of a child on the spectrum, could lead to me doing something that would be useful and rewarding for me. I just don't know what yet.'

'Sounds like a good start,' said Riley. Her expression turned serious. 'Do you think I'm on the spectrum?'

Hafsa's head dropped to one side. 'What makes you ask?'

'Chegs said I don't think like a normal person. He says my head's on wonky.'

'Normal?' Erin spluttered. 'Wonky?' Maybe her policy of waiting to be asked for her opinion shouldn't apply in this case. Riley deserved to be admired, not denigrated by someone who was meant to love her. If Erin told her what she thought, maybe Riley would see that idiot boyfriend of hers for what he was – an entitled dick.

Riley straightened. 'He didn't say it like . . . he says he doesn't understand my thought processes and he thinks I'm probably autistic, or something.'

She sounded defensive, and Erin knew she had to tread carefully. She wanted to tell Riley she thought she was being intentionally diminished, gaslit by a man who wanted to control her. Instead, she said, 'You are very creative, but surely not all creatives are on some kind of spectrum?' She turned to Hafsa for confirmation.

'If you're worried about anything, you could always see your GP, but I would say that, unless you are finding areas of your life unmanageable and think a diagnosis would lead to you getting the support you need, then I wouldn't give it too much thought. Are you struggling?' Hafsa asked gently.

Erin could imagine her in her surgery giving sage advice and making patients feel like nothing was too much trouble. Maybe she should open up about her anxiety. Hafsa had probably come across plenty of anxious people in her time. She instantly dismissed the idea. Hafsa wasn't her GP, and the poor woman had enough to worry about without Erin burdening her with her issues too. A niggling voice told Erin she'd also probably suggest she went to her doctor and asked for medication to help her deal with her waspish thoughts, and she didn't want to do that. Her worries were circumstantial. If she wasn't so stressed about money and Jack, she would be absolutely fine, and no amount of pills could deliver a substantial income or a fulfilling career for her son.

Riley stuck out her bottom lip. 'Nah, I'm not. He thinks my brain is weird, but I quite like living in my head.'

'That's what matters,' said Erin. 'I'm not sure I know many people who like living inside their own heads, so I'd say you're in a better position than most.' She'd certainly like a holiday from her own brain once in a while. She'd also like Riley to have a holiday from her idiot boyfriend. A permanent one. It occurred to her that at least Chegs was financially secure, so when she had to let Riley go, she would have him as backup. The thought made her feel sick. The last thing she wanted was for this lovely young woman to have to rely on a man whose treatment of her was questionable at best. Erin couldn't bear to entertain that line of thinking so she took the opportunity to change the subject. 'What book have you brought?'

Riley's face brightened. She dipped her hand into a canvas bag with The Bookmark logo by her side, and brought out a blue book. She held it out for them all to see. Erin read the title, *Natives: Race & Class in the Ruins of Empire*. 'This is epic. Akala starts by explaining his ideas using his own experiences then widens them to examine social, historical, and political factors and then he comments on how we got to the fucked-up world we live in now. If I want to make a living doing spoken word, I need to have something to say, so I'm reading books by people I think are changing the world for the better. Akala's incredible. Has anyone read this?'

'I remember Jack talking about it,' said Erin. 'Is the author a musician as well?'

'Yeah, he's a hip-hop artist. He founded the Hip-Hop Shakespeare Company.'

'I'll have to look that up,' said Joe. 'Hip-hop sounds like my kind of music, although I might be more likely to fall into the hip-op category at my age.' Tybalt stirred as Joe's body shook with laughter.

As they all laughed along with him, Erin wondered how many other seventy-five-year-olds would be interested in learning about hip-hop. She paused to consider that thought. Now information was available on the internet, people didn't have to be stuck in the echo chamber of their immediate surroundings, and that was a good thing. Some change was good. She glanced around the group, loving that they were a mix of ages, ethnicities, and socio-economic backgrounds. Joe was the only man, though. Adam had evened that out a little, but he still hadn't arrived and, annoyingly, now the group felt less balanced because of it.

She turned her phone over and her heart rate quickened when she saw a notification on the screen. It was a reply from Adam. She lifted it and opened the message. 'Adam's replied,' she said to the group. 'He says he's sorry he couldn't come tonight.' She glanced up. 'He says something unexpected cropped up.'

'Fair enough,' said Susan. 'At least he hasn't left us for good.' She viewed Erin. 'Has he?'

Erin glanced back at the message. 'Don't think so.' It was pointless trying to pretend she wasn't drawn to this man. Despite her best efforts, he'd already taken up too much space in her head to ignore. With a mixture of anticipation and nerves, she reread the second part of the message silently to herself.

> I could do with a chat. Don't suppose you're free for that walk tomorrow? 12pm any good?

Chapter Fourteen

Erin didn't reply to the message straight away. She thought about it as she stacked the cups in the dishwasher, and when she locked the door after the other members of book group left. The pros and cons swirled in her head as she crossed Royal Parade and she still hadn't decided when she arrived at Dartmouth Grove, or when she walked up the flight of stairs to her flat. As she put the key in the door she wondered whether Adam would be able to tell she'd read what he'd sent. If it was WhatsApp, two blue ticks would have appeared, but she didn't know if iMessage was the same. She didn't want to leave him on read, but she also seemed completely incapable of deciding how to respond, because if she went along, that could be the start of something, which scared her.

'How was book group?' asked Jack. He was sitting on the sofa in jogging bottoms and a crumpled T-shirt, scrolling through his phone. He yawned, stretching his arms over his head. His T-shirt rode up and she saw his lower ribs protrude over his concave stomach.

'Fine, thanks.' She poked him in his middle and he

curled inwards, groaning and pulling down his top. 'You need plumping up.'

'Body shaming, much?' He pouted and laid his phone down on the cushion beside him.

'I'm your mother. I worry about you.' Still, the shame of knowing he was right made her regret her words. Doing the right thing as a parent was impossible, and she'd always felt double the pressure since she was the only parental influence Jack had growing up. Every misplaced word or sentiment could have an unintended impact. He was a sensitive soul, infected by her anxiety. She needed to do better.

'I've been living on chickpea curry for three years, remember? I promise to eat you out of house and café now I'm home, if that helps?'

'It does. Thank you.' She smiled at her gorgeous boy. Would she ever stop worrying about him?

'Was Adam there tonight?'

He was looking at her with benign interest, but she kept her face impassive so he wouldn't see there was anything significant about the question. 'Oh, no, he wasn't.' Why did she add the 'oh'? It sounded weird, like she'd practised it.

'I hope he's all right.' Jack opened his mouth and stroked down the edges of his moustache.

He didn't seem to have noticed she was acting strangely. That was good. Maybe he could help her decide what to do about the message. 'He's asked me to meet him tomorrow for a walk,' said Erin, nonchalantly.

It was all she could do not to scan the room, feigning disinterest.

'So he hasn't been knocked off his bike and laid up in hospital or anything. That's good. Say hi from me tomorrow.'

He made it sound like a given that she would agree to meet this man they barely knew. It wasn't as simple as that. Adam made her feel things she didn't want to. Her life was unstable enough right now; the last thing she needed was a risky romance. As soon as the word romance occurred to her, she felt like a fool. He probably just wanted to discuss that article. Internally, she berated herself for all this conjecture. She didn't need the wobbly emotions that came along with wondering if someone liked her. Liked her? Jesus, what was she turning into? 'I'm not sure if I'm going yet.'

'Why wouldn't you? Me and Riley are on the morning shift. You're not due in until two.' His top lip rose to show his pink gums. She wondered if his moustache tickled his nose when he did that.

'I know, but . . .' But what? She could hardly tell her son that Adam was the first man she'd found genuinely attractive in decades. He certainly wouldn't want to know that her attraction to his father had clouded her judgement for far too long, and that she wanted to avoid making the same mistake again. The plain fact was that if she had feelings, then those feelings could get hurt. They probably would. Things ended, and she was terrified of endings for very good reasons.

'You haven't got a good reason, have you?'

She bloody well did. 'I'm not sure.'

'Mother.' His voice was firm. 'He's a nice bloke, you said so yourself. He hasn't asked you to go sky-diving, or micro-dosing mushrooms, he's suggested a walk in the park down the road. If you're overthinking that then you need to have a word with yourself.'

Had she said he was nice? She didn't remember saying that. And why had micro-dosing mushrooms occurred to Jack? Her head went back to that awful time he was taken into custody, before she shook the thought away. He was older and wiser now. But he was right, it wasn't that big a risk.

Adam might not even find her attractive. She might be imagining his lingering looks, and that flirtatious smile of his. She should stop flattering herself. The message said he wanted to chat about something and chat was a casual word – more casual than talk, or discuss. It was probably to do with that article after all. She should stop going around in circles and get on with it. Added to that, she didn't want to model being a scaredy-cat to her son. 'All right then, bossy boots. I'll go.' She'd said it now, so she had to. Her stomach fluttered like she'd just placed an enormous bet on the Grand National and the horses were already frothing at the mouth, straining for the start of the race.

'Good.' Jack yawned again, tugging down the bottom of his T-shirt as if shielding his stomach from her poking finger. 'Right, I'm knackered and since my slave-driver boss expects me in work at 6.30am tomorrow, I'd better get to bed. Night.'

'Night, love. Sleep well.' She watched Jack wander off to his bedroom, opened up the message and forced herself to type.

See you at the park gates on Charlton Way at 12.

Chapter Fifteen

Erin stood by the pedestrian gate at the top end of Greenwich Park, the yellow stone pillars topped with ornate gas lamps at her back. She fiddled with the hem of the white blouse she'd teamed with black linen trousers. She'd considered her outfit for longer than usual, keen to look her best, but not appear to have made too much effort. Ordinarily, she wore jeans and a polo shirt with The Bookmark logo for work, and only swapped that out for a Breton T-shirt outside work in the summer, and a sweatshirt in the winter. The last time she'd given an outfit this much thought was when she and Jack were invited to the Buckingham Palace garden party to celebrate him achieving his Gold Duke of Edinburgh Award. She'd bought a floral dress for that, and spent the whole day sucking in her stomach and checking her cleavage wasn't on show. The dress had hung untouched at the back of her wardrobe ever since.

The day was bright, and she was glad she had an excuse to wear sunglasses. She felt like she could scour the road and the heath beyond for Adam without looking like a desperate woman who'd been stood up. A quick check of her watch told her he was already five minutes late. Not a great start. She would wait until ten past, then go home, she decided. He'd probably forgotten. She was an idiot for putting so much stock in this arrangement. It was a stroll in the park not an episode of *First Dates*. She smiled to herself as she imagined the maître d'hôtel on the dating series, Fred Sirieix, greeting them both as they arrived at the rose garden, and leading them to a table set with silver cutlery glimmering in the June sunshine.

She caught the daydream in a mental butterfly net and threw it back out into the world. This was not a first date in any way, shape, or form. If she seriously thought it was, she would have declined. She'd spent wakeful hours contemplating it last night and decided she definitely wasn't in the market for a relationship. Not that one was on offer. This was a chat, nothing more. As she was reminding herself of that, she saw Adam approaching from across the road. He was grinning and waving. She waved back and smiled, as her lurching stomach betrayed her.

He looked good in a cream knitted T-shirt with a collar and a zip which was partially open, showing a patch of salt and pepper chest hair. It was smarter than his grey or black band T-shirts, and his jeans were less faded than the worn Levis he usually turned up in. A baker-boy cap covered his hair and, with his dark glasses, she couldn't help but think he looked like one of those older models you saw on posters above the tills in the men's department at M&S.

'Hiya,' she said, as he reached her. She didn't know what to do with her hands. Did they hug, kiss on the cheek?

He put a hand on her shoulder. It was heavy and warm. 'I'm sorry I'm late. Have you been waiting long?' He took his hand away.

'No, not long.' She turned towards the park. 'Shall we?' He followed her inside the gates and past the cars parked in the shade of the trees. 'Haven't seen you around for a while.'

'No, it's been . . . anyway, I'm glad I was missed at book group.' He shoved his hands in the front pockets of his jeans as he took long strides. She could be imagining it, but he seemed a little nervous. He was wearing white trainers in place of his chunky biker boots today. It occurred to her he might have made the same level of effort she had.

She resisted the urge to say it was Mercy who told her to type that they were missing him. Instead, she blurted, 'Joe wasn't happy about having to fly the flag for the men all on his own again.' Why did she say that? Joe had never expressed any thoughts about being the only man in book group. He was happy in his own skin, and took people as he found them, regardless of gender or any other attribute.

'I've missed the chat,' he said, looking at her for a long moment. Did she imagine the inference that it was her he specifically missed speaking to? 'I plan to be back next week, all being well.'

She noted the caveat and wondered again what kept him away. It felt impertinent to ask right away. She hoped he'd come to it soon enough.

'What book did you ruin this week by reading the last page?' There was amusement in his voice and when Erin glanced at him, his lips were pinched in a suppressed smile.

'We didn't *ruin* any books, actually.'

'Okay, okay. Which did you pick?'

'None, seriously, since you came in and shook things up with your questions, things haven't run the way they usually do. Everyone brought in a book that relates to what they're writing in their last pages, so we haven't chosen one to read together.'

'I take it you still haven't forgiven me for shaking things up, then?' He turned his head to her, and she wished she could see his eyes. His voice was light and gently teasing.

'Hm, I'm working on it.' She aimed for blithe and hoped it landed okay. They were at the top of the hill with the Royal Observatory to their left. The view ahead was awe-inspiring. They both stopped to take in the panorama of the London skyline beyond the Royal Naval College, to the skyscrapers of Canary Wharf glistening in the sunshine.

'Forgive me for prying, but it's been playing on my mind, why do you need to know the ending before you start a book? I still don't really get it.'

Erin took a step down the path, trying to remember what she'd said to him when he first challenged her about this. 'I like to know how things will turn out. It makes me feel . . . safer.'

'So, you always need to know where things are heading?' He walked by her side, keeping his eyes on the view. 'Is there a reason for that?'

She glanced up at his face. 'You really are a journalist through and through, aren't you?'

He held out his arms and laughed. 'I'm interested in people. You can't blame me for that. People are endlessly fascinating.'

Erin smiled. From what her friends who were on the dating scene told her, most men their age were deeply incurious, much more inclined to talk about themselves than anyone else. A couple of women who were recently divorced had held a competition to see whose date would go on longest before the man asked the woman a single question. One claimed the whole date went by without the man inquiring about anything beyond what she wanted to drink, and then had the gall to act surprised when she didn't accept the invitation to go home with him. 'They are. And I have my reasons.'

'Sorry,' said Adam. 'Forget I asked. I didn't mean to overstep.' His tone was serious and Erin felt him shift a little further away from her on the path.

She had the feeling she'd made a mistake. She wanted the flirtatious tone back, and to feel his proximity, their arms almost touching as they walked side by side. She took a deep breath and decided to tell him the truth. 'No, it's fine.' She swallowed. 'I thought I knew my ending, once upon a time, if you'll pardon the cliché. Then it all went wrong, and I never regained my trust in things working out, I suppose. I need to know where something is going before I embark on it, or I don't do it. The fear is too much for me.'

'Fear?'

How lovely it must be to not understand the fear that rumbled inside her all day everyday, making her agonise over every decision she made. The energy she put into planning for what could go wrong, mitigating for every eventuality, was exhausting. 'I suppose I'm an overthinker.'

'Don't feel you have to tell me, but—'

'What derailed my happily ever after?' She watched a very small boy tottering alongside a young man who was grinning down at the child. The boy tripped and there was a brief hiatus before his wails rang out across the park. The man scooped the boy up and held him close to his chest before examining his face, then kissing his wet cheeks. Soon the boy was giggling at something the man said, and he set him down to resume his toddling amble across the grass. Erin pointed at the pair. 'I expected that would be Jack and Andrew. Andrew is Jack's father. We got together when we were at sixth form, and no one expected us to last through uni.' She laughed. 'No one except us, anyway.' She sighed. 'We proved them wrong, and when we graduated we both moved back home and got jobs, and as soon as we could afford it, we got married and bought a house.'

She couldn't help but smile when she remembered Andrew carrying her over the threshold of their home. Her smile faded when she thought about the years that followed. 'We planned to start a family . . . but things didn't quite go to plan.'

'But Jack . . .?'

She thought of her gorgeous son and her heart filled with gratitude. 'Yes, in the end the final round of IVF worked, thank God, and we got our little bundle of joy. But it was a brutal process and by the time Jack came along, I suppose the cracks were already there. I don't know if I ignored them, or if I was too caught up in finally having it all, the happy ending I'd dreamed of. Either way, when Jack was still a tiny baby, Andrew told me he didn't want any of it anymore. Not me, not the house, not even his beautiful baby boy.' She sniffed back the tears that threatened. 'So, you see, I thought I had my story's perfect ending. We'd overcome adversity and were on track for our happy ever after, then boom, plot twist.'

'That's quite a plot twist,' Adam said. 'I can see why you were thrown.'

Thrown didn't begin to describe it, but she didn't need to tell him all the gory details. 'And since then, I've avoided anything that might throw me a curveball. I like life to be calm and predictable. I like to know exactly where my life is heading.'

'But surely you can't account for everything?'

'I can try.' She lifted her face to the sun and closed her eyes, breathing in the smell of the grass until a teenage boy with a pimply face passed, breathing out the artificial scent of a fruity vape and spoiling it.

'But life has so many variables. Other people for a start. You can't control how other people behave, so you can't truly manage how things will turn out.'

She was about to say that's why she never had relationships, but she was oddly comfortable in this man's presence, more comfortable than with any man since Andrew, so she said. 'True, but I do my best.' She was surprised to see a frown creasing his brow under his hat. 'What's up?'

'I'm just thinking about you having to bring up your son on your own.'

She lifted her shoulders. 'I didn't plan it that way, and there was a time early on that I didn't think I could do it, but we muddled through, and I think we did more than that in the end. We've done okay.'

'He seems like a good lad.'

The praise blossomed in her chest. 'He is. He's the best. His dad's missed out on so much by not being present. His loss.' She wasn't about to disclose the grim episode with the cannabis. That reflected badly on Jack as well as Andrew and she didn't want to sully Adam's opinion of her lovely boy.

'Do they have any contact at all?' Adam's voice was serious.

'Not really. Jack doesn't think much of him, to be honest. At least, that's what he tells me. I used to worship Andrew, I thought he was the most gorgeous man on earth, but I don't know what I ever saw in him now. He hasn't amounted to much. Whatever grand plan he had when he left us to regain this life of freedom he was so desperate for, it seemed to peter away pretty quickly. He's a middle-aged man with a paunch doing a boring office job somewhere in Hertfordshire. No more, no less.'

'But . . .' Adam licked his lips. 'I suppose he had his reasons for not being around while Jack was growing up.'

Erin stopped. 'Nothing that justified hurting his son.'

Adam scratched underneath his chin, the stubble making a rasping sound under his nails. 'There are loads of reasons why fathers aren't involved in their kids' lives.'

Erin huffed. 'You sound like you think it's okay for a dad to simply bugger off if they decide the responsibility doesn't suit them. I mean, what about the women? Imagine if women took off at the first sign of trouble, like some men do.' She shook her head, knowing how rarely that would happen. Nothing could have compelled her to leave her son. She was besotted with him from the first moment she knew of his existence. Even during those troublesome teenage years, she still loved him ferociously.

'I'm not saying that.' Adam rolled his shoulders, looking decidedly uncomfortable.

‘What are you saying?’ She blinked up at him. The sun was behind him, giving him a bright halo, but an unwelcome silent voice whispered to her that maybe Adam was no angel.

‘It’s just that individual circumstances should be taken into account when—’

‘Do you have children, Adam?’ Even as she asked it, she knew the answer could change everything. She held her breath.

Adam took off his cap and ran his hand over his cropped hair. ‘I have a grown-up son.’

A buzzing started in Erin’s ears. The next question would be make or break for them. ‘And were you involved in your son’s upbringing?’ She read the answer in the grimace on his face. ‘I’m going to go,’ she said, unwilling to let him see the disappointment engulfing her. Meeting him today had been a mistake. She should have listened to her instincts.

She turned to walk back up the hill, feeling like a fool for ever hoping it could have ended differently.

Chapter Sixteen

Erin marched across the heath towards the village, her heart pounding with the exertion. Sweat dripped down her back and soaked into her bra strap. Her shift didn't start for another hour and a half, but she didn't want to be alone in the flat. She knew her thoughts would spiral if she wasn't distracted, and she didn't need to berate herself for having let her guard down any more than she already was. As she passed a young couple walking arm in arm across the grass, she tried to work out what her predominant feeling was.

Disappointment was definitely top of the list. She'd felt attracted to Adam, she'd stopped trying to deny that, but the only reason she'd gone against her own rules and her instincts was because something about him told her he was a good man. Now she'd discovered he was an absentee father, and she couldn't think of a single viable excuse for that. Surely no one with a truly good heart could desert their own child?

Her breath came fast when she arrived on Brigade Street, so she stopped to regain her composure before she entered the café. Jack came into view, a tea towel thrown over his shoulder again, like some kind of waiter in an American movie. He turned towards Riley, who was next to another table, moving her hands as she spoke, then he threw his head back in a guffaw that reminded Erin of her father. This was what she needed, to be around true friends and family: people she loved and trusted. People who would never let her down.

Jack did a double take when she came through the door. 'Thought you were going for a walk with Adam?'

'I did,' said Erin. 'Just a short one, and now I'm back.' Customers' conversations buzzed around the room and her shoulders instantly dropped a notch at the cheerful atmosphere. The sun shone through the far window, its yellowy beams catching the vase in the grate, spreading dappled rays of colour across the wall and floor. 'Glad to see we're busy.'

'It's been a good morning.' He glanced around with a satisfied smile and Erin wished her mother was there to see his pride in the place they all loved, before remembering how little time was left before she was forced to tell them the truth.

'That's what I like to hear.' She spied Joe sitting in one of the leather armchairs, Tybalt on his lap, his gaze on the pages of a book. 'Can you bring me a ham salad sandwich and a tea over there?' She pointed at Joe's table. 'And whatever Joe's having.'

'On it.'

She picked her way over, stopping to pet a spaniel

who was lapping from one of the bowls of water they kept for visiting dogs. 'Hi Joe.'

He raised his head, a grin instantly lifting his crinkled cheeks when he saw her. 'Erin, how are you?'

'Good, thanks. Mind if I join you?'

'I'd be heartbroken if you didn't.' He sounded like he meant it and she was even more grateful than usual for having this gentle father-figure still in her life. He would have made a wonderful dad if he and Nuala had been able to have children. Erin often thought she was the one who benefitted most from their childlessness. They'd practically treated her as their own, which meant she hadn't felt entirely untethered when her mother died, bereft as she was. Friends of hers described feeling orphaned when they lost their last parent, even in their fifties. She still had Joe, and he was a firm foundation in this rocky world.

She sat in the adjacent chair to his. 'What are you reading?' He slipped the dog-eared envelope he was using as a bookmark between the pages and closed the book, before turning a cover with soft purple, pink and green hues to show her. '*Love After Love*,' read Erin. 'Any good?'

'It's heartbreakingly beautiful. It's all I can do not to wail like a wounded moose,' he said, his Irish accent sounding strong with the emotion in his words. 'I'm nearly at the end.' He turned the book to show her how few pages were left after the ad hoc bookmark.

'I can leave you to finish it, if you like.'

'No.' Joe put a hand out to stop her. 'You stay where you are. I suspect it might be better for me to read the last bit in the privacy of my own home. No one wants to see a fine, strapping young man like me sobbing in a public place.' He stroked Tybalt's back and the cat began to purr.

'If you're sure?' She raised an eyebrow. 'You're your own worst enemy, you know? I have no sympathy for you. You should have followed book group rules and read the last page first, then you'd know what was coming.'

He chuckled. 'You're not wrong. I could have saved myself all manner of pain.'

'Is it that emotional?' She eyed the book, wondering whether she should read it herself. It was sometimes cathartic to have a good cry over a fictional story rather than her own.

'It's a fine story, to be sure. It's about an unconventional family in Trinidad, and how a secret drives them apart. It's hopeful too, thank the Lord. It came up as a suggestion when I was searching for books to go alongside my last pages.'

'What did you search up?'

Joe dropped his gaze. 'I'm a bit embarrassed to say.'

Erin nudged him with her elbow. 'I won't judge you. You know that.'

He glanced up, a shy smile lifting one side of his mouth. 'Love in later life. Do you think I'm an old fool?'

'I think you're brave and wonderful,' she said. 'And

I think you deserve to be happy more than anyone else I know.'

Riley appeared by the side of the table, then flopped into a chair beside them. 'Don't look now, but that blonde girl over there gets right on my tits.'

Erin couldn't help but turn around. She recovered herself and swiftly turned back to Riley, but not before she saw a wiry girl with thick hair and a sour expression, shoving a purse into her bag. 'Who is she?'

'Teagan, a friend of Chegs'. She's such an entitled cow. Honestly, she seemed gobsmacked when I gave her the bill, as if the fact she went to some posh knob school with my boyfriend meant she expected me to give her freebies.' Riley scowled over at the girl, who was now making her way to the door. 'Why is it that the more people have, the more they expect to get for nothing? Her parents own half of Keston, apparently, so she can afford to pay for a bacon buttie and a chai latte.'

This was exactly what Erin imagined friends of Chegs to be like, but she didn't say so. 'She certainly doesn't seem like your kind of person.' She'd met some of Riley's friends and they were as sweet and quirky as she was. She wondered what they made of her idiot boyfriend. Maybe they were keeping their thoughts to themselves like she was, although she was finding it increasingly difficult to do so.

'She isn't my bag at all. I've got to be nice to her, though, because she's only just moved home after a few years travelling South America, so Chegs has taken her under his wing. He asked me to be kind to her because none of her friends live locally anymore.' She rolled her eyes. 'Even her accent grates on me. She's got one of those posh voices with a hint of American that International School kids get, which is stupid because she was brought up in Southeast London, like the rest of us.' She jutted out her chin and said, 'Yeah, I've been on a gap year,' in a mash-up of RP and US.

Erin laughed, despite being desperate to point out that Chegs had a similar affectation. But Riley seemed blind to all his flaws, so she kept her mouth shut. Riley waved Jack over. 'Can I get a mint tea, please?'

Jack dropped his head to one side. 'Aren't you meant to be working?'

Riley covered her mouth, a snigger escaping from behind her fingers. 'I am, aren't I?' She shook her head. 'As soon as I sat down, I forgot.' She stood. 'I've had my break and everything. What am I like?'

Erin grinned at her. 'Back to work, you.' She mimed cracking a whip and Riley saluted and wandered back to the kitchen with Jack. 'She's ditsy, that one, but I do love her.'

Joe leaned forwards and spoke in hushed tones. 'I don't know what she sees in that Chegs fella. He's a right daffodil.'

'Me either,' said Erin smiling at Joe's unique term for someone he didn't respect, and glad she wasn't the only one with reservations. 'It's been two years now. I expected her to see through him after a couple of months.'

'I didn't mind him at first,' said Joe. 'I could understand what she saw in him. He's a good-looking lad, if you like the foppish type.' He mimed pushing hair off his forehead. 'And he's confident, right enough, and he's clearly got a bob or two. All very attractive traits, objectively.'

Her thoughts went to the new rental amount. How freeing it must be to not have the constant tap of calculator keys going on in the back of your head. 'Objectively, yeah, but you know Riley. She isn't motivated by money. I just don't get why she's stayed with him when he clearly doesn't make her feel good about herself.'

'That could be the appeal, in a perverse sort of way,' said Joe, quietly. 'She had a tough upbringing, didn't she? She was never the centre of anyone's world. That's got to leave you feeling like you don't deserve much love and attention. Maybe she has a low opinion of herself, and so she doesn't expect much from anyone else.'

Erin observed Riley, who was standing behind the till by the cakes, taking a card payment. Her cropped hair, which was growing back a little more each day, accentuated her sharp cheekbones, and made her eyes appear enormous and innocent. She was a beautiful soul and deserved to be cherished. 'I wish she could see herself the way we see her,' she said. 'Then she'd know her own worth.'

Joe smiled and patted the back of her hand. 'Don't we all feel like that about the people we love?'

She took his hand and squeezed. The door opened and the post woman came in, wearing combat shorts and a red Royal Mail T-shirt. Her eyes searched the room before alighting on Erin. She strode over and handed a wadge of letters to her. 'Hope they're not all bills,' she said. 'See ya.'

'Thanks,' said Erin, leafing through the envelopes. Her fingers paused on one with *Galmouth Estates* printed across the top. That would be the new lease for her to sign, only she couldn't sign it, because she couldn't afford the rent. In a matter of weeks she would have to give notice to end the tenancy. The time was fast approaching that The Bookmark would have to close.

Chapter Seventeen

Erin's self-imposed deadline for telling everyone about the café's fate was now only days away and she knew that once she'd said the words out loud, it would become hideously real.

In the meantime, she needed to be distracted from the turmoil of her churning thoughts, so when Susan sent a cryptic message asking her to join her in London for an afternoon out after her morning shift in the café a few days later, she agreed. She presumed Susan wanted to go shopping, or to a gallery. Her request for an itinerary only yielded the time of the train Susan wanted them to be on, and Erin hadn't felt able to ask again without seeming like a weirdo. Now Erin stood outside Blackheath station in the chilly afternoon air, wishing she'd worn something warmer than her denim jacket. Despite it being late June, the blue skies of recent days had gone, and heavy clouds sagged with the promise of rain.

Five minutes before the train was due to depart, a tap on her shoulder made her turn to see her friend, dressed in a smart blue suit. She should have known she was nearby by the gorgeous floral fragrance that wafted up her nostrils a second before.

'You're all dressed up,' Erin said, glancing down at her jeans and trainers. Jack had convinced her double denim was fashionable again, but she still felt like an older, less attractive member of the nineties pop group, Bewitched, whenever she tried it. Their song, 'Blame It on the Weatherman' had played in her head for her entire walk to the station.

'Only because I'm nervous.' Susan patted her hair with both hands, which indicated double the concern.

'Nervous about what?' said Erin, starting to feel unsettled herself. 'I presumed we were going to Oxford Street or something.' The muscles in her shoulders contracted. She didn't like surprises. Susan should know that.

Susan turned and peered at the orange lettering on the departures board. 'I'll fill you in on the train,' she said and marched towards the barriers, a disgruntled Erin fast on her heels.

Minutes later they were sitting side by side on a train rumbling towards London Charing Cross. 'Right, spill,' said Erin. 'What have I let myself in for?' She tried to sound jovial, but her need to clutch her bag tightly to her middle would have told any observant onlooker that she was feeling decidedly uncomfortable.

'We're going to make perfume.'

'We're doing what now?' Erin turned to examine Susan's face. Surely she couldn't have heard her right?

'I've booked us on to a ninety-minute taster course to learn how to make perfume. I didn't tell you because I knew you wouldn't come unless I let you pay for yourself.'

'You were right,' said Erin, loosening her grip on her bag. Perfume making was an odd choice of activity, but it didn't sound like it held much peril.

'And that wouldn't have been fair because you're not interested in making perfume.'

'I might be,' she said, trying to work out whether she was or not, which was difficult because the concept had never crossed her consciousness before.

'You're not,' said Susan, defiantly. 'And I didn't want to go on my own, so since Bella and Sophia are both teaching during the week, I roped you in. Selfish, I know, so the least I can do is pay for you.' The brakes squeaked as the train pulled into a station. The doors whooshed open and passengers embarked and scanned the carriage before choosing seats furthest away from anyone else. 'I feel foolish for not having the confidence to go along on my own. I'm so sorry for hoodwinking you into coming with me.'

'I forgive you . . . I think. Although I reserve the right to retract that. I'm flattered you want me to come with you.' Now the idea was sinking in, she was curious. 'In fact, I haven't experienced a single urge to jump off the train and get the next one home. I don't like surprises, though, so please don't do it again.'

Susan pinched her lips, seeming unconvinced. 'I'm

not sure I'd be so kind if you dragged me along to a barista course, or something like that.'

'What can I say? I'm just an easygoing kinda gal.' Erin grinned, releasing her grip on her bag so far it almost fell off her lap. She righted it. 'And I'm quite excited now I know what we're doing. I'm all for a new experience.'

'You are not,' said Susan, a little too quickly for Erin's liking. 'Sorry, that came out wrong. I meant, you usually give things a lot of thought before committing. That's why I was deliberately vague about this afternoon.'

'Sneaky,' said Erin. 'I feel properly hoodwinked now.' She crossed her arms and pouted. She was pretending to be offended, but in truth she was unsettled by Susan's insight into how she came across. No, that wasn't the problem. The unsettling thing was that it was true. She'd become someone who didn't try new things and whose friends didn't trust her to support them without running it through her internal risk assessment process. That didn't show her in a great light. 'Why are we doing a perfume course, anyway?'

'It's for my last pages,' said Susan. 'I'm doing something for me.'

'Good for you,' said Erin, intrigued. 'What's the plan, then?'

'First, I'll see how today goes, and if I like it, I might book myself onto a longer, more intensive course.' She saw Erin's concerned expression. 'Don't worry, I won't try to rope you into that. If I decide to do it, I'll have to pull my big girl pants on and get on with it.' She lowered her voice. 'The one I've got my eye on is quite pricey. It would feel a bit indulgent to do it, but Stewart said I should. I'm still only sixty. He said I should live a bit and do something for me.'

Erin put her hand over Susan's. 'He's absolutely right, bless him.' Susan's other half might be a workaholic, but he was a kind and loving husband when he was around.

'And, you never know, if I manage to make something that doesn't smell like a stink bomb, maybe I could take a stall at Blackheath Market on a Sunday.'

'Get you and your entrepreneurial spirit,' said Erin. 'I love that idea. And even if you're crap at it, then I'm sure there's a market for stink bombs. I know there was when I was a kid.'

'You make a good point,' said Susan, an unusually childlike grin on her face. 'We're winning either way.'

***

Even at the start of the session, it was clear Susan wasn't crap at creating beautiful scents. Erin was. She'd listened carefully to the instructor, Serena, who spoke slowly, catching the eye of all fifteen people sitting around the enormous table in the clean, white room that looked like a laboratory. She wore a serious expression and a blinding white lab coat when she explained the safety protocol. 'You'll be handling a variety of chemicals, some of them dangerous,' she said. Erin had never considered that concocting something you put on your skin would be a dangerous activity.

That made her vigilant and caused other worries to sneak through her brain to the front. She was glad when they got to the practical part, because at least then her mind was occupied by not blinding anyone or causing an explosion, both of which seemed strangely probable from what she could gather.

'On the paper in front of you, please write down the name of the person you're creating the scent for, your ideal customer, if you will,' said Serena. 'Then write down the words which best describe the aroma you'd like to create for that person.'

Erin held the pen in her hand, but her mind was blank. Susan scribbled feverishly. Erin peered across at her paper and read, *aromatic, with hints of sweet vanilla*.

'How do you know what to write?' she whispered.

'I'm making it up,' said Susan. 'I'm my ideal customer, so I'm writing down which scents I prefer.'

'I like Lenor Summer Breeze fabric conditioner. Does that count?' said Erin, the urge to giggle strong.

'Write fresh and floral, then.' Erin did, but couldn't think of anything else. Susan said, 'What about earthy?'

'Like mud?' said Erin, unable to stop her laughter then.

Susan smiled and shook her head. 'Behave yourself.'

Erin tried. She listened to the next steps about top, mid and base notes, then dutifully donned the blue latex gloves and safety goggles but found managing the pipettes to take tiny amounts from the glass jars almost impossible. The gloves were thin, but not thin enough for her to be dexterous. Then her goggles kept steaming up.

'Did you take in all that information about the raw materials and essential oils and stuff?' she whispered to Susan, when the instructor was helping someone at the far end of the table.

'Yes,' said Susan, picking up a small brown bottle and peering at the label. 'Didn't you?'

'I failed O level chemistry,' Erin said. 'And now I remember why.'

Susan's eyebrows made a stricken triangle. 'I'm sorry for making you do this.'

'God, no,' said Erin, 'I'm having a ball. Just because I'm rubbish at it, doesn't mean I'm not enjoying it. And I'm looking forward to saying I was there at the start of your global perfume empire.'

'Imagine,' said Susan, dipping a scent stick into the bottle then waving it under her nose, then Erin's.

'Musky,' said Erin, nodding as if she knew what she was talking about. Something in the scent reminded her of Adam and her heart tilted. She opened her mouth to tell Susan about how disappointing he'd proved to be, but closed it again. He might be a disappointment, but he'd shared the news about his son, but hadn't given her permission to tell anyone else, so she couldn't spread it any further. It wouldn't be right, and she knew wrong from right, even if he didn't.

'You're learning,' said Susan. She let out a long, satisfied sigh. 'I'm going to do the long course,' she said, decisively. 'It's time I did something for me.' She focused on Erin. 'Thank you for coming along today. You helped me to be brave. If I can ever return the favour, just say the word.'

Erin was touched. 'I will.' But the words felt hollow in her mouth, because she didn't believe she had the capacity to be brave, even with the help of her dear friends. The things she had to tackle were insurmountable. Change was coming and even the thought of the future made her toes curl inside her shoes.

'I think we all have a lot to thank Adam for,' said Susan. 'Him coming to book group and questioning how we did things has led to all of us thinking about what we want for our next chapters, hasn't it?' She dipped another scent stick in a bottle and brought it to her nose, breathing in the fragrance with her eyes closed. 'I don't think I'd be doing this if he hadn't come along, and I haven't been this excited about something for myself, rather than the girls, for as long as I can remember.'

Erin was glad her friend wasn't watching her, because she didn't think she could disguise her disappointment in Adam. She didn't feel like she had anything to thank him for, other than reminding her that taking a risk never, ever ended well.

Chapter Eighteen

The flat was quiet when Erin got home. Susan had insisted on buying them dinner on the way back. She said it was a thank you for accompanying her on the course and refused any financial contribution from Erin. Despite her insistence, and the truth that she could probably afford the bill far more easily than Erin could, Erin still felt like she'd taken advantage. Next time Susan ate at the café, it would be on the house.

Jack was sitting on the sofa, staring at a laptop screen, when she walked in. 'Hiya,' she said.

'All right?' He didn't look up, which was odd.

'Don't let Susan get the bill next time she eats at the café, okay?' She removed her jacket and laid it over the sofa arm. 'She paid for me to go on this perfume-making course today and then insisted on buying dinner as well. I owe her big time.'

'Hm?' He was still staring at the screen, eyes narrowed.

'And when a giraffe walked in and offered us a ride on its back, I said why not? Susan wasn't keen, though. She wanted a go on the elephant.' She stopped talking and waited for Jack's nose to crinkle in incomprehension. Nothing. 'Jack, are you listening to a word I'm saying?'

He glanced up, but his eyes remained serious. 'Sorry. I was reading through this.' He turned the laptop towards her, and she saw the title on the Word document: *Save The Bookmark*. Her list of doom. Nausea swilled in her stomach when she remembered Jack messaging earlier in the day to ask if he could borrow her laptop. His was playing up after an update was installed. She hadn't given it a second thought. Now she could see she should have.

'Oh,' she said. Why hadn't she hidden that document under some random file name, like Mum's favourite porn? Jack would have left it well alone then. At least, she hoped he would.

'So, The Bookmark's in financial trouble?'

She opened her mouth to deny it, but the title was pretty explicit and her list of advertising plans and cost cutting exercises were there in black and white. 'The building's been sold to a new company and the lease is ending soon. The rent's going up by eight grand a quarter.'

He moved the mouse to point at the last thing on the list. He read it out, 'Try to negotiate the rent increase down.' He gazed up at her. 'The new owners are increasing the rent by thirty-two thousand pounds a year? Is that even legal?'

She shrugged, defeated. Any remaining energy she had seeped out through her feet into the floorboards.

She was so very, very tired of thinking about it all the time, and even though he hadn't got a job to fall back on, she couldn't hide it from Jack any longer. 'I don't know. They sent a load of examples of comparable properties and what they pay in rent, and it looks like we had a very good deal before. I knew it was cheap for the area, but never questioned it because I thought we had a good understanding. I never bothered them with maintenance or anything, and kept it in good condition, and I was never late with the rent. I suppose I thought we'd keep ticking along like that until I retired, or sold the business, if anyone was daft enough to take it on. To be honest, I hadn't thought that far ahead.' She attempted a smile. 'You know me, not a fan of looking forwards.'

He didn't smile back, so she carried on, 'It looks like it's the end of the road for The Bookmark.' Her voice cracked and before she could stop them, tears tumbled from her eyes. She put her hand to her mouth, appalled at herself for breaking down in front of Jack. He was her child. She was supposed to shield him from worry, not add to it, but saying it out loud to another person made it all agonisingly real.

He dropped the laptop on the cushion, jumped up, and wrapped his arms around her. She hated herself for sobbing into his bony shoulder but once the tears had started she couldn't stop them. She was weak and pathetic. Who behaved like this with their child? She'd always seen her parents as strong and capable people.

Even when her mother was sick at the end of her life, her vibrant personality didn't diminish. She never crumbled like Erin was now.

'Why didn't you say anything?' said Jack.

'You've got enough on your plate looking for a graduate job.'

'Oh, Mum. It's okay,' he said. 'We'll sort it out.'

She lifted her head, summoning her last vestige of strength. 'I honestly don't think it's something that can be sorted out, and anyway, this isn't your problem to solve, it's mine.' She extricated herself from him, took a tissue from the box on the table and wiped her face with hard strokes in an attempt to feel something other than the surge of fresh tears climbing up her throat. 'You concentrate on getting a job you'll enjoy, and I'll work out what to do about The Bookmark.'

He scratched his cheek and pulled his lips tight. 'You can't afford to employ me, can you?'

She viewed the soggy tissue in her hands. 'I, erm . . .'

'I'll look for bar work tomorrow,' he said. 'There's no point giving me a salary when you don't have to. I'm sorry I asked now. I thought you'd enjoy having a bit more time off. I had no idea I was putting you under more pressure.'

Now he was beating himself up over something that was entirely her fault. Her lovely, lovely boy. 'You have nothing to be sorry for. I wanted you there. It's a family business. It's your grandma's legacy.' The image of her mother's face when Erin told her she wanted to run the café came back to her. She'd looked so proud of her, and now she was letting her whole family down.

'Sit down,' said Jack, his voice firm. Erin sat, feeling like a child about to get a ticking off from an exasperated parent. 'You keep talking about this legacy thing.'

'It's important,' said Erin, dabbing at a teardrop sliding down the side of her nose. 'Mum worked so hard to build the place up, and I feel like she's still there, in a way. She started the wall of books, and she was the one who encouraged people to borrow and swap them. It's her record player in the corner, her LPs in the cupboard underneath.' More sobs gathered as she remembered Mary closing her eyes and listening to the first few notes of one of her favourites. She clenched her jaw to stop the strangled sounds escaping.

'If you kept it going, would you want me to take the café over?'

That seemed like a strange question. She frowned. 'What do you mean?' They'd talked about this. It wasn't what either of them wanted for him.

'If it was still running and anything happened to you, would you want me to take over The Bookmark?'

She tried, but couldn't picture him in the café as an older man. He was a creative at heart. He wouldn't be fulfilled by a career in hospitality. She blew her nose. 'There won't be anything to take over, anyway.'

'That's not the point,' said Jack. 'If nothing else was at play, would you want me to take over the family business?' There was an urgency in his question.

‘Only if you wanted to.’

‘Exactly,’ Jack said, with a sweep of his hand. ‘You want me to do what’s right for me.’

‘Of course I do. I’m your mum. I want you to be happy.’

‘That’s exactly my point. Grandma would only want you to do what was right for you.’

Erin knew that was true, but he was missing one crucial fact. ‘Carrying on her legacy does make me happy,’ she said. It did, at least, before all this rent rise business. But there was more to a legacy than profit. She sniffed. ‘I feel close to her in that room.’

Jack shifted the laptop and sat next to her, putting an arm around her shoulder. ‘I get it. I do too. But the grim fact is, legacy or not, if it’s not working, something has to change.’

Chapter Nineteen

Erin was surprised and a little put out when Adam arrived at book group on time the following day. She hadn't slept well after her talk with Jack, and she was utterly drained. Now he knew, there was more urgency to tell Riley and the others, but every time she thought of it, tears bubbled inside her. She was going to miss her self-imposed deadline because she was too weak to get the words out without crying. Was it any surprise her business had failed with a coward like her at the helm?

As if sympathising with her mood, the weather was still miserable and Adam's biker jacket was shiny with rain when he came through the door, smiling and greeting everyone like old friends. Everyone except her, at least. They just nodded at each other as he took his coat off and dropped it over the back of his chair, rubbing his wet head as if his hand was a towel. At least he hadn't taken Riley's empty armchair. She hadn't yet arrived. Erin sneaked a glance at Adam's long-sleeved T-shirt with *Red Hot Chili Peppers* written in a circle around a central red asterisk. She'd seen the band at the O2 a few years ago. She found herself wondering if Adam had been there too, before catching herself. She needed to stop allowing this man into her head. He might be all smiles, but underneath he was not a trustworthy person.

'Good to see you, young man,' said Joe.

'We missed you,' said Mercy. There she went again, thought Erin, telling him he was missed, when really, things were no different with him around. She corrected herself. Things were better before he came along and changed things up. Much better.

'How's everyone getting on with their last pages?' he said, and Erin wanted to scream. This was her book group, not a writing group. She'd started it ten years ago, before anyone had heard of Adam Bloody Darling.

Susan's face lit up. 'I've made a practical start,' she said. 'Yesterday Erin and I went on a perfume-making course.'

'Is that right?' There was delight in Adam's voice and Erin could feel him turn to look at her. She kept her eyes on Susan.

'It was brilliant,' Susan gushed. 'I feel like I've found my calling.'

'Amazing,' he said. 'I'm impressed.' Erin dug her nails into the soft flesh of her palm. Who was he to praise her friends? She wanted to put a spike in their adulation of him right now by telling them all what he was really like. He was cut from the same cloth as Andrew. He wasn't the fine, upstanding man everyone thought he was. He was a feckless deserter of children, a man who put his own selfish needs above those of his son and the woman who raised him.

'And I'm thinking about booking my first trip.' Mercy sounded like an excited child who wanted some of the teacher's praise for herself. The delight in Mercy's voice melted Erin's fury a little. She had to concede, albeit reluctantly, that the writing exercise had done some good when she saw how Susan and Mercy were glowing. 'I'm planning to go to Kenya in September.'

'Kenya, wow,' Erin said. Mercy had played it safe all the time Erin had known her, and now she was jetting across the world. It sounded terrifying, but that made it all the more impressive. 'That's fantastic.'

'I'm thinking, go big or go home,' Mercy said, chuckling. 'My parents talked so fondly of their birthplace, and I have relatives I've never met, so I thought, why not start my adventures there?' Her face turned serious. 'I wanted to read a few books to give me a feel for the place, so I went to see Jakub at the library.' She sat back and crossed her arms over her soft chest. 'You wouldn't believe how hard it is to find a novel set in Kenya that isn't written by a white author. Can you think of any?'

Erin glanced across at the wall of books, hoping for inspiration, but nothing jumped out. After a quiet moment, she viewed the group's perplexed faces and realized none of them could either. 'I can't, I'm afraid. That's not good, is it?'

'The only books set in Kenya I can think of are *Out*

of Africa, and *Born Free*.' Susan grimaced, 'Which rather proves your point, doesn't it?' The others mumbled in agreement.

The broad smile returned to Mercy's face. 'Jakub has sent me on a mission to find the best books by local authors recommended by the people I meet when I'm travelling. He's going to set up a corner of the library with books from around the world. He's going to call it Mercy's Corner.' She slapped her hands down on her thighs and rocked forwards, her glee palpable.

'That's incredible,' said Erin, tears pricking at the corners of her eyes. 'You're fulfilling your dream and you're creating a legacy here in the UK that will benefit so many other readers. I feel quite emotional about that.' She had to stop herself from gazing around at her mother's legacy, her heart aching with the knowledge it was slipping through her fingers. She used to think of the café as somewhere people could get away from the stresses of the world and find comfort. Now, as she took in the prints on the walls that needed dusting, and thought about the coffee machine that needed descaling, she felt exhausted, and that was before she even considered what was coming. The weight of it all was crushing.

'And I'll have my blog,' Mercy said. 'I'm going to have a book section on there.' The pride in her eyes was a joy to see. She'd always been a lively, positive woman, but now she had this new purpose, she seemed to literally glow.

The door opened and Riley walked in, followed by Tybalt, who stopped to shake droplets of moisture from his fur. 'Sorry I'm late.' There was an unusual slouch in her gait.

'You okay?' said Erin. She went to the kitchen to get a towel, then caught Tybalt and rubbed him a little dryer before he jumped onto Joe's lap. She threw the towel to Joe, who carried on drying the cat as Tybalt batted the cloth away with his paw.

'Yeah. It's been a good day.' Her flat tone suggested otherwise. She flopped into the empty armchair.

'Are you sure?' said Hafsa.

'I was buzzing earlier,' she said, smearing raindrops across her claret faux-leather jacket. 'A promoter's been in touch about getting me some gigs.'

'That's fantastic,' said Erin. This was Riley's dream. 'So, why the glum face?'

'I went around to Chegs' to tell him, but Teagan was there. Apparently, her parents have kicked her out for trashing their place when she was coked up with her mates, so she's staying at his for a bit.'

'Oh.' Erin thought back to the entitled girl who'd expected to eat at the café for free. 'You didn't know she was staying with him before you got there?'

Riley shook her head. 'And she was wearing this tiny little pyjama suit thing that was practically underwear.' She glanced up. 'I mean, I'm not slut-shaming her, or anything. She can wear whatever she wants, it was just a surprise to find her on my boyfriend's fucking couch like that.'

‘Understandable,’ said Susan. ‘Was Chegs at least happy about your news?’

‘Chegs?’ asked Adam.

‘My boyfriend’s called Lawrence Chegwin, but everyone calls him Chegs,’ Riley said, before turning back to the group. ‘After I told him, he googled the promoter and said he’s not that big in the industry, so that took the edge off it a bit.’

Erin would quite happily have smacked Chegs in the mouth. ‘But he approached you. That’s amazing. It could be the start of something very exciting.’

Riley’s eyes brightened. ‘Maybe.’

‘And one gig will lead to another,’ said Hafsa. ‘When everyone sees how good you are.’

‘Soon, you’ll be booked up every night. You’ll be going on world tours,’ said Mercy. ‘I’ll come and see you in cities around the globe.’

Erin imagined Riley going on a world tour. That would be incredible. It occurred to her that it would also mean Erin wouldn’t have to tell her that she had to let her go. That would be a huge relief. She gave her head a shake. What a wimp she was.

‘Will you still speak to us little people when you’re famous and on Letterman, and such like?’ said Joe, and Erin loved each and every one of them for giving their friend the kind of boost she deserved.

‘Shut up,’ said Riley, squirming in her seat. She glanced up, shyly. ‘It is pretty fucking cool, isn’t it?’

‘It’s brilliant,’ said Adam. ‘There’s nothing like

making your living from something you love. The creative industries are tough, but it's totally worth it.' He paused. 'And I hope I'm not speaking out of turn, but shouldn't your boyfriend be your biggest cheerleader? Correct me if I'm wrong, but he sounds like a bit of a . . . well, a bit of a dick.'

That was rich, thought Erin. It was all she could do not to say, *takes one to know one*.

Chapter Twenty

To Erin's disappointment, Riley spent the next few minutes telling the group all the things she loved about Chegs. 'He keeps me grounded, because I can get, like, pretty over-excited, and that's not cool.' It sounded very much like she was justifying her relationship to herself as much as everyone else. 'So, he's actually really good for me,' she said in conclusion. Erin wanted to tell her what she'd described wasn't the basis of a healthy, loving relationship. As Adam said, Chegs should be her greatest fan. Instead, she seemed grateful he liked one in five of her videos and showed her he loved her by having the odd jealous tantrum. But then, what did Erin know? She'd only ever had one long-term relationship, and look how that turned out.

'I apologise,' said Adam. 'I was completely out of order. I had no right to say what I did.'

'S'all right,' said Riley. 'No worries.' Luckily for Adam, Riley wasn't the kind of person to be easily offended or hold a grudge. That's why Erin was surprised about her response to Teagan. The girl must've really ruffled her to elicit that level of negativity from Riley, who was now scanning the group, back to her normal, cheerful self. 'What have I missed, people?'

They filled her in on Susan and Mercy's news and she high fived them both before turning to Joe. 'And what's your news, old man?'

'Less of your cheek,' said Joe, grinning at her. 'I do have a snippet, actually.' He lay his hands flat on the chair's arms as if bracing himself. 'I've joined a dating site.'

'No way?' Riley lifted out of her seat, her hand aloft. She slapped her palm against Joe's. 'Go you.'

'It's called London Seniors and when I say I've joined, I've downloaded the app on my phone and paid the subscription. I haven't added my profile yet. I was hoping you lot might help me with that.'

'Hell, yes,' said Riley, shifting to the edge of her seat. 'What's your handle going to be?'

'I was thinking about Jazz-hands Joe. It has a nice ring to it, and it says something about me, don't you think?'

'Hm.' Riley glanced around the group. 'Are you looking for women, or men?'

Joe frowned. 'Women. I have nothing against men, but I have no attraction to them physically.'

'Then maybe leave off the jazz-hands.' Riley screwed up her face. 'It sounds a bit queer, which is cool, but if you're not into—'

'Queer?' Mercy said, her expression confused. 'That's a slur, isn't it?'

'Not anymore,' said Susan, with authority. 'It's been reclaimed by the LGBTQ+ community. Bella and Sophia both identify as queer. They explained it to me as having a sexual identity that isn't heterosexual and maybe a gender that isn't . . .' She tapped her temple. 'What is it? Cisgender, or something.' She sounded less sure now. 'Anyway, we're allowed to say it, as long as we don't mean it negatively, apparently.'

'Right,' said Mercy. She turned to Joe. 'You don't strike me as queer.'

'I'm a bit old to start trying all that,' he said. 'Better to stick with what I know.' He tickled Tybalt under his chin, and addressed the cat. 'Wouldn't you agree, my friend?' Tybalt clearly enjoyed the scratch and stretched his neck so far it looked like he might fall over backwards.

'Maybe jazz hands isn't ideal, then,' said Erin. 'It reminds me of Jack in that sitcom, *Will & Grace*.' She had an idea. 'What about Bass-notes Joe? That's quite masculine, if that's what you're after.' It seemed odd to be talking about what sounded queer or masculine on a dating app with a man who was like a father to her. Maybe she wasn't as comfortable with the idea of him looking for love as she thought she was. She had a quiet word with herself. This wasn't about her. If it was what Joe wanted, then she would support him all the way.

Joe's eyes twinkled. 'I like that.' He brought a folded piece of paper and a pen from the breast pocket of his shirt, rested it on the chair arm, and began to make notes. He raised his head. 'What should I say about myself?'

'Widowed is probably relevant,' said Susan. 'I imagine people would want to know your relationship status.' She turned to Riley. 'Is that what you call it?'

Riley nodded. 'And list your interests.'

'Okay. Jazz music, double bass, reading.' Joe wrote in spidery handwriting that Erin recognized from years of birthday and Christmas cards. Nuala and Joe were the kind of people who always wrote thoughtful messages, rather than letting whatever was printed inside the card do the talking for them. Erin had kept each and every one. They were in a box alongside those from her parents in the bottom of her cupboard. 'Book group. What else?'

'You're already doing better than most,' said Erin. 'I remember trying to write my personal statement when I was applying for university. I was one of those saddos who wrote reading, swimming, and socialising. That's why I made Jack try out all the extra-curricular activities he could. Gold Duke of Edinburgh sounds a lot better than socialising on a CV.' She sighed. 'Not that it seems to be doing him much good at the moment.'

'The job hunt isn't going well, then?' said Hafsa.

'Nothing's come up yet.'

'Oh, love. You never stop worrying about them, do you?' said Joe.

Erin swallowed. 'Sorry, I didn't mean to change the subject. Let's get back to your profile.'

Joe folded the paper up and tucked it away in his pocket. 'You've set me on the right track. I'm going to give it some more thought and perhaps run it by you before I make it live, if that's okay?' he said.

'Totally here for that. And take a look at what other nannas have put on theirs,' said Riley, winking at Joe, who gave her a pretend hard stare. 'That'll give you an idea of what people are looking for.' She turned to Erin. 'I'll miss Jack when he gets a full-time job. I've loved working with him. He's a right laugh. Even though I'm only a few years older than him, I thought of him as a scrawny kid when I started working here, and now he's a fully fledged grown-up. Makes a girl feel old.'

'Imagine how I feel,' said Erin. 'In my head he's still a little boy, and now he's talking about his future career prospects.' Images of Jack as a toddler, holding his pudgy hands out when he wanted to be lifted into her arms, stopped her in her tracks. What she wouldn't give to be able to lift him up and cradle him now. But that was wrong. He was a man, and she knew in her heart of hearts she wanted to cling to him partly because she was frightened of the future, and that wasn't right.

'He's probably getting a bar job in the meantime,' she said. Maybe she was strong enough to tell them about The Bookmark's future. She opened her mouth to speak, but felt tears well in her eyes. Bursting into tears would be embarrassing, especially with Adam there. And they were all feeling positive about their next steps. Now wasn't the time, she decided. She told herself it wouldn't be fair to bring the mood down by telling them how dire the next chapter of her own life looked, when really she knew it was cowardice, not consideration on her part. 'He needs more hours than I can give him.' She felt an urgent need to shift the focus away from her. 'Talking of kids, Hafsa, how's Zahra doing?'

'Not bad at all,' said Hafsa. She was as beautifully dressed as ever, in wide-legged trousers and a boat-necked black top with white stitching detail around the bottom hem and sleeves. 'In fact, I think we've come to a new understanding. I've shared the stuff I've learned through reading up on what it's like to be a teenage girl with autism, and she's been more open about what's going on in her head.' She smoothed out an invisible crease in her trousers. 'I asked her to write some of it down and she stared at me like I'd lost my mind. But that evening I was watching our famous friend—' she gestured to Riley, who gave a little bow '—on Tiktok, and then a video of a woman who looked to be in her early twenties came up. She was talking about getting an autism diagnosis recently and started to list all the traits she wished she'd known about years ago, like the fact that loads of people with ASD are good with words, even though people presume they're bad at communicating.'

'I didn't know that,' said Adam. 'I thought that was an issue if you were autistic.'

'Me too,' said Susan.

'You see, this is where it gets complicated,' said Hafsa. 'Hyperlexia, the ability to read early and a strong interest in letters and numbers, isn't that uncommon in autistic kids, but it can mean they don't understand the meaning as well, or what the words are meant to communicate.' She took a breath. 'Or it can mean they're gifted in reading and comprehension and incredibly articulate. This is the trouble. Everyone's experience of the condition is different.'

'Blimey. There's a lot to learn,' said Susan.

'So much,' said Hafsa. 'And the more people share their experiences, the more we can start to understand, so I asked Zahra how she felt about making a video diary.' She held out her hand. 'Not for public consumption. We won't be sharing it anywhere, but to help her make sense of the way she experiences the world, and to help me and Amir and the rest of the family understand her a bit better.'

'That's a great idea,' said Riley. 'Completely understand why you don't want to share it, though. The trolls on my page are vile.'

'You get trolled?' Erin was shocked. It had never occurred to her to scroll through the comments on Riley's posts. She'd always presumed everyone would be as impressed by her friend's talent as she was. Now, she realized how naive that was. She lived in a bubble of her own making and had done for years.

Riley snorted. 'All the fucking time. You'll be surprised to learn not everyone in the world is a big fan of outspoken feminist voices being amplified.'

'Idiots,' said Adam. 'Keyboard warriors are the worst. I get plenty of nasty comments online whenever my stuff's posted too. Some people shouldn't be allowed access to the internet, not without passing some kind of moral compass test first.'

He was a fine one to talk about moral compasses. 'What happened to that piece you were writing about Lebanon and Terry Waite, the one you asked me about?' She felt brave for reminding him he had asked for her help and not followed up on it. Men in glass houses, she thought, piously.

'I put it aside when . . . actually, I wanted to talk to you about that,' he said. 'Could we have a chat after book group?'

That? Was he talking about the article, or the thing he'd wanted to chat about when he asked her to go for that walk in Greenwich Park? She tried to keep her mind from wandering as the others discussed the books they were reading to help with their last pages, but it was no use. Adam had piqued her interest, damn him.

Chapter Twenty-One

Erin moved to the side as Adam brought the last of the cups through to the kitchen and hovered, as if asking where to put them. The patterned porcelain teacups looked tiny and fragile in his enormous hands. Everyone else had gone, and she became hyper-aware of being on her own in the small space with this big man. She took the cups from him and put them on the top of the dishwasher. 'Why don't you wait for me out there?' She pointed out to the room, noticing the light was fading outside and fresh rain spattered the windows. The uplighters on the walls made the café appear cosy and warm, and a surge of affection for the space was followed by a scooping out in her middle. 'I'll be done in a minute.'

'I'm happy to help,' he said. 'Being a single man has its benefits. I'm fully competent in all things domestic.' Did he want a prize for doing tasks every woman on the planet performed daily without a word of praise? 'Point me in the direction of the dishwasher.' He scanned the various chrome appliances.

'I wouldn't thank you for it,' said Erin, forcing

humour into her voice. 'I'm a tyrant when it comes to loading.'

'Ah, you're one of those, are you?' He pointed at her. 'I saw a meme that said in every couple there's one person who loads the dishwasher like a Scandinavian architect, and one who loads it like a raccoon on meth.'

'Scandi as charged,' said Erin, opening the front and bowing down to reorganise the top rack. She wanted to shove her head inside and put it on a boil wash when she realized she'd unintentionally implied they were a couple. But she couldn't backtrack without making it into a thing. She spent longer than she needed to re-stacking the delicate cups, before standing and moving to the sink to wash her hands. She kept her back to him when she said, 'What was it you wanted to talk about?'

She heard the soles of his boots shift on the floor. 'I wanted to explain . . . I think I gave you the wrong impression when we went to the park last week.'

'About what?' She turned off the tap and dried her hands on a tea towel before folding it neatly and hanging it over the handle of the oven.

'About my son. If you'd hung around long enough to hear—'

'It's really none of my business.' Erin walked past him into the body of the café and began to tuck chairs neatly under tables, annoyed at the hint of irritation in his voice. He was in no position to tell her what she'd done wrong. She wasn't the one who'd abandoned their family. Quite the opposite, in fact. She shoved a chair hard, its legs scraping loudly on the floor.

'No, it isn't,' he said. His exasperated tone made her bristle. Why had he bothered staying behind if that's what he thought? 'But for some unfathomable reason, I feel the need to explain myself to you, because, again, for reasons I find utterly baffling, I care what you think of me.'

She turned to face him, surprised by his candour. 'You don't owe me an explanation.'

'I know.' His fingers curled inwards. 'God, you really are infuriating.'

'Me?' That was rich. 'I'm not the one who infiltrated a perfectly functioning book group and turned it on its head.'

'Infiltrated?'

It did sound a bit strong when repeated back. 'No one asked you to change things.'

'Everyone else seems happy with what's going on. More than happy.'

That might be the thing that annoyed her the most. 'Well, I'm not.' There, she'd said it.

'That's because you're terrified of anything upsetting your finely balanced ecosystem. Heaven forbid anything should ever change.' He tucked a chair under a table so hard it clunked against the wood, then looked sheepish and took more care with the next one. 'Change isn't all bad, you know. Sometimes things change for the better.'

She needed to get to the crux of what bothered her

the most. 'Well, you can't change the fact of having a child. You can't just walk away from a living breathing person, not without harming people, if you do. Children are precious. You can't be in their lives one minute and not the next. It's not fair on anyone. Parenting is hard, but that's what you agree to when you bring a new life into this world, you sign up to do the hard work and to put them first.' Even as she spoke, she knew her words were really meant for Jack's father, more than the man standing in front of her now.

Adam raised his eyes to the ceiling. 'I didn't even know I had a son until a month ago. That's what I wanted to talk to you about. If you hadn't been so busy deciding who and what I was, judging me and finding me guilty in your personal family courtroom, you might have worked out that I wanted help. I needed help.' He said the last words slowly, and the emotion in them made Erin turn and stare. What she saw wasn't a confident man who travelled the world in search of a scoop. His shoulders were hunched, and pain showed in the deep creases beside his eyes. 'I thought I could talk to you because I saw how kind and compassionate you are with everyone at book group, but I made a mistake. You haven't given me a fair hearing.'

'You didn't know you had a son?'

'Not a clue.'

Head suddenly light, Erin pulled out a chair and sat. Adam did the same.

'I had no idea until I got an email about four weeks

ago asking if I was willing to do a DNA test. A twenty-six-year-old man had been told that I was his father, and he wanted to know if it was true.'

'He'd only just been told?' That sounded brutal. Jack might not have much of a relationship with Andrew, but he knew his genetic heritage, at least.

'Yep.'

'His mother . . .?'

'Someone I had a brief relationship with in my late twenties. We were both journalists covering the election. We were on the campaign trail together, sharing the tour bus, staying in the same hotels. We hooked up for a couple of weeks, but agreed it was never going to go anywhere. She was a home-bird, mostly working on local news, I wanted to travel.' He gazed at her earnestly. 'I swear to you, it was a mutual decision. Neither of us left the other. It was fun while it lasted, but that was it.'

'And she never told you she was pregnant?'

'No.' He rubbed his face. 'If she had . . . I think . . . I'm sure I would have wanted to be part of his life, I mean, half his DNA is mine, for God's sake. I was nearly thirty. I wasn't a kid. I would have done the right thing.'

There was such sincerity in his voice that Erin believed him. She'd judged him, and she was wrong to do so. She was getting everything wrong these days, and this time she'd walked away when someone needed her help. That was against everything she stood for. Blood rushed up her neck as it dawned on her she was the one who'd behaved unforgivably, not him. 'Why do you think she didn't tell you?'

'I honestly don't know. Maybe because she knew I was ambitious and didn't want to be tied down. That's one of the reasons we decided not to try to make a go of it. If we'd really fallen for each other, maybe things might have been different, but, like I said, it was just . . . nice. She was a couple of years older. I got the impression she wanted the husband and kids, the semi-detached house in the suburbs and all that. But there were no hard feelings, honestly. I didn't use her and abandon her. Oliver knows that.'

'That's his name, Oliver?'

'Yes.' Adam's face brightened. 'It's a good name, isn't it?'

'It's a lovely name.'

'His mum married his stepdad when he was two, and he calls him Dad, so it's not like he's missed out on having a father figure. Not from what I can gather, anyway.'

'So why has he got in touch now?'

He sat back, eyes wide. 'He's going to be a dad himself.'

'Whoa.' Erin couldn't stop it coming out. 'You're going to be a grandad?'

He laughed. 'No need to look like that.' Erin closed her mouth, when she realized it was hanging open. 'That call I got, when I left book club that time, it was Oliver. That was the first time I'd spoken to him. The DNA tests came back positive, so there was no doubt I was his dad, genetically I mean, and now he's going to be a father himself, he wanted to reach out and see if I was willing to meet up.'

'That's massive.' She tried to imagine meeting Jack for the first time as a fully grown adult. She couldn't.

'Yep.'

'What's he like?' Jack was an intrinsic part of her. Being his mother was a significant element of her identity. She couldn't begin to imagine not having witnessed him growing up, it was simply inconceivable.

Adam raised his palms. 'I haven't met him yet.'

Erin calculated the time that had passed. 'But it's been a couple of weeks since that call. Does he live far away?'

'Only Market Harborough.'

'Then . . .?'

Adam dragged his nails across the underside of his chin. 'It's a big decision.'

'Is it?' Erin couldn't imagine anything on earth keeping her away from her son. The pull she felt towards him was visceral, magnetic.

He dropped his eyes to the table. 'It is for me. I'm not like you, Erin. I've seen what you're like with Jack. You're a great mum.'

Erin warmed at the praise. 'And you could be a great dad.'

'I'm not sure I'm cut out for it. You've got all this.' He gestured out to the room. 'You've got foundations, people you've been friends with your whole life, it's all solid and tangible. I've never put down roots. I travelled, I made friends, I moved on. I've never really committed to anything except my career, and even then I've always been freelance. I haven't even said a solid yes to a job.'

'So, you're a commitmentphobe, is that what you're saying?'

'You make it sound like I'm taking it lightly. I'm not. I just need to know I'm making the right decision.'

'I don't understand what decision there is to make,' Erin said, unable to keep the exasperation from her voice. She was truly confused as to why he wouldn't leap at the chance of having a relationship with his boy.

Adam stood. 'I'm sorry. I shouldn't have bothered you with this.' He marched to grab his coat from the back of the chair.

'Is this what you always do? Run away when things get hard?' Erin was beginning to wonder if he'd lied. Maybe he knew about his son all along, but didn't want Erin to know that.

'That's rich, coming from you.' Adam shoved his arms into the sleeves of his jacket.

'What's it got to do with me? I brought my son up myself. I didn't bugger off when things got real like his dad did.' She stood facing him and leaned against the table, arms crossed tightly.

'You can't judge everyone by that metric, Erin. You're tarring me with the same brush as him, and that's not fair. I thought you'd understand. I was wrong. I get that you were hurt, but you've let that make you blinkered and stuck in the past. Forget I ever said anything.' He strode towards the door, his boots clonking on the wood.

'You thought I'd understand what? Not facing up to your responsibilities? Does that sound like me? I've got responsibilities coming out of my bloody ears.' Her voice cracked. 'I'm drowning in them.'

He flung the door open. 'I thought you'd understand how hard this change is for me. What it feels like to be terrified you'll fuck up and get things wrong.' A breeze blew in from the street, making the hairs on Erin's arms stand on end. 'I thought if anyone would get that, it was you.' He stepped into the night and closed the door behind him.

Chapter Twenty-Two

Erin stood, frozen to the spot, her heart pounding in her chest. Adam wasn't trying to shirk his responsibilities. He was scared. He was frightened of this huge change and of messing up when the stakes were so high. He cared about getting it right with his son, and he was right, she'd been so blinkered by her own experiences that she'd blocked him when he reached out for help. As if jolted awake by an electric shock, she sprang towards the door and wrenched it open. 'Adam,' she yelled. She ran to the end of Brigade Street and looked left and right along the parade, but he wasn't there.

Directly ahead, a tall figure was marching across the heath. All Saints was lit up to the right, its walls illuminated like a beacon in the gloom. She rushed across the road and yelled again, 'Adam, stop.' The figure turned. Through the drizzle and half-light, she could see his shoulders curled inwards. What an idiot she'd been. 'Wait.' She ran across the uneven grass towards him. 'I'm sorry.'

'Don't be,' he said. 'Forget it.'

A raindrop landed on her eyelashes. She blinked

it away. 'I don't want to forget it. I feel like I wilfully misunderstood what you were trying to tell me.'

His lips lifted a fraction. 'It did feel like that, actually.'

She stared at her feet. Mud clung to the sides of her white trainers. 'I have a particular dislike of commitment-phobes.'

'I get that . . . and I might have been guilty of that in the past, but that's not what this is.'

'I understand that now.' Water seeped through her shirt onto her skin, making her shiver. 'Come back to the café. Let's talk.' Adam hesitated. 'Please.' She put her hand on the slippery leather of his sleeve. He nodded and, to her relief, followed when she turned to walk back to The Bookmark.

Erin kicked her wet shoes off at the door and Adam did the same. The wooden floor was cold through her damp socks as she went through to the kitchen. She unhooked the tea towel from the oven door and offered it to Adam. 'You need that more than I do,' he said.

He wasn't wrong, her white shirt was soaked through and when she glanced down, she was mortified to see the lace of her bra was clearly visible. She turned around and patted at the cotton, then pulled it away from her skin, cursing herself for changing out of her polo shirt before book group. 'I'm going to put something dry on,' she said, grabbing her tote from where it hung on the peg. 'Don't go anywhere.' She rushed to the ladies and changed quickly back into the creased polo shirt. Adam was sitting in an armchair scrolling through his phone when she came out. 'Fancy a cuppa?'

'No, I'm fine, thanks.' He lifted his phone. 'Want to see a picture of Oliver?'

This was more than she deserved. She took the seat next to him and looked at the photograph of a young man on the screen. He had broad shoulders, and soft grey eyes. 'I'm not sure you needed that DNA test,' she said. 'He's your double.'

'He's the spit of my dad when he was his age,' Adam said, his voice wavering. 'The Darling genes are strong, apparently.'

Erin thought again about how much Jack looked like Andrew. At least his personality came down her line. She knew him so intimately, and Adam had only just heard his twenty-six-year-old son's name. It was beyond her comprehension. 'How does that make you feel?'

Adam stared at the screen until it went dark. He swallowed and Erin could feel the emotion he was trying to manage. 'Weird.'

'Come on. You work with words; you can do better than that.' She spoke softly, aware she had some making up to do.

He gave her a wry smile. 'I feel the inexorable march of multitudinous, labyrinthine, and discordant emotions. That better?'

A laugh spurted from her. 'Now I don't know what you're on about. Tell me what they are, these discordant emotions.'

'There's the fear, but I feel like we've covered that.' He scratched under his chin and Erin realized she liked this familiar tick of his. It felt very him. 'It's not the most masculine thing in the world, is it?'

'Pah,' she said. 'Societal gender norms are so last century.' He cocked an eyebrow, and she grinned. 'I got that from Jack.'

'Nice.' His smile dimmed and he sighed. 'Regret's definitely one. Apart from the obvious, not seeing him grow up, I regret not providing my parents with a family, especially now I know there might have been a possibility of that, if I'd known about Oliver.' He traced the grain on the tabletop with his fingernail. 'I was in Sumatra covering the tsunami when my dad died. I hadn't been home for over a year. I kept putting it off, thinking there was plenty of time. He wasn't that old, so when a pulmonary embolism killed him out of the blue it was a real shock. I beat myself up over it for years, and I've tried to do better, visiting Mum, but she's in a care home now, and she's got dementia, so I'm not sure how much she takes in when I'm there.' He brought the phone screen back to life and the young man grinned back at them. 'She would have loved being a granny.' He glanced at Erin with sad eyes. 'I always felt bad for not giving her that chance, and now I feel worse because it could have happened.'

'I understand that, but it wasn't your fault it didn't. And I'm sure she's proud of the life you made for yourself.' Erin hesitated then said, 'I googled you.'

Adam glanced up, a smile lifting one side of his mouth. 'Did you now?'

'Just once.' That wasn't true. She'd kept going back until she'd read most of what came up in the search, but she wasn't about to admit that now. 'I bet your parents were bursting with pride.'

'I hope so. I kept telling myself you can't live your life for someone else. But now I feel like I've needlessly denied Mum all that potential joy.'

'If you didn't know . . .'

He huffed out a breath. 'I could have contacted Lucy, Oliver's mum. I could have checked in on her.'

'Do you usually check in on people you've had relationships with?'

His nose creased. 'I don't have relationships, really. Not long-term ones anyway. I've always been a bit of a free spirit. Lucy would have known that. I didn't exactly keep it a secret. I was the bloke with the motorbike and a backpack, always off on a new adventure. I was a bit of a cliché, back then, now I think about it.' He barked a short laugh. 'I'm just an older version of that now, aren't I?' He ran a finger over the moisture that lingered on the sleeve of his jacket. Erin was glad when he didn't look up, expecting her to confirm or deny, because she could see what he was saying, but that didn't mean she didn't find it attractive. She did, even though it was the opposite of what she thought she wanted for herself. Perhaps that was why. *They say opposites attract.*

'I imagine that's why she never tried to tell me she was

pregnant.' He shook his head. 'She probably thought I wouldn't step up.'

'And would you have?' She was invested in his answer.

'I like to think so, but . . .' He raised his shoulders. 'We'll never know.'

She'd wanted him to be more definite, but quickly realized his truthful answer was better. The world wasn't full of absolutes, much as she wished it was. It was full of flawed people doing the best they could. 'And what's stopping you now?'

'It's such a huge thing. At the moment I'm just a name and a set of DNA. We've talked on the phone a couple of times, and he seems like a great lad . . . but it's not him I'm worried about. What if I'm a disappointment? What if I am nothing more than a cliché? What if he invests in me and I let him down? I don't know if I'm cut out to be a dad. I haven't got a great track record for putting the time and effort into relationships.'

'But you can make a choice to do this right.'

'How, though? I decided to put down roots here in Blackheath, but I still couldn't bring myself to buy a place. I'm a coward. I rented because in the back of my mind I know I want the option to move.'

A wave of sadness passed through Erin. Maybe Oliver would be better off not expecting anything from this man. Maybe she would too. 'Well, you know yourself better than anyone else.'

He stared deep into her eyes. 'But I've surprised myself recently. I haven't got itchy feet at all.'

'At all?'

He moved his head side to side. 'Not even slightly.'

'Then maybe you can make relationships work, if you put your mind to it.' She kept her gaze locked on his.

'I'd like to. Change is hard, but I'm thinking it might well be worth it.'

'Change is hard,' said Erin, slowly. 'And scary. But if you do decide to be part of Oliver's life, you can make a conscious decision not to let him down. And relationships work two ways. If both of you want the same thing, then you'll find a way to make it work.' As a flame lit in her core, she knew she wasn't only talking about Adam's relationship with his son. And by the intensity in his eyes, Adam knew it too.

Chapter Twenty-Three

Adam waited on the wet cobbles as Erin locked up the café. When she turned the key in the lock, she heard a familiar mewling sound. She opened the door again, but Tybalt wasn't inside. 'Can you see Tybalt?' she said to Adam. 'I could have sworn he left when the others did, but I can still hear him. He doesn't usually like to be out in this weather.'

She followed the sound, taking a step towards the empty unit next door. She peered through the glass door and saw Tybalt, paw raised, his mewling louder as if shouting at her to let him out. 'How did you get in there, you silly creature?' she said. Adam joined her and peered over her shoulder at the cat. 'I'd better get Victoria to let him out, although I'm not sure she'll still have a key. Don't landlords usually change the locks when a tenant moves out?' It occurred to her that soon she wouldn't be able to open the door of The Bookmark anymore and she wanted to cry.

'Someone must've opened up for him to get inside,' said Adam, 'Surely?'

Erin cupped her hands to the side of her face and

squinted past the rain splattered glass to the back of the dark shop. A sliver of light was visible at the rear of the building from a crack in the door leading to what used to be Victoria's stockroom. 'There's a light on back there,' she said.

Adam pushed down the door handle and it creaked open. Tybalt rushed past their feet, and Erin turned just in time to see him disappear through the cat flap in Victoria's front door. 'You're welcome, pal,' she said, turning back when the sound of voices came from the lit room at the back. She paused, skin prickling, wondering whether they might be intruders. Should she call the police? Last time she did, it was only Jack, and she wasn't in a hurry to repeat that mistake. She was glad Adam was by her side. She felt safe with him, and she hadn't felt that way with anyone for a very long time. She glanced his way. He was standing still, listening too.

'I don't reckon her next door will be able to afford the thirty-two grand rent hike,' said a deep voice with a London accent. 'I'm expecting an email telling me she's packing up by the end of next month.'

Erin froze at the mention of the rent. She strained to hear more clearly.

'Do you think I can get the builders to do a reckie before that? I want to start knocking through as soon as she's out. I want the restaurant open before the end of the summer,' said a higher, younger-sounding male voice.

'All in good time, son. There's still some work to do

on getting the planning application through. You know what people round here are like. They want artisan, local shit. They think they're too boho for burger franchises, bunch of snobs. We can't rush things. We don't want people getting wind of any preferential treatment.'

Erin felt Adam's hand on her arm. He put a finger to his lips, and led her back from the door and into the mouth of Brigade Street. Once they were out of earshot, he said. 'Do you know what that was about?'

Erin glanced back towards the old gift shop, her brain replaying what they'd overheard. 'Whoever was in there knows that the landlord is putting my rent up in two months' time.'

'By over thirty thousand?'

'Yep.'

'Wow,' said Adam, his voice raising an octave. He frowned. 'They seemed to think you can't afford that.'

'I can't,' said Erin, looking down at the shiny cobbles under her feet. There was no point hiding it any longer. 'I've spent the last month trying to pluck up the courage to tell Riley and everyone that I've got no choice but to pull the plug on the business. I've tried, but I can't make the figures work, not with that kind of increase. I've got four weeks until I have to give notice under the terms of the lease.' She nodded towards the old gift shop. 'And it sounds like whoever's in that building is counting on me leaving. They were talking about knocking through and opening a burger place, as if it's a fait accompli.'

Adam's face was full of concern. 'Are you really going to give up The Bookmark?'

She turned to view the café that had been part of her family's history for four decades, fury taking over from the anxiety that had plagued her. 'Honestly, I thought I had no choice, but hearing those two talking about it as though it was a done deal has shifted something in me.' As she spoke, she realized it was true. It was as though a fire had been lit inside her, burning through the liquid worry that had been her constant state. 'What right have they got to profit from the devastation of my livelihood, my family business? And for what, another faceless bloody burger joint? How would more takeaway saturated fat benefit people around here?' She saw a smile creep onto Adam's face and felt the fire inside her burn even brighter.

'Good point, well made.'

A new, urgent resolve made Erin's spine straighten. 'Maybe I shouldn't give up without more of a fight. I've got a month left before I have to make it official. There's got to be something I can do.' She understood now that she'd accepted defeat without truly exploring all options. Surely, if there was any way of avoiding the change she'd been dreading, she owed it to her mother to try? The café was so much more than a place to eat and drink. It was part of the local community, and with the new fire burning in her belly, she knew that she had to try to preserve it, for her, for her family, and for everyone else who walked through that door.

Chapter Twenty-Four

The blazing fury that someone was planning the downfall of Erin's beloved café for their own gain raged during that night, and she used the time she tossed and turned to try to devise a way to make enough money to thwart their plans. But one thought kept trying to extinguish the flames of hope; it didn't matter how strong her will to survive was, if she didn't have the money for the rent, she didn't have a business. But she was damned if she was going to give in without exploring every available option. It was time to be brave. Change was coming whatever happened, and she had to try, at least, to make that work in her favour. She thanked her lucky stars that she didn't have an early start, because she didn't manage to drop off properly until the morning light began to creep into her bedroom.

Hafsa didn't usually have the time to come into the café during the day, so Erin was surprised to find her sitting in one of the armchairs reading a book when she started her shift that afternoon. 'Hello,' she said, taking in Hafsa's cream flares with matching waistcoat. 'Good to see you. You're looking gorgeous, as ever.'

'This old thing?' said Hafsa, grinning and tugging at the bottom of the waistcoat. 'I was hoping to see you today. Do you have time for a chat?'

'Course,' said Erin. The only viable solution she'd come up with during the night was to call the bank to try to arrange a bigger overdraft to give her some time to build the business up again. The thought of taking on more risk terrified her. She would do it, but she wasn't looking forward to that conversation and was happy for the distraction. She glanced around the room, at the woman with a toddler in a highchair holding a chewed rice cake between her fingers, and the young man with a half-finished toastie on a china plate in front of him, so engrossed in the book he was reading, he seemed to have forgotten to finish his lunch. The smell of coffee and grilled cheese filled the air, and Erin felt more certain than ever that she shouldn't let this oasis of calm slip through her fingers. She sat next to Hafsa. 'What's up?'

Hafsa put her book down on the low pewter-topped table. 'I wanted to talk to you about the last pages. I haven't done mine yet. Have you?'

'I haven't even started,' said Erin, more than a little relieved she wasn't the only one who was behind on the assignment. 'It's not homework, though. We're not going to pass or fail if we don't do it.' If she and Hafsa both decided not to write anything, no one could make them. On top of everything else she had to worry about, the pages had been constantly tapping away at the back of her mind, like a teacher knocking their red pen against a desk, and now maybe it could disappear from her endless to-do list, and her lungs seemed to have the capacity for more air.

'I'm such a swot,' said Hafsa. 'I've never not completed a piece of work on time in my life.'

'You do give off head girl energy,' said Erin. 'I don't suppose you get through medical school if you're a slacker like me.' She wasn't really a slacker, but she imagined Hafsa tried her utmost at everything she put her hand to, so it didn't feel right to put herself in the same category as her impressive friend. 'I imagine it's harder for you to renege on this than me, but if we both give up on it, then at least we're failing together.'

'Failing. Urgh.' Hafsa shuddered. 'I don't like the idea of that.'

'Okay, not failing. Choosing to spend our precious time on other things.' Erin should not have used the word failing with someone who probably ironed their duvet covers. That was one of her metrics for how efficient someone appeared to be. Ironing your duvet cover was top level – performing to high standards even when other people weren't looking. But you could go too far. If she thought someone probably ironed their knickers, then they had too much time on their hands or were utterly bonkers. Erin aspired to iron her duvet covers but never had the time.

Hafsa watched Riley move around the room, stopping to chat to customers, then scatter dog biscuits in a bowl for a cute French bulldog before disappearing into the kitchen. 'I feel like I'd be letting Riley and the others down,' she said, thoughtfully. 'And it's not even about failing.' She pinched her lips. 'Although that's not a word I'm familiar with.'

'Of course,' said Erin, with mock seriousness. 'Perish the thought.' Her chance of having a partner in crime was fading away.

'I think I'm struggling with it because I really want to do it, but I'm not sure how. I haven't pinpointed what I want my next chapter to look like. And that's new for me.' She picked up the book she'd been reading. 'I know I want it to involve supporting young people with autism, so I've been reading around the subject, like the good little student I am. This book's brilliant.' Erin read the title: *Strong Female Character*. 'It's Fern Brady's memoir and it's so funny and so sad at the same time. She wasn't diagnosed until she was an adult, and her life was so much harder because of it. I know Zahra's lucky because she has parents who'll advocate for her and support her, but so many kids aren't. I feel like I want to be part of making it easier, but . . . well, how?'

'What does your heart tell you to do?' Even as she said it, Erin knew that question had a multitude of answers. Added to which, what Hafsa wanted to do and what she was able to do with all the different variables in her life could be two vastly different things. She was struggling with that little conundrum herself. God, decisions were hard.

'That's the trouble. I don't know. Every time I think about it, my brain kind of freezes. I've been on one path my whole life. I did everything expected of me, and I'm not saying I minded. It made things simpler, if anything. I knew I was expected to do well in my exams, and get to medical school, and I was okay with that. I met Amir in my third year, and since he was training to be a medic as well, things just slotted into place. Since we wanted a family, we decided I would be a GP because it was the most regular hours, and then we had the kids and I thought we'd carry on . . . but Zahra's diagnosis, then Riley and Adam asking us to think about our futures, together those two things have set my head spinning in a different direction.'

'So, your last chapters are different to what you thought you'd be writing?' Erin could relate to that.

Hafsa bit her lip, her expression uncertain. 'I thought I knew my trajectory, and now I'm not so sure, and that's been destabilising, to say the least. We have a mortgage and three kids. Amir is supportive. If I do want a career change, he'll help, but he's getting frustrated with me vacillating the way I am. He wants to know what my plans are, but like I said, whenever I try to give it proper thought, my brain refuses to play ball. It's like my neural pathways shut off.'

'Because it's too scary to think about change?' Erin found it hard to believe someone as put together and academically brilliant as Hafsa had the same response to the future as she did. She thought back to the conversation with Adam last night. He was frightened to make changes too. Maybe her responses to uncertainty were more normal than she thought.

'Yes. What if I make the wrong choice? It's not that I'm unhappy in my work, and it can be fulfilling, but I have a hankering to make a real difference, and I think if I could decide on how I'd like to go about doing that, I could be more useful to young people like Zahra.'

'So, are you thinking about retraining?' Should Erin retrain? Even the thought of it made her sag. She was in her mid-fifties, running out of time to turn her hand to something new. And where would she find the money for any kind of training, or the time for that matter? No. The Bookmark was where her heart was. She was good at the job she already had, she just needed to try harder to make it work.

'Maybe.' Hafsa curled her lip. 'See, I'm all over the place. I half wish this had never come up so I could carry on plodding along with my head in the sand.'

'You and me both,' said Erin, with feeling.

'And there's something else that's bothering me.' Hafsa picked a hair from where it had stuck to her dark red lipstick. 'If I do leave medicine, I'm scared my parents will be disappointed with me.' She took up a napkin from the table and wiped a red stain from her fingers. 'How pathetic is that? I'm a forty-two-year-old mother of three, and I'm still worried about what my parents think.'

'I don't think we ever stop wanting validation from our parents,' said Erin. 'Even though my mum's not around anymore, I still always wonder what she'd make of my decisions.' She turned her gaze to the record player, and wished with all her heart that her mother was there to choose the next track, to decide whether to change the fruit and vegetable supplier, to tell Erin how to earn enough for the rent rise. Her heart ached for her. She wanted to be a child again, so that all the hard choices were someone else's to make.

'I get that. What people think of us matters, doesn't it? I mean, parental approval is one thing, but it's not just that. When new patients come into my treatment room, I know they make an immediate assessment about whether they can trust me or not. That's partly why I dress like this.' She gestured to her beautiful outfit. 'I feel as though looking like I'm put together is important for my job.'

Erin listened in fascination. She'd always presumed Hafsa just *was* put together. She thought life came easily to her because that's the impression she gave off. 'Really?'

'Yes. I mean, I like fashion and love nice clothes, but I always make sure my outfits match, that they fit well, and my make-up's perfect. When people come to see me, they're already in a vulnerable position. They're generally worried about something and they hope I can fix it, or at least refer them to someone who can. I decided they'll feel safer with someone who appears to be on top of their life than they would with someone with a crumpled shirt and food on their chin. But it's all a mask, isn't it – a conscious decision? I'm trying to be perceived in a certain way. This exercise has made me think about that too. What does it matter what I look like as long as I can do the job?'

'I'd never considered any of that.' Erin felt like she was getting a peek behind the scenes of Hafsa's life, and it surprised her.

'It's probably me overthinking it.' Hafsa leaned in. 'Amir thinks it's post-rationalisation. He says I've made my theory up about people feeling safer to justify shopping for new clothes, and he might be right. The brain is a clever thing, isn't it? It will serve up thoughts to make us believe what works for us, even when there are convincing arguments to the contrary. The stories we tell ourselves make us feel safe, don't they? That's why we believe them. That's why we cling on to them so tightly.'

That was a new concept to Erin, but it made perfect sense. She chewed it over as Hafsa continued to speak, wondering what thoughts her brain was serving her to make her beliefs stick. Knowing the inside of her head, it wouldn't be anything good. She only seemed able to hold on to thoughts with peril attached. 'I mean, rationally I know someone's professional competence has absolutely nothing to do with their outfit. And we're all different, aren't we? If Zahra was judged and dismissed on what she likes to wear, then no one would ever get to know how extraordinary her brain is. She'll only ever wear black or grey T-shirts and jeans when she's not at school, but that's irrelevant to the fact she's one of the most brilliant mathematicians I've ever met. And she's only thirteen.'

Pride radiated from Hafsa. 'I dismantled my own argument there, didn't I?' She laughed. 'It's turmoil inside here at the moment.' She hit her temple with the flat of her hand. 'I think my point was that I've learned a lot from being Zahra's mum. She genuinely wouldn't understand why I care what other people think of me. It wouldn't cross her mind to dress for anything but practicality and comfort. And in future, I don't think she'll make choices based upon what Amir and I want for her because that wouldn't be logical to her when she's the one who has to live her life. Maybe I should take a leaf out of her book and stop thinking about other people's expectations of me.'

'That all makes so much sense. I think my brain might need a bit of Zahra-ing too.' Erin's worries about the café were on the tip of her tongue, but she clamped her mouth closed. She reminded herself that Hafsa had concerns enough of her own. It wouldn't be fair or kind to burden her with Erin's too, not before she'd come up with a more tangible plan. 'Is there anything I can do to help?'

Hafsa smiled. 'That's such an Erin question.'

'Is it?'

'Yes, you're always a good sounding board.' She touched the back of Erin's hand. 'Thank you for always being there. Not many people listen without judgement, and I know how hard it is not to try to fix things. I appreciate it. I think I just needed to get the thoughts straight in my head. Talking to you has helped, thank you.'

Erin didn't deserve the praise. She'd judged Adam unfairly without knowing the full story and she'd even had an agenda when this conversation started. She'd wanted Hafsa to be a rebel to make things easier for her and she felt terrible about that now. 'Any time. Any time at all. Are you coming to Joe's birthday party tomorrow?'

'Yes,' said Hafsa. 'Wouldn't miss it.'

There was no way of getting out of doing those bloody pages, but she could at least delay it until she'd solved her more pressing issue. 'All the others will be there, so why don't we ask for an extension on our assignments? If we can shift it back by a couple of weeks, maybe we'll have a better idea of where we're heading?'

Hafsa's brown eyes were hopeful. 'I've never asked for an extension before.' She bit her lip. 'This is already a whole new experience for me.' She shimmied her shoulders. 'I feel like a badass. I might take up smoking and snogging inappropriate boys behind the bike shed.'

'I think Amir might have something to say about that,' said Erin, delighted to see the light back in Hafsa's dark eyes.

'Yeah. Maybe I'll stick to ordering a coffee in the afternoon. That's a big enough risk for me. I never usually have caffeine after twelve.'

'I could make you a decaf?' said Erin, standing.

Hafsa laughed. 'Yeah, make it a decaf. Let's not go too wild.'

Chapter Twenty-Five

Erin and Riley were standing next to each other in the kitchen, putting together an order for afternoon tea, when Erin felt Riley stiffen beside her. She turned to follow her gaze and saw Chegs pulling out a chair for Teagan, and her smiling coyly up at him through bat-wing-like eyelashes as she sat down. They were obviously flirting. But why come to Riley's place of work to do it?

'You okay finishing this?' asked Riley, unceremoniously dropping two scones on the top tier of the pretty cake stand.

'Yep,' said Erin, grabbing two tiny pots of strawberry jam and putting them beside the scones. When she turned to get the clotted cream from the fridge, she couldn't stop her gaze from following Riley to the table. Chegs' head was bowed over the laminated menu, his foppish hair falling over his face, but Teagan was gazing up at Riley with a sickly-sweet smile. Erin continued to watch as Riley took their order, then turned and made her way back to the kitchen. When Riley's back was turned, Teagan extended her foot and tapped her Converse against Chegs' trainers. She whispered something and

Chegs roared. Riley turned at the sound, and they both glanced at her, then quickly away. Her cheeks were flushed when she reached the kitchen.

Erin seethed. How dare they come into her café and make Riley feel small? 'All right, love?' she said.

'I don't like that woman.' Riley gritted her teeth, making the muscles in her jaw protrude. The movement made the hollows under her cheekbones even deeper, and Erin wanted to take a photograph to show Riley how truly beautiful she was.

'She looks more like a daft teenage girl than a woman to me,' said Erin, taking in her cut-off denim shorts and the edge of red lace visible where her shirt was unbuttoned. 'Like a mean girl.'

Riley sniggered. 'You've always got my back, haven't you?'

'Always,' said Erin. 'Is she still staying with Chegs?'

'Yeah. Apparently she's paying rent now, so it looks like it's a long-term thing.' She slammed around making coffee.

That was not reassuring news. Erin might not like Chegs, but as long as Riley did, she would continue to hope for the best for their relationship. Failing that, she at least kept her thoughts to herself and hadn't yet given in to the urge to spill boiling tea down the front of his trousers. She was the model of self-restraint. 'And how do you feel about that?'

The steam from the coffee machine hissed in accordance with Riley's expression as she glanced back at the table, where Teagan was giggling, head thrown back in an exaggerated display, long hair trailing behind her. 'I wouldn't mind if she was a bit more real, but everything she does seems contrived. Look at her now, all, *Oh, you're so funny, Chegs. You make me laugh so fucking hard.*' She used a high-pitched voice and screwed up her face.

Erin couldn't help but laugh, but underneath she was even more concerned for Riley than usual. She agreed with her assessment of Teagan, and that she was now a permanent fixture in Chegs' flat didn't bode well. 'Didn't he talk it through with you first?'

'No, but there's no reason why he should, is there? It's his flat. He's just being a good friend. It shouldn't make a difference that she's a girl, should it? It makes me seem like I don't trust him if I make a big deal about it.'

I wouldn't trust him, or her for that matter, thought Erin. They looked like a toxic combination to her, but she could see Riley's problem. Jealous girlfriend was not a good vibe. 'Would he like it if you moved a lad from school into your place?'

'That's never going to happen, is it?' said Riley. She wiped milk from the frother with the cloth hanging over the wand. 'My place is barely big enough for me.' Riley lived in a room in a shared house. She didn't have her own bathroom, and the original sash windows and Victorian fireplace allowed the wind to whistle through her room. If Jack hadn't always maintained he wanted to move home after university, Erin would have asked Riley if she'd like to live with her. Not that she necessarily would. Living with a woman the same age as her mother probably wouldn't appeal any more than a place where the bathroom floor was spongy with mould.

'Were you hoping you'd move in with Chegs?' Erin asked softly. Despite how she felt about him, she could see how the life Chegs might offer would be attractive to someone who'd always had to worry about their finances and never had a stable family or home. She didn't for one minute think Riley was with him for his money, but he represented a world that Riley had never been a part of, a life that appeared a lot easier to live than her own.

Riley shrugged. 'It's been a couple of years, so I suppose I thought he might ask me to move in eventually, but I'm not sure I would have said yes, even if he did. I like having my own space, even if it is a shit-hole.'

Erin squeezed her arm, both saddened and reassured by her response. 'A shit-hole of one's own,' she said, intentionally misquoting Virginia Woolf. 'What else can a girl ask for?' A dozen answers instantly sprang to mind, but she chose not to say any more. They both winced when Teagan's giggles rang out again, loud and performative. 'What did they order?' said Erin, 'and where did I put those laxatives?' She tapped her chin thoughtfully before joining in with Riley's authentic, throaty laugh.

'Tempting,' said Riley.

'Very,' said Erin. 'But we're better than that. We'll rise above and choose not to poison either of them.'

'But we could,' said Riley. 'And that knowledge sustains me.' She lifted her chin.

'We are in a position of power,' said Erin. 'But we are good, honest people.'

'Not even a little bit of poison?' Riley whispered, narrowing her eyes.

Erin searched her face to see if she was serious. Maybe her joke was rash. She didn't want to give Riley ideas, not when she was channelling a woman scorned, and she certainly didn't want a court case brought against her on top of everything else. That would finish her. 'No. Not even a sprinkling.'

'Spoil sport,' said Riley, grinning.

Erin kept an eye on Teagan and Chegs all the time they were there, her discomfort growing when she noted Teagan's shoe edging towards Chegs' more than once. Was she trying to play footsie with him in full view of his long-term girlfriend? When Riley stood by their table as they finished their drinks and chatted with them for a while, Erin allowed the tight muscles in her neck to loosen. She seemed fine. There was no need for Erin to be hyper-vigilant. Riley was twenty-four, not twelve. She could look after herself.

Erin gave the pair a convivial smile and a wave when they made their way out of the café five minutes later. Riley whistled along to 'The Girl from Ipanema' which was playing on the turntable as she took their cups through to the kitchen. Something made Erin keep her eyes on the pair as they sauntered up Brigade Street. Her stomach balled when she saw Teagan move closer to Chegs, then slip her hand into the back pocket of his jeans. He grabbed her hand and moved it, before turning his head to gawk back at the café. Erin turned away, hoping he hadn't seen her watching. But whether he knew it or not, she had seen that over-familiar gesture, and now she had to decide what to do about it.

Chapter Twenty-Six

That evening, Erin was already in her pyjamas when Jack came home. She'd been watching the clock, memories of those dreadful teenage years replaying in her mind. She knew that was ridiculous now he was a grown man who'd put his life back on track years ago, and survived on his own for three years in Birmingham, but did a mother ever stop worrying when their chick was out after dark? In some ways, it'd been easier when he was at university, because she had no idea if he was in or out, so she could con her brain into believing he was safely tucked up in bed when she was trying to sleep herself.

She popped her head out of her bedroom door and greeted him. 'Hello, love. Been anywhere nice?' She'd been planning to tell him about her new determination to try to save The Bookmark, but she could tell by the looseness of his limbs that this wasn't the best time to have a sensible conversation about finances.

He hung his jacket on a hook in the hall and swaggered towards her. 'Just out and about securing paid work, like the legend I am,' he said. He'd clearly had a drink or two. He pointed to himself with both hands. 'You are now looking at the newest employee of The Crown, Blackheath's finest hostelry.'

'Well done,' she said, making sure her voice and expression stayed bright. Despite the necessity, she didn't want Jack to work at The Crown. She wanted him to be at The Bookmark with her. 'You don't mess about.'

'You know me, Mother, a go-getter to the core.' He laughed, because they both knew that wasn't true. He was an overthinker like her and that often stopped him from acting. 'To be fair, they've lost someone because he forgot to renew his work visa, so he had to go back to Oz, so the fact I'd worked there before and could start immediately made me a very attractive proposition. Right time, right place. Boom.' He pulled his fist into his middle, wobbling as he did so.

'I'm very proud of you. I take it you celebrated the win with a few pints?'

'It was important to test the wares, so I know what I'll be selling,' he said, grinning. 'It was the responsible thing to do.' He peeled one trainer off with the toe of the other foot. It thudded as it hit the skirting board. 'I'm quite looking forward to being back there. It will be like being at sixth form again, only with more facial hair and student debt.' He sighed as he removed his other shoe. 'At least the wages are so bad I won't have to pay any of that back for the foreseeable. Every cloud.'

'Every cloud,' she repeated, wanly. Erin was one of the last cohort to get an entirely free university education, and she really felt for young people today, graduating with tens of thousands of pounds of debt around their necks before they earned a penny. How she envied parents who could afford to pay for their children's education. She'd failed in that respect, and now Jack was back working at the same place he had been before his degree because she couldn't manage to employ him. The guilt threatened to overwhelm her.

'What's up?' He walked towards her, concern etched on his face.

She didn't want to burden him with her guilt, so she scrabbled around for something to explain her low mood. 'I'm worried about Riley.' It wasn't a lie. She'd been torturing herself about whether to disclose her suspicions to her friend. 'I think I saw Chegs and another girl acting . . . inappropriately.'

'Inappropriately how?' He passed her and wandered into the kitchen.

Erin followed and leaned on the door frame, watching as Jack fed two slices of bread into the toaster. It really was as if they'd gone back in time. This was his routine when he came in from a night out before he went to uni. He was the eldest in his school year, turning eighteen at the start of his last year of A levels, so, as long as she was convinced he wasn't doing drugs again, she didn't complain about him going out drinking with his friends, especially when he got the job serving behind the bar at The Crown. But she couldn't stop herself from watching out for signs he was drinking too much, and was always relieved to hear his key in the lock, and to smell the toasting bread that meant he was safely home. 'Chegs and that Teagan, the one who's moved in with him, seemed to be flirting when they were at the café earlier, and when they left, she put her hand in the back pocket of his jeans.'

'Whoa, that's some familiar move. What did Riley say?' He searched in the cupboard, found a jar of Marmite, trying and failing to open the lid.

Erin took it from him and ran the cap under the warm tap until it unstuck. 'I don't think she saw.' She handed the open jar back to Jack.

'Did you tell her?' The toast popped up and he picked it out, then flung it on a plate, shaking the heat from his fingers. He plunged a knife into the jar and hooked out a gloopy black mass before spreading it on the bread. Erin wanted to remind him to go easy because of the salt, but she managed to stop herself.

'I didn't know what to say.' She'd agonised about telling Riley from the moment it happened, but hadn't come to a decision by the time they closed up, so came home feeling like she was carrying a hand grenade in her tote bag along with the soiled tea towels. 'Do you think I should have said something?'

Jack took a bite and chewed thoughtfully. He wiped crumbs from his moustache. 'I think I'd want to know. Wouldn't you?'

Erin pondered the question. When Andrew left, some of her friends speculatated about whether he was seeing someone else. In some ways, she'd hoped he was. At least then there'd be a reason beyond her and her son being so unworthy of love that he would rather live without them. If he'd fallen in love with someone so deeply he couldn't bear to be without them, then it would feel like a different kind of tragedy, one there was at least a point to. But she'd never found out exactly why Andrew left. All he would say was that he didn't want the life mapped out for him. She hadn't discovered an affair, and he hadn't begun another relationship soon after leaving them, as far as she was aware. If he had cheated on her, she was pretty sure she would have preferred to know. 'I think I would.'

'Then, I suppose you should tell her.' He took another bite. 'That Chegs is a dickhead. She's way too good for him.'

'She is,' said Erin, the contents of her stomach curdling at the thought of breaking her young friend's heart. 'You really think I should tell her?'

'You wouldn't want her to find out further down the line, then work out you knew all along. Rip the plaster off. She'll probably thank you for it in the long run.'

He was right. Of course he was. But there was no guarantee Riley would thank her for it. There were so many ways this could play out. This felt like another pressure on top of her worry about the café. Why, oh why, did every decision come with such high risks?

Chapter Twenty-Seven

Riley wasn't due in until lunchtime the following day, and by 11 a.m., acid was threatening to burn through Erin's stomach lining. She distracted herself by scouring the wall of books to find stories that matched her mood. She pulled out a slim novel by Jeanette Winterson. She'd read *Written on the Body* when it first came out and remembered it was about a woman's affair with the unnamed narrator. She considered giving it to Riley to read in the hope she might get the gist but dismissed it as the coward's way out. She dropped the book on the nearest table and waited, indigestion gurgling, until Riley arrived. When she sauntered in, her arms were heavy at her sides, her usual energy nowhere to be seen.

'You okay, flowerpot?' Erin watched Riley pull her pale arms from her denim jacket with Frida Kahlo's face painted on the back and hang it on the hook on the back door of the kitchen.

Riley puffed out her cheeks. 'S'ppose.'

'Can we have a—' Erin's sentence was cut short by the sound of a voice calling Riley's name. She turned to see a bright-eyed man with an expansive afro, wearing a beige crew neck jumper and thick-framed glasses.

'Riley Moore?'

'Who wants to know?' said Riley, moving to the kitchen doorway.

The man wiped a hand on his chinos, then extended it. 'I'm Gavin Adesina. I'm a big fan.'

Riley shook his hand, her spine straightening. 'Thanks.'

'Hope you don't mind me tracking you down.'

Erin's ears pricked up at the word *tracking*. She'd watched *Baby Reindeer* with Jack and now she knew about stalking, she had something new to worry about. 'How exactly did you track her down?' she said, coming to stand by Riley's side, legs wide, arms crossed.

'Sorry, I should have introduced myself properly.' He dug into the pocket of his trousers and brought out a business card, which he waved in front of the women, clearly unsure who to offer it to, the woman he'd been looking for, or the one who appeared to be her bodyguard. Riley took it. 'I'm the promoter who sent you the DM.' He pointed at the card in Riley's hand, as if that proved it. 'Like I said in my message, I follow you on TikTok, and I saw you'd filmed one of your posts on Blackheath. I'm local, well, I live in Deptford. I was going to ask where to find you, but thought that might come across as a bit weird. I asked around and the fella in Montpeliers sent me here. Thought it might be better to meet in person.'

Beads of sweat sprung up on his brow and he was blustering. Erin got the impression he really was a fan but wasn't sure if that made him more or less dangerous. 'Where abouts do you live?' she said. If he knew where to find Riley, it was only right she should have the same information about him.

A 'v' appeared between Gavin's eyebrows, as though the question confused him. 'On Blackheath Hill, Deptford end.'

Erin nodded in acknowledgement.

'Anyway,' Gavin said, turning his attention back to Riley. 'Since I first got in touch, I've started working with the people who are running the community spaces down in Kidbrooke Village.'

'Kidbrooke Village,' Erin said, with a derisive laugh. She couldn't stop herself. She'd lived in the area all her life and remembered the Kidbrooke of old, when it was dominated by the Ferrier Estate, before the ugly social housing was demolished and replaced with bougie apartments that no one who'd previously lived there would be able to afford in a million years. Some of her favourite customers had been displaced by the new development. 'They add Village to the name and suddenly there's a couple of zeros on the end of the property prices.'

'I know,' said Gavin, his face turning serious. 'I grew up on the Ferrier. We were moved to Hackney, and it's taken me years to get back to the area. I don't recognize the place now.'

Erin softened. If he'd survived the Kidbrooke of old, he deserved their time. 'It's different all right.'

'They're trying to get some of the community spirit back,' said Gavin. 'They've approached me to sort out some local talent to perform down there.'

'Local talent,' said Erin, now willing to believe he was who he said he was. She bumped Riley with her hip. 'That's you, that is.'

Riley grinned, a flush blossoming on her cheeks. 'What kind of gigs are you planning?'

Gavin scrunched his lips to the side. 'It's all a bit vague at the moment. The guys down there are trying to set up a community space, but they haven't got any firm plans yet. I know what I think they should do, and they're listening, but—'

Erin was distracted from the conversation by a mother with a toddler in a highchair waving for her attention. She mouthed that she wanted the bill. 'Sorry.' Erin shuffled past Riley and Gavin and took the bill and the card machine over to the woman, who was trying to distract her crying toddler with a rice cake. He pushed it away with a pudgy fist, while rubbing his tear-filled eyes with the other. 'Naptime, is it?' Erin said.

'Hopefully,' said the woman, crossing her fingers before holding her phone to the end of the card reader. 'Sorry for the mess.' She grimaced at the table strewn with soiled napkins and half-chewed rice cakes.

'Don't you worry about that,' said Erin. 'We've all been there.' The woman hoisted the crying child from the chair and onto her hip. Another customer gestured Erin over and she took his order, then swiped up a pair of empty cups on her way back to the kitchen, where Riley and Gavin were still chatting.

'Sorry, I'm keeping you from your work,' said Gavin.

'Don't worry,' said Erin. She meant it, but she couldn't stop to earwig, however much she wanted to, because she had an English Breakfast tea to brew and a sausage sandwich to make.

'I've got your number,' said Riley. 'I'll give you a call at the end of my shift, okay?'

'Great,' said Gavin. 'Thanks for your time. Bye, then.' He called into the kitchen. 'Bye!'

'See ya,' said Erin, over the sound of the sausages already sizzling in the pan.

Riley's blue-green eyes seemed to glitter for the rest of the afternoon. Erin would have loved to talk more about Gavin's plans, but for the first time in ages, The Bookmark thrummed with customers, and they were both rushed off their feet. Even Zita had to sit at a different table to usual. Erin noticed her check out the sugar bowl and scowl at the meagre contents. The temptation to leave it as it was was overridden by Erin's mother's voice in her head, and she greeted Zita as usual, and refilled the bowl with small white sachets. It was empty the next time she passed.

'That was a good day,' she said to Riley, when she locked the door and turned the sign around to closed. 'We could do with a few more like that.' If they did, maybe she'd be able to hold on to the business. She tried to stop her mind from doing the maths, but it wouldn't be told. It presented her with the sad truth that she'd need to fill every chair in the place all day, every day for the sums to add up to what she needed for the rent increase.

Riley dropped into an armchair. 'Yep. Exhausting, but good.'

Erin sat next to Riley, gearing herself up for the difficult conversation. 'What's that Gavin got planned for you?'

'Not sure yet.' She tugged at the hair behind her ear, which was growing back at a surprising rate. 'But it's a buzz to be approached out of the blue. Makes things seem possible, you know? Like what I'm writing in my next chapters isn't just fiction.'

'I can imagine,' said Erin. 'What do you think Chegs will say?'

Riley's smile dropped. 'Huh. Probably nothing. He's only interested in what Teagan has to say these days.'

Erin clenched her buttocks. 'About that.' She made fists and dug her nails into her palms. 'I try not to get involved in other people's business unless I'm asked to, but . . . I saw something yesterday that I thought I should mention.'

Riley's brow furrowed. 'What?'

'I can't be sure . . .' She paused. 'Actually, that's not true. I am sure I saw Teagan put her hand in the back pocket of Cheg's jeans when they left yesterday.'

Riley sat up. 'Like, taking something out of his pocket?'

Erin dug her nails in deeper. 'No, like she was kind of putting her arm around him, in a . . . well in a way that made them appear to be . . . close . . . a couple, maybe.'

'What did he do?' Riley's chin puckered and Erin wanted to take it all back. Being the cause of her pain was agonising. She braced herself. She was not the cause of Riley's pain. Chegs and Teagan were.

'To give him his due, he sort of pushed her hand away, but the way he looked back in here, it seemed more like he wanted to make sure he hadn't been caught. I didn't get the impression he was surprised, or upset with her, if you know what I mean?'

Riley stared down at her hands. 'You think there's something going on between them?'

'I don't know. But if I were you, I'd be asking questions.' She reached for Riley's hand. 'I'm sorry, love. I've been dreading telling you. I didn't know what to do for the best.' She almost added that Jack told her to share what she'd seen but thought better of it. Riley might be feeling humiliated, and knowing Jack knew before she did could add to that. 'I just thought that, if it was me, I'd want to know.' Riley gave a tiny nod. A tear dribbled down her cheek onto her black satin skirt, and Erin's heart broke for her. 'It could be nothing.'

'I've had my suspicions,' Riley said. 'And, even if they're not shagging, I've been wondering what I'm doing with someone who chooses to spend their time with someone like Teagan. She stands for everything I'm opposed to. She's an entitled leech.' She took a napkin from the holder on the table and wiped her cheeks. 'When we got together, Chegs made all the right noises. He said he admired my politics and my creativity and all that. He was so supportive, but recently, he hasn't been interested in what I'm doing. If anything, he seems annoyed that my stuff is getting noticed. He likes to be the star of the show. I think he liked having a quirky girlfriend with tattoos and piercings and who dresses differently and thinks differently to the people he grew up with.' She glanced up and Erin's insides clenched at the sadness in her eyes. 'But I've been wondering for a while whether he was only ever with me to piss his parents off, or to prove he was down with the plebs, or something.'

'Don't say that,' said Erin. 'You're not a pleb. You're a beautiful, talented, caring, and downright impressive woman.'

The corners of Riley's mouth lifted minutely. 'Thank you. But I suspect I've been the opposite of a trophy girlfriend. Chegs fancied being seen as alternative, and I think I've been unwittingly fetishised.'

'Unwittingly fetishised. Sounds painful.'

'It is painful.' Riley's voice cracked.

'Come here, love.' Erin wrapped Riley in a hug and held her tightly as she cried. 'We don't know the facts yet. There might be a perfectly innocent explanation.'

'Even if there is,' said Riley, through her tears. 'I think

it's the end of the road for us. I'm not sure I even like him that much anymore, so I don't know why I'm so upset.'

'Because it's not the ending you wanted, and that's always going to be hard. We go into relationships full of excitement and hope, and it's so disappointing when it all comes to nothing, especially when it's not for want of trying.'

Erin envisioned Adam sitting at the table across the room when they'd talked. Excitement and hope had bubbled inside her and she was almost certain he felt that too. But she'd been foolish to let her guard down, and the girl crying in her arms was testament to that. This was how love stories ended, with tears, hurt and recriminations. She held Riley close, whispering, 'It's all right, sweetheart. You'll be okay.' Maybe everyone's better off on their own, she thought. At least then they're the ones who decide what happens next. As Riley sobbed into her shoulder, a new wave of fear for the future of the café surged through Erin. If Chegs was out of the picture, Riley needed this job more than ever, and it was up to Erin not to let her down.

Chapter Twenty-Eight

Erin had put together platters of sandwiches and cakes for Joe's birthday gathering, as she did every year. Since she was a child, she'd been attending the small party Joe insisted on holding to celebrate another trip around the sun. 'Life is hard,' he always said, 'So we should celebrate every win, large or small.' He'd even had everyone around when his birthday fell soon after Nuala's death. 'She wouldn't want me to stop celebrating being alive, just because she's not here with me,' he'd said, although it was a subdued affair, and Erin suspected he regretted trying to carry on as normal when his world had a fresh, un-stitchable tear in it.

Now, five years on, Erin and Jack arrived at Joe's thirties semi, set back from the road that connected Blackheath and Kidbrooke, half an hour before everyone else. She averted her eyes from the house attached to the other side. She'd grown up in that house and it pained her every time she noticed a change to her family home's exterior. When the family who lived there now had replaced the front door, she hadn't been able to stop herself from weeping. It was as though the imprints of her parents' hands had been discarded, like their very existence meant nothing. She knew it was irrational, but she couldn't help feeling like every new coat of paint on the window frames, covered up a part of their past. She'd learned it was easier to look away.

They unloaded the trays of food from the boot of Erin's trusty old Ford Focus, and knocked on the door. Joe threw it wide and greeted them with open arms. From the second she walked into Joe's hallway, Erin felt like she'd gone back in time. She was nine years old again, following her father as he greeted Nuala with a hug and a loud kiss on the cheek. She could almost smell Nuala's floral perfume and hear her mother's laughter as Joe recounted some story about the gig he'd played the previous evening. The music was still the same, soft jazz filling the air now, just as it always had.

Turning, she was almost surprised to see her own adult son beside her. Back in the moment, she followed Joe through to the kitchen at the back of the house and lay the trays down on the spaces on the worktops that weren't already filled with glasses and bottles. She took in the various spirits, some of which had labels that looked older than her. 'Blimey, Joe, are you expecting hoards of drunken sailors this year?'

'That lot was in the back of the cupboard,' he said. 'I need someone with better eyesight than me to read the expiry dates on the labels.' He patted Jack on the back. 'Go on, son.'

'Does alcohol go off?' said Jack. 'Isn't it a natural preservative?'

'If it's been opened it does,' said Erin. She'd been on enough food safety courses to know exactly how poisonous out-of-date food and drink could be. She lifted a bottle of rum with a sealed cap. 'This one should be all right, but definitely not this.' She tapped the neck of a half empty bottle of Martini Rosso, which was more brown than red.

'That was Nuala's favourite,' said Joe with a long exhalation.

'Sorry, Joe, but if she was the last one to drink it, then I think it needs to go down the sink, along with this, this, and this.' She lifted other questionable bottles and moved them over to the aluminium sink.

'Let me smell it before you chuck it away,' said Joe. The cap scratched as he unscrewed it. He put it to his nose and breathed in, his expression turning wistful.

Erin put her arm around him. 'You okay?'

'I'm grand.' He tipped the liquid into the sink and the fruity, spicy scent drifted up to Erin's nostrils. She remembered hugs and kisses that smelled like that after evenings dancing as Joe and his friends played impromptu concerts in their front room. A longing to go back to that time tightened around her waist like a belt.

She released Joe and took a parcel wrapped in bright paper from her bag. 'Here's your present.'

Joe turned it over in his hands, then shook it near his enormous earlobe. 'I wonder what this could be?' he said, winking at Jack, who knew as well as he did that it would be a book. It was always a book. Mary always let Erin choose a novel from a local bookshop for all their friends for their birthdays, and Erin had carried on the tradition.

'Open it and see,' said Jack. He watched them as he moved around the kitchen, peeling cellophane off the top of the sandwich platters and rolling them into a ball between his hands.

Joe unpicked the sellotape and revealed a blue cover with a yellow gate and an inverted teardrop shape with *You Are Here* printed in the middle. 'David Nicholls,' said Joe. 'Lovely. Thank you.' He embraced Erin and pulled Jack in too. Erin breathed in the smell of his hair gel mixed with the familiar, fresh laundry scent of her son and in that moment she could almost believe all was well with the world.

'I hope you like it,' she said. 'It's tender and funny and the characters are spot on. I absolutely loved it. One of my top five reads of last year.'

'Does it have a happy ending?' Joe asked.

'Why don't you start at the end and find out, like a normal person?' Erin laughed, then thought about Riley and stopped immediately. 'Has Riley been in touch?' Riley had promised to perform a poem for Joe's birthday, but she probably didn't feel much like performing or celebrating after their talk earlier.

There was a knock at the door and Jack left them to answer it.

'No, why?' said Joe.

'I'm not sure she'll make it tonight because—' She stopped speaking when Riley appeared in the kitchen, looking stunning in a vest and a black tulle skirt so full it nearly touched both sides of the kitchen at once. 'Hello, love. How are you doing?'

Riley plonked a bottle of wine on the counter. 'I am a single woman once again.' Beyond the darker than usual eyeliner, her eyes were watery.

'So . . .?'

'Yep, Chegs and that skank are getting it on. He tried to deny it, but she was all like, "Don't you think she deserves to know the truth, Lawrence?"' She did a perfect impression of Teagan's irritating voice.

Erin watched her, waiting for a return of the tears from earlier, but she seemed fortified, somehow. 'I'm so sorry.'

'The boy's a fool,' said Joe. 'He doesn't know a good thing when he sees it.'

'Thanks,' said Riley.

'Prick,' said Jack. 'Drink?'

'Hell, yes. Let's get this party started.' Erin watched her as she took the glass of white wine from Jack, and was reassured that, even if she wasn't okay now, she would be. She was resilient. She'd had to be, poor kid.

The others arrived soon after, along with some of Joe's old friends and ex-bandmates. Erin was nervous about seeing Adam after the moment of connection she'd felt when they were alone in the café and afterwards in the street. The sensation of being safe when he was beside her had felt good at the time, but in the intervening days, she'd realized it wasn't ideal. It made her vulnerable. She shouldn't need a man to make her feel safe. One reason she'd almost rolled over and given up on the café was because she was too cowardly to fight. She needed to be stronger in her own right, more like her mother. Seeing Riley's relationship implode added to her resolve, so she needed to put a spike in it now. Saving The Bookmark would take up all her focus and energy, and she couldn't let anything derail that.

She said a quick hello to him when she bumped into him in the hall, then made her excuses and busied herself offering drinks and food to the people gathering in the long room Nuala had knocked through to give the house more light. She wanted to ask if he'd made any decisions about Oliver, but wasn't sure how to be around him after what passed between them without giving him ideas, so she decided avoidance was her best strategy. He seemed happy enough chatting with Susan and Hafsa, so she left them to it.

Before long, a collection of elderly men and women opened instrument cases and sat on dining chairs at the back end of the room, which had started out as a dining room. The other party-goers gathered at the end that was the sitting room, drinks and sandwiches in hand, ready for the traditional performance by some of the best jazz performers of their time.

Lulu, an octogenarian singer with a voice so tender

it always made the hairs on Erin's neck stand up, waved her arms to shush the group. She always wore sparkly dresses, and the red and black number she wore today kept falling off one bony shoulder. She'd lost a lot of weight since last year's party and Erin wondered if she was unwell. The thought made tears gather behind her eyes. Why did people have to get sick and die? Why did everything have to change? 'Before we start the musical shenanigans,' said Lulu, her voice notably huskier than Erin remembered it, 'we've got a special guest performer,' she said. 'Where's Riley?'

Riley moved next to Lulu. 'Hi, everyone.' Her fingers furled and unfurled at her sides. 'I had planned to write something fitting for the man of the hour.' She met Joe's eye and they shared a smile. 'But circumstances . . .' She put her hand to her mouth and whispered, 'Dumping cheating, shit-head boyfriend, got in the way.' The crowd made various noises from sympathetic 'ahhs' to a shout of, 'Want me to kill him for ya?' from a man with a pork-pie hat and a trumpet dangling by his side.

Riley bowed to the man, and mouthed 'thank you', before turning her bright eyes back to the group. 'So, I'm afraid I can only offer something I wrote on the bus on the way here. You are worth so much more than this, Joe, but I hope it's better than nothing.' She took a breath, then narrowed her eyes. 'What makes a man?' She tapped her chin. 'That's a question for our time, I'll explore it now, in the medium of rhyme. It's not flesh, it's not blood, those are animal traits. It's not going down the pub, drinking beer with your mates.'

'Isn't it?' said the man in the hat, chuckling. He looked cowed and put a finger to his lips when Riley arched an eyebrow in his direction.

'It's in here.' She put her hand on her chest. 'It's in here.' She cupped her scalp. 'In your heart and your head. It's not what you can lift, or get up to in bed. We've lost sight of the things that matter, that are true, and those things, my dear friend.' She pointed at Joe. 'Are what we all see in you. You are gentle, you're kind, and you fight for what's right. You value laughter and love, that's why we're all here tonight.' She crooked a finger for Joe to join her. He stood and moved to her side, a shy grin on his face. Riley put an arm around him and continued, 'Because, Joe, my friend, you're the very best of men, and like everyone here, I'm proud to call you my friend.' She kissed his cheek and the crowd whooped and applauded.

Erin jumped at the sound of a sharp whistle near her ear. She turned to see Adam at her shoulder and immediately flushed at the proximity. He opened his mouth to say something, but she gave him a quick smile and rushed forwards to embrace Joe and Riley. The warmth that flowed through her from just standing next to him was a worry. If she was going to protect herself, then she would need to stay as far away from that man as possible.

Chapter Twenty-Nine

The performers bowed out one at a time, finally leaving the man in the pork-pie hat playing his trumpet alone. Erin could remember a time when the band would play into the early hours, Lulu singing one track, then someone else taking over as she danced with Nuala and Erin's parents. Joe would play his double bass, breaking now and again to twirl Erin around the patterned carpet. Contemplating the same room, with its ancient flock wallpaper and carpet worn out by decades of dancing feet, the exhilaration of being allowed to stay up in adult company and feeling grown up and mature was still easy to recall. How she'd longed to be a real adult. Little did she know how hard being a grown-up with real responsibilities truly was.

She caught sight of a photograph on the mantlepiece above Joe's ancient gas fire. In it, her parents and Joe and Nuala were sitting around a table at The Bookmark. Erin had taken that picture on the day the café opened. They'd all been so proud of Mary. She'd always worked in hospitality and dreamed of opening her own place. They'd remortgaged the house next door to furnish the room and buy the equipment, much of which Erin still used today. Tears filled her eyes when she thought of what her mother achieved, and how desperate she now was to keep it going.

She felt a hand on her shoulder and turned to see Joe, his eyes on the same photograph. 'Seems like yesterday,' he said.

'It does.' Erin leaned her head against Joe's. Didn't he used to be much taller than her? Now their heads rested together perfectly. 'I wish—' Erin was interrupted by Lulu, now wearing a huge fur coat over her sequined dress.

'I'm off,' she said, kissing Joe on the cheek and leaving a smudge of bright red lipstick. 'If I don't make it to next year, I'll see you on the other side.'

'Don't say that,' said Joe.

'Gotta face the facts, old man, the Grim Reaper's coming for all of us.' She cackled. 'See ya, pal. It's been a blast.' They hugged for a long minute, then she stalked off, singing 'Ev'ry Time We Say Goodbye' by Cole Porter, as she made her exit.

Erin swallowed, finding it hard not to cry. How could Lulu be so sanguine? Joe turned to her and pinched her cheek. 'Cheer up, kid. She's going out singing.'

'But I don't want her to go out at all,' said Erin, sounding pathetic.

'It's the way of the world,' he said. 'It's sad, but when you get to our age, and you've lost as many people as we have, you make peace with the inevitability of it. At least, you do if you try to stay positive. Reality would become unbearable otherwise. I make a conscious choice not to dwell on what's coming my way. I didn't count the people who weren't here this evening, even though they meant the whole world to me.' His eyes trailed back to the photograph. 'I counted the ones who were.' He glanced across at Adam, who was standing with the other members of book group. 'And there's always one or two new faces to bring up the numbers, like your man over there.' He took her elbow. 'Come on, let's not be maudlin. It's a celebration.'

The group opened up to allow them in. Erin found herself next to Adam again. He was wearing the smart T-shirt with the zip he'd worn when they went for their truncated walk. She noted that this was what he wore for an occasion, concluding he'd given his outfit as much thought as she had that day, then got annoyed with herself for thinking about it. It wasn't relevant because she was not going to start a relationship of any form with him. His arm brushed hers and the urge to move closer was almost overwhelming. Instead, and with more effort than it should take, she moved her weight onto her other hip, so she didn't feel the repeated electricity of his touch.

'Hafsa and I were talking about our pages,' she said, when there was a break in conversation. 'Would it be okay to give ours in in a couple of weeks?'

'It's not homework,' said Susan, brusquely.

It bloody well felt like it. 'No, I know, but we wanted

to check you lot were all right with it, rather than not . . . handing it in.' She stared at Hafsa, willing her to add something, but she looked down at her glass. 'Didn't we, Hafsa?'

'Yes,' she said, raising her eyes briefly. 'A bit more time would help, I mean, if it's okay with you?'

'I don't see why we need a time limit on getting them done. We haven't decided what we're going to do with them when we've finished,' said Joe. 'Any ideas?'

'I think we should read them out,' said Riley.

'Spoken like a true performer,' said Mercy. 'I'm happier writing than I am speaking to a group.'

'It's only us, though,' said Riley. 'And there's something really special about sharing your words with people you trust.' She bounced her knees. 'Oh, go on. I really think you'll get a lot from it.' She pouted. 'And I'm sad, so you have to do what I say.'

Erin laughed. 'You're not above a bit of emotional blackmail, then?'

'Not even slightly. Seriously, though, when I've done poetry workshops, the most moving times are when people make themselves vulnerable by sharing their work. It connects you in a way you don't expect. Trust me.'

'I only heard the word vulnerable in that sentence and I'm telling you now, that is not my most favourite feeling.' Erin meant every word. Feeling vulnerable was one of the things she actively expended energy avoiding.

'I get what you're saying,' said Adam. Erin turned

to him, grateful for the support, but his eyes were on Riley. 'There is something special about reading your work out to a group. I've done it a few times at writing retreats, and it can be pretty emotional.' He glanced at Erin. 'In a good way.'

'Writing retreats?' said Riley. 'Say more.'

'Oh, there's not much to tell. I thought I had a novel in me once upon a time, like every journalist, I imagine, so I went away with a few other writers to try to tease it out.' He shoved the hand not holding his drink deep into his pocket. 'It refused to be shaped into anything but garbage, so I gave up.'

Riley frowned. 'You don't look like a quitter to me, Adam Darling.'

'Looks can be deceptive,' he said. 'Anyway, the point is, I'm happy to read my pages out when I've written them . . . which I haven't yet . . . so yes to an extension on the time frame too, please and thank you.' He put his beer bottle to his lips and drank, as if needing to plug his mouth.

'So, that's decided,' said Riley. 'We bring our pages along whenever they're ready and share them with the group.' She lifted her glass, and Erin felt obliged to hold up hers and clink it against everyone else's. At least the time frame was vague. That was something.

Chapter Thirty

Late that night, Erin was woken by sounds coming from Jack's bedroom. She heard his voice, then a higher one. He had a girl in there. Erin pulled her duvet over her ears, wishing they'd been quieter, or that she'd remained obliviously sleeping. Since he'd become an adult, she'd asked that he was at least in a committed relationship before what they'd both called 'sleepovers', for want of a better expression. Since he wasn't in a relationship, whoever was in there was clearly someone he'd met when he and Riley had gone on to The Crown after Joe's party, and that seemed a bit quick to already be performing bedroom shenanigans to her.

Feeling like a prude, and disliking herself for it, she eventually fell back to sleep. Grogginess made her eyes scratchy when she dragged herself out of bed at six the following day. She walked blearily into the kitchen, stopping abruptly at the sight of Riley standing next to the sink, her tulle skirt touching the units on both sides of the narrow room. Erin's mind put the noises from last night and Riley's presence in her kitchen together, and the result made her brain stutter. 'Morning,' she said. It was all she could come up with, and was certainly better than, what on earth were you two thinking?

'Morning boss.' Riley sucked air through her teeth. 'Might be a bit late in this morning, unless you want me working in this?' She fingered the black netting. 'I'm just grabbing a quick glass of water before I get the bus home. I'm parched. We caned it last night.'

'Righto,' said Erin, still unable to quite get her head around her friend and her son spending the night together.

'Morning.' Jack appeared in the doorway, his hair sticking up in all directions. It reminded her of when he was a small boy, and he used to want to brush his own hair before playgroup. He'd only ever brush through the front, leaving the back like a dark bird's nest. How had that little boy grown so quickly into a man who brought a woman three years his senior home after a late-night drinking session? Erin watched to see how the pair interacted. Was this the start of a love affair?

'Right, I'm off.' Riley glugged the last of her water. 'See you later.' She left the kitchen, and walked past Jack, saying, 'Thanks for last night, it was exactly what I needed.'

When she heard the door close, Erin widened her eyes at her son. 'Was that a good idea?'

He dropped his gaze to the floor and laughed. 'It felt like a good idea at the time.'

Erin was disappointed by his response. 'Christ, Jack. I hope you—'

'It's no biggie,' he interrupted. 'She feels exactly the same way I do.'

'How do you know? She's probably all over the place. She only came out of a long-term relationship yesterday. Yesterday,' she repeated.

'I am aware.' He pointed in the direction of the door. 'But you heard her say that was exactly what she needed.'

Erin did not want to think about what *that* was. 'She's three years older than you.'

Jack came into the room and switched on the kettle. 'To be fair, that was only relevant before I was a grown-arsed man myself.'

'Yes, well . . .' Erin paused, not quite sure what to add. She just knew she had an uneasiness in her gut about this. 'How does it end?'

Jack turned and leaned back against the sink. 'I don't know.' There was exasperation in his voice. 'It might already be over. It probably is. I'm happy to be her rebound guy for one night. Not everything has to be an epic saga. Some things are short stories. Some are poems. Hell—' he lifted his arms '—this might even be a haiku.' He grinned at his own cleverness. 'And I'm pretty sure we're both okay with that.'

'But I worry—'

'You worry about everything,' he said. 'But please believe me when I say you don't need to worry about this. I'm fine. Riley is fine. Nothing is going to change.'

He'd said the magic words and they helped. 'Okay. As long as you're sure no one is going to get hurt.'

'No one will be emotionally damaged. I promise.' He smoothed down his moustache and gazed down at his feet. 'We were pretty drunk, though, and . . . I might have said something I shouldn't.'

Erin tensed. 'What's that?'

'She was asking why I'd gone back to working at The Crown and I have a hazy recollection of telling her you couldn't afford to keep me on at The Bookmark. I think I let on that the café is in trouble.' He bared his teeth. 'Sorry.'

'Bloody hell, Jack.'

He held a hand up. 'I know, I know, I'm an idiot. I'm sorry.' He stepped forwards and hugged her. 'I am sorry, but I do think it's time you stopped trying to carry the worry about that on your own. People want to help. You should let them.'

'I've got no choice, now, have I?' said Erin, her mind whirring. How would Riley feel now her job was in jeopardy so soon after the end of her relationship?

'No.' Jack stood back and looked her in the eyes. 'And I think that could be a good thing. I'm not just saying that to get out of trouble. I think you should talk to the others at the next book group.'

Erin saw the sincerity in his bloodshot eyes and found it hard to be cross with him. He was right. The burden of anxiety was too heavy to carry on her own. She would share her load with the others.

Chapter Thirty-One

Erin meant to bring up what Jack had disclosed with Riley before the next book group. She must be worried about her job, and on top of everything else going on in her life, it wasn't ideal timing. But despite Jack's reassurances that his night with Riley wasn't a big deal, she felt like Riley was avoiding her, always finding an excuse to leave the kitchen if they were in there together, and moving to wipe down tables at the other side of the room that looked suspiciously clean, whenever Erin got close. When she left quickly at the end of her shift on Wednesday and only returned when book group was due to begin and the others were all seated, Erin was sure that either she had an issue with Jack or with her, and she wished she'd tried harder to have a conversation when it was just the two of them.

When they were all settled, Erin tried to formulate the words to share her plans for the café when Susan blurted, 'I've finished my pages.' The words came out loud and rushed, like water released from a dam. She brought a notebook with a black and white leopard on the cover out of her bag and placed it on her knee. 'It's probably very badly written, but it's done, and I can't tell you how helpful it was. I feel like a new woman since starting this exercise.'

'Well done,' said Mercy. 'I know what you mean. I feel like I've been injected with a shot of adrenaline every morning, now I have things to look forward to.'

'That's so cool,' said Riley. 'I fucking love this for you guys.' The energy had returned to her voice and Erin relaxed a little.

'How do you feel about reading it out, Susan?' said Adam. He sat in his usual chair, his leather jacket slung over the back, a cup of black coffee on the table beside him. 'I'd love to hear what you've written.'

Susan ran her fingers over the notebook. 'Nervous,' she said. 'But I've been trying to gear myself up to it all day.'

'You're a brave and brilliant woman,' said Joe. 'Come on, let's hear it.'

Susan shifted in her chair. 'I don't even know if I've done it right.'

'There's no right or wrong when you're doing something creative,' said Riley. 'And what Joe said is true. It's very brave to bring your work here, and we all appreciate you starting us off, don't we?' She viewed the group and they nodded their agreement. Erin wasn't proud to feel relieved Susan's last pages would delay her having to share the disastrous nature of her current situation.

'Okay, then. Here goes.' Susan opened the notebook

and started to read. 'Motherhood changed me.' She glanced up. Erin focused on her, hoping to convey positive vibes. Susan dropped her gaze back to the page. 'I know it sounds strange, but I feel like all my senses had been transferred to my baby girl. What I mean is, I can see now that, soon after she was born, I started to see things through her eyes. When she stared up from her pram at the leaves on a tree fluttering in the breeze, I did too, and I saw those leaves afresh, their greenness, the carefree way they moved in the wind. Things I had grown accustomed to became new again, and I noticed the beauty of the world for the first time in years. It was like an extra gift, the cherry on top of the cake of becoming a mother. When I was teaching her to speak, it was as if I heard the way vowels and consonants merged together to create words for the first time, and then when she began to dance, I felt the beats of the music through her movements.' She raised her eyes from the page, her lips pinched tight. 'See, I've done it wrong. It's meant to be about the future, but I've written about the past first.'

'It's context,' said Erin. 'That's totally relevant.'

'The future is always moulded by the past,' said Joe.

'Yep. Where you come from will always inform where you're going,' said Adam. 'You're not doing it wrong. This is lovely. Go on.' He gestured to her notebook and Erin was moved by his kindness.

Susan took a breath before carrying on, reading a little more slowly. 'I've always had a keen sense of smell. I think I'm more sensitive to smells than most people, but even the way I experienced scents changed after I had Bella. What smelled good to me became irrelevant. Bella didn't like the taste or smell of overripe bananas. She loved strawberry shampoo, but not coconut. As time went on, I chose to cook food according to my daughter's tastes, because life was easier that way, and isn't that what mothers do?'

Erin smiled encouragingly as Susan glanced around the group before turning to the next page. 'I was happy to hand over my senses. I derived an enormous amount of joy from experiencing the world through Bella's eyes, but I think I might have made a mistake in giving myself over to someone else so completely, even if it was my own child. Because children don't remain children forever. The kisses that used to leave your face wet and sticky, are all too soon bestowed elsewhere. The hands that used to reach up to hold yours are eventually filled with phones, or someone else's fingers, and your hands are empty. Your home is empty, and if you are not careful, your life will be empty too.' Her voice wavered.

She coughed and turned the page. 'I didn't realize how empty my life had become because, even twenty-eight years on, I was still trying to fill it with Bella. Her wife, Sophia, has the patience of a saint, but looking back, I imagine I have been the mother-in-law from hell.' She paused as the group tried to stifle their laughter. 'And that's not okay. What's even less okay is that somewhere along the way I had lost my own identity. I'd given myself away, and it was only when I started to think about what I wanted for my future that I realized I didn't put myself front and centre in any of my plans. I thought about Bella and Sophia's IVF, I thought about my role in their experience and about potentially becoming a grandmother to their child. But I hadn't thought about me. Now, I want that to change.'

'Whoop,' Riley shouted, flicking her fingers above her head. 'That's what I'm talking about.' Tybalt, who was in his usual position on Joe's lap, raised his head at the noise. He kneaded the fabric of Joe's trousers, retracting his claws when Joe gently lifted his paw away from his leg.

'I've always been told I smell nice,' Susan continued, through smiling lips. 'I became proud of the fact I could choose a perfume that suited me and that people would invariably comment upon. I took enormous pleasure in selecting the right diffuser for the right room at home and loved that everyone who came into my house commented on the aromas. So, smell was the first sense I decided to reclaim when I thought about rebuilding myself as an individual. Because that is what my last pages are about – me becoming me again. I am actively reclaiming myself and my senses. I've made the first small steps by doing the perfume taster session with Erin, and I've booked the longer course which starts in September. I'm toying with the idea of selling a bespoke range at Blackheath Market one day, but that's a way off. For now, I'm embracing the glorious potential of it all. In conclusion, my last chapters will still very much include my family, but with their love and their backing, from now onwards, the main protagonist in my story will be me.'

Erin was too choked up to speak. Susan had said as much when they were on their trip to Central London, but to hear it again in such a thoughtful and considered way made her heart swell with pride for her friend. She leaned forwards and grabbed Susan's knee, and the two women smiled at each other with tears in their eyes.

'That was very well written, if you don't mind me saying,' said Adam. 'It's a great concept too, the way you've pinpointed your trajectory and illustrated it using the senses. Clever.'

'Thank you.' Susan looked as though she was struggling to contain her pride. 'That means a lot from a professional writer.'

'Very moving,' said Mercy. 'The perfect coming of middle-age story.' She gave a wink.

'I love that you're embracing change like that,' said Riley. Her gaze moved to Erin, and before Erin shifted her eyes away, she saw kindness there. 'Change is fucking hard,' Riley continued. 'But it can be for the best, can't it?'

'True,' said Mercy. 'That's certainly how I'm feeling about it.'

'What about you, Erin?' Riley's voice was soft, and Erin knew she had her best interests at heart. But that didn't stop her from wanting the ground to open up and gobble her into its burning core.

‘Oh, I’m still lurching from one idea to another,’ she said, hoping vagueness would get her out of disclosing the facts. She didn’t want to say anything anymore. She wanted to stay with Susan’s pages. Hers were hopeful. Erin’s very much were not. ‘Haven’t quite pinned down my future yet.’

‘Do you envisage it being here, at The Bookmark? Jack seemed to think the future of the business might be in question.’ She’d only gone and said it. Erin’s cheeks reddened as all sets of eyes turned to her.

‘Is that right? Are you having difficulties?’ said Joe, his voice full of concern. ‘Why didn’t you say?’

The urge to minimise it was strong, but instead, Erin let the breath leave her lungs in a long sigh. ‘Passing trade has been down since the gift shop closed,’ she said. ‘And when the lease ends in a couple of months and the rent goes up by an enormous amount, we’ll be in real trouble. I’ll be in real trouble.’ This wasn’t anyone else’s fault but hers. Her mother had managed to keep things going in a way that looked effortless, and no one else in that room was to blame. The failure was hers, and hers alone.

‘Are you thinking of closing The Bookmark?’ said Joe. He gazed around the room and Erin’s heart broke when she imagined all the beloved scenes replaying in his mind.

She let her eyes move from the prints on the wall, to the blue candlesticks, and the bright vase in the fireplace, her vision blurring with collecting tears. ‘I’m desperate not to,' she said. 'But unless I can find a way of bringing the profits up, then in four weeks' time, I'll have to give notice. I won't have any choice.' She couldn't stop tears from spilling onto her cheeks. This building was such a huge part of her life. Not only that, it was also her only income. She had the bills on their flat to pay, and all the expenses of living in an affluent area of South London. If she lost the business, she'd inevitably be left with debts, and she couldn't imagine getting a job that would pay enough to keep her and Jack afloat. Losing the business would mean her life would have to change beyond all recognition. The last time that happened it left her a broken shell. 'I was trying to pluck up the courage to tell you,' she said to Riley. 'I should have let you know as soon as I found out about the rent increase. I'm sorry.'

'So, you really think it might close?' said Riley, a wobble in her voice.

'Initially, I thought I had no choice, but now I've decided I won't go down without a fight.'

'Good,' said Riley. 'I like a good fight.'

'We've got to do something,' said Mercy. 'We've got to save The Bookmark.'

'We'll do whatever it takes to help,' said Susan. It was her turn to squeeze Erin's knee.

'I've already done everything I can think of to cut costs,' said Erin. 'I've got an appointment at the bank, but that's all I've come up with so far.'

'Time to brainstorm,' said Riley. 'Operation save The Bookmark is go.'

Chapter Thirty-Two

A new energy crackled in the room, as they brainstormed money-generating ideas. 'I've been thinking about what's going on next door,' said Adam.

'Next door?' said Joe. As if aware that his old haunt was the topic of conversation, Tybalt peered around the group. 'What's happening there?'

'We overheard a couple of fellas discussing the rent rise the other night, and saying they planned to knock through from the empty shop and make this one big unit.' Adam scratched under his chin, thoughtfully.

'What are they planning to do with all that space?' said Susan.

'Open some kind of burger chain,' said Erin, glumly.

'Another fast-food place?' Susan sounded disgusted, 'Instead of your lovely café? That's awful.'

'We can't let that happen,' said Joe. 'Those places are soulless. This café's part of the local community. A fast-food outlet couldn't offer anything like as much to the area.'

'Well, if they can afford the rent and I can't, then . . .' Erin lifted her hands and trailed off.

'They said another couple of things that got my

journalistic antennae twitching, though,' said Adam, propping his elbows on his knees and leaning forwards. 'I think the two of them might be related. The one with the older-sounding voice called the other one "son", and when they talked about the planning application . . . I don't know, something just struck me as off.'

'So, you're saying it might be another family run business?' It occurred to Erin that if that was the case, then maybe it would make losing the café more bearable.

'That's not the impression I got,' said Adam 'And they talked about how people around here were too snobby to want a burger chain, so even if it was, it would probably have a different ethos to this place.'

'Charming,' said Susan, crossing her arms, seemingly oblivious to the fact her indignant tone and pious expression did little to disprove the point.

'It felt more like the older man was pulling some strings, and a third party was involved somehow.' Adam ran his tongue over his lips. 'I'm wondering how he knew the exact figure of the rent increase. Have you told anyone except Jack?'

Erin shook her head vigorously. 'No one. Even thinking about it made me feel sick. I put my head in the sand when I first got the letter. I was paralysed by fear, I couldn't think about it, never mind talk about it. I only mentioned it to Jack the other day, and the only person he told was Riley.'

'Oh, love. I'm so sorry you've been going through this.' Joe gripped her hand tightly. 'I wish you'd said something.' He turned to Adam. 'You think there's something fishy going on?'

'I certainly think it's worth looking into. Leave it with me.'

'Thank you,' said Erin, choked by all the kindness, but painfully aware of how little time she had left to make this work.

'Does anyone have any ideas about how we can get profits up?' said Susan. 'Fast?'

'I could try to pull a few strings and get you a feature in one of the local papers,' said Adam. 'And maybe some advertorial at a discount.'

'Thank you,' said Erin, blown away by how proactive he was being. 'That's really kind. I've looked into advertising, but it's so bloody expensive. And it would have to be a series of adverts, wouldn't it, to shift the dial? Don't you have to see something seven times or something like that for it to permeate?' If that was the case, three and a half weeks was nowhere near enough time, even if she could afford it.

'You just need to get someone to taste your superior coffee and experience your superlative customer service once and then they'd be a customer for life,' said Susan, her tone suggesting she was taking the news of the café's demise as a personal affront.

If only it were that simple. 'The only people I can guarantee will be customers for life are you lot and Zita, and she costs me more in sugar than she contributes to profits.'

'I'm never filling her bowl up again,' said Riley, slumping back in her chair and crossing her arms. 'And you can't make me.'

'Fair enough.' Erin stared out of the café's window at Brigade Street beyond. The scene was so familiar. It broke her heart to think she would lose that on top of everything else.

'You need a USP,' said Riley.

'I thought we had one.' Erin turned to view the wall of books behind her, the spines adding a trove of colour to the room. 'Maybe people aren't interested in sitting quietly with a book anymore. Perhaps they'd rather scroll on their phones. Things don't stay the same, do they?' Oh, how she wished they did.

'That's so sad,' said Mercy. She examined the wall of books. 'I suppose it's the way of the world, though. When I was at the library, I admit I was reluctant to embrace changes when they came along. I was up in arms when they introduced digital books to borrow. I thought it was fine that we had the cassette versions, then the CDs, because visually impaired readers needed stories too, but when they brought in ebooks and audio downloads, I thought it would be the death of what I considered *real* books and the library system as we knew it. But I was wrong. It evolved, people kept reading, and I learned the library is so much more than somewhere people come to get physical books. It's a community space, and that has a value all of its own. I feel a similar way about this place, too.' She gave a deep sigh.

'I do love an audiobook,' said Adam. 'When you're travelling, it's a lot easier to carry headphones than a hardback.'

'I still remember my first audiobook.' Mercy grinned. 'It was the *Orwell Collection*, narrated by Stephen Fry. Sixteen hours of pure brilliance. I never looked back. I know now that it doesn't matter how someone reads, or listens, the story is the same, and every reader will have their own takeaway from the book, however it finds its way into their head. The fact is, the old ways aren't always the best. They're just old.'

Much as Erin wanted to argue that the old ways did matter, she had to admit Mercy made a very good point. She'd recently listened to *In Memoriam* by Alice Winn on her walks to and from work, and playing it while she cleaned the kitchen and prepared food had made the mindless tasks dissolve as her brain was entirely transported by the poignant, heartbreaking love story set against the horrific conflict of the First World War. She would never have time to sit and read all of the books she wanted to. Being able to listen to some was a welcome addition to her life. With this in mind, she had to reluctantly concede that not all change was bad.

'What about applying for a license and turning this place into a café-bar?' said Riley.

'We'd have to overhaul the menu and offer different food, buy in all kinds of alcohol, hire staff.' She lifted her hair from her neck, which had grown sticky at the last suggestion.

'We could turn it into a venue,' said Riley. 'You could have live music or spoken word events. I could ask that promoter Gavin if he's got any ideas.'

They all peered around the room, and Erin could imagine them all thinking the same things; the café was just about big enough for the comfy chairs they were sitting in, and the smattering of tables, but there was nowhere for anything resembling a stage. The corner where the record player stood would be big enough for one person and a microphone stand, but an amp would be a push. Erin eyed her mother's record player and tears stung the corner of her eyes. She couldn't do away with that. It was part of what made the place special. She didn't want anything about The Bookmark to change. That wasn't true. She did want it to make money again. 'I don't think it's big enough,' she said. 'It's a shame, because the events coordinator in me loves the idea of holding things like readings and spoken word gigs here.'

'I still think it's worth getting Gavin to take a look. He might have some ideas.'

'Okay,' said Erin, more to appease Riley than because she thought anything would come of it. It would take too much time to implement any of these changes, and time, along with money, was far too short.

'I'll give it some thought, too,' said Adam, decisively. 'And I'll let you know what I find out about what's going on next door. This place is the closest I've ever had to a local. I don't want to lose it.' The others murmured their agreement, and while Erin was deeply moved by his words, a layer of guilt added to the misery of potentially not being able to keep hold of the business.

Adam offered to stay behind at the end of book group and help her tidy up. It would have been churlish to refuse, especially since her grounds were that her feelings for him were getting stronger, despite her best efforts, and that wasn't what she wanted. Instead, she agreed, and rushed around to get the jobs done as quickly as possible, so she didn't act on the magnetic pull she felt whenever he was near.

He paused in the kitchen doorway. 'I've arranged to meet Oliver,' he said. 'We're going to an exhibition at Tate Britain.'

Erin grinned properly for the first time that evening. 'That's great news. How do you feel about it?'

'Nervous.' He scratched the stubble under his chin. 'But excited. It's weird. I'm not usually a worrier, but I keep thinking of all the things that could go wrong.'

Swallowing the urge to say, *welcome to my world*, Erin said, 'Like what?' as she powered down the coffee machine and checked all the other appliances were turned off.

'What if he doesn't like me? I mean, what if he expects a proper father figure, a bloke in a suit and tie, and I turn up like this.' He gestured to his slightly crumpled We Are Scientists gig T-shirt, and faded Levis. 'I'm an overgrown kid. I ride a motorbike and don't have a regular job. I don't even own my own place. That's hardly stable father material, is it?'

'You're fine as you are,' said Erin, thinking to herself that he was worrying because this mattered, really mattered. Perhaps he wasn't lucky for his ability to breeze through life. Maybe she was the fortunate one for having people she cared so deeply about that their welfare kept her up at night. And she wanted to tell him he was more than fine. He was clever and interesting and kind. 'And he's an adult himself. He's probably not looking for a traditional father figure. In my view, authenticity is the best thing you can offer anyone. Don't pretend to be someone you're not or try to fit some kind of mould. That's all artifice and you can't make proper connections if you're pretending. He'll want to know the real you, and the real you is all right, from what I've seen. A bit annoying, obviously, but generally passable.'

'High praise.' Adam gave a short laugh. 'Annoying but generally passable. I'll put that in my bio.'

'You do that.' Erin couldn't remember when she last had this easy banter with a man. 'And you're putting down roots, aren't you? You've got a local café. That's a start.'

'I have.' He bowed. 'Thank you.' He took in a breath. 'I wanted to talk to you about that, actually. When I said this place felt like a local, I didn't mean to add any pressure. It's not just the café that makes it feel like that, it's the people.'

Goosebumps rose on Erin's skin. 'I appreciate that, thank you.' His words permeated through the layers of anxiety and lodged deep in her mind, because what he said was true. The people she loved happened to congregate at The Bookmark, but the building mattered too. It felt like part of her, it was so tied up in her memories and her family history.

Adam insisted on walking her home, and she was glad to have his solid presence by her side. As the roads got quieter on their approach to her flat, she realized they'd become comfortable enough in each other's presence to walk in companionable silence.

'Thank you,' she said, when they arrived at Dartmouth Grove.

'No problem.' He stood with his hands deep in his pockets. 'Any time.'

She had the urge to roll onto her tiptoes and kiss his cheek, but would that be too intimate? She imagined the feel of his stubble against her lips and a shiver ran through her. Resisting her instincts, she reached out and squeezed his forearm. 'Night, then.' Embarrassed, by her odd gesture, she turned and marched towards the building, hearing him echo her words back at her, and feeling the cold leather of his jacket somehow hot on her palm.

Chapter Thirty-Three

Erin spent a restless night dreaming she was on the back of Adam's motorbike, clinging on to his jacket for dear life as the countryside whizzed past at a terrifying rate. His jacket became slippery, as though coated in cooking oil, and she was finding it increasingly hard to keep hold. She eventually lost her grip, and the tarmac of the road rose up to meet her. She jolted awake, hair stuck to the sweat on her neck and gasping for breath. The dream left her with a new sense of unease, and she was tired and grumpy when she arrived at the café. She scanned the shelves for weepy books and, with a surge of satisfaction, she found *Me Before You* by Jojo Moyes. She sat and reread the ending before setting up for the day, letting the tears flow freely.

'What's the matter?' Riley rushed to her side when she came through the door. 'Has something happened?'

Erin held up the cover for her to see. 'All the uncertainty is getting to me. I just needed a good cry,' she said.

'That book will do it,' said Riley, squeezing her shoulder. 'Feel better?'

‘Yeah.’ Erin wiped her face. ‘A bit.’ She gazed up at Riley’s lovely face. ‘I’m sorry things are up in the air at the moment. If you want to look for somewhere else to work, I’ll completely understand.’

‘I won’t have that kind of defeatist talk,’ said Riley. ‘We’re not beaten yet. Gavin’s coming at eleven. He might have some ideas.’

‘True,’ said Erin, trying to sound more hopeful than she felt. A vision of her and Jack standing in their flat surrounded by their all worldly possessions packed in boxes, as they listened to the sound of bailiffs’ boots approaching their door scored across her brain. She blinked it away.

Riley wound the hem of her T-shirt around her finger, looking suddenly bashful. ‘I wanted to talk to you about the other night. About Jack.’

Erin lay the book on the table and stood. ‘It’s none of my business, lovely. You’re both adults.’

‘I know, but it must’ve been pretty fucking weird to find me in your kitchen.’

It was far more weird hearing the two of them in the bedroom next door, but Erin didn’t mention that. ‘A bit.’

‘And I know you worry, so I wanted you to know we’re cool. We’ve talked and both agree it was a one-off, no biggie and we’re still mates. It’s all good.’

‘Pleased to hear it,’ said Erin. ‘Thank you.’ Jack certainly didn’t seem to have been negatively impacted. He wasn’t pining for Riley after the encounter, so hearing she was fine too was reassuring. Young people did things differently to Erin when she was their age, but that didn't mean it was wrong if no one was hurt.

When Gavin arrived at The Bookmark at 11 a.m., the café wasn't busy so both Erin and Riley had time to chat.

'Do you think we could make this into some kind of daytime venue,' said Riley, after making him an oat milk latte. Erin's heart clenched at the sight of her wide, hopeful eyes. Despite her optimism, she must be worried sick about her job since she didn't have a wealthy boyfriend as a safety net anymore. Not that she'd ever have viewed him in that way, but Erin knew firsthand how hard it was to only have yourself to rely on.

'What kind of gigs?' said Gavin, adjusting his glasses and peering around the room.

'Dunno. Maybe like open mic, or poetry readings? Things that might bring in return customers.'

'There's not a lot of free space for performers.' He rolled his lips over his teeth. 'Maybe if you got rid of the armchairs, that would free up an area over that side.'

Erin took in the lovely old brown leather seats her mother bought decades before. Four of the six were occupied now. 'The trouble is, they're the most popular seats,' she said. 'I can't imagine getting rid of them. If we did, then we'd have to put in more tables and chairs, otherwise we might not have enough seating.' More expense, more risk, for no guaranteed return.

Gavin turned to take in the empty tables behind them, and she could see why he might be sceptical. 'How do you think your regulars would respond to live events?'

Erin had no idea. It was something she'd worried about herself. A few people still came into the café to work, and they would almost definitely find somewhere else to have their coffee and cake if there was a performance going on. Every change she thought of implementing had potential pitfalls. That was one of the problems with change, it could go many ways. 'No idea.' She needed a crystal ball so she could see how various scenarios would play out. She needed a crystal ball full stop. Or did she? She'd always craved being able to predict what was coming, but if the future was as bleak as she anticipated, now she thought it might be better not to know.

'It could bring in a crowd, though,' said Riley.

'It could,' said Gavin, doubtfully.

'We won't know unless we try,' said Riley, her voice rising in pitch.

'There'd have to be some changes before you gave it a go, and you'd need to do a fair bit of advertising.' Gavin's voice didn't sound hopeful.

Erin slumped into a chair at an empty table. 'I've got to give notice soon.'

Gavin pulled out a chair and sat, and Riley did the same. 'You could give it a try, see what works.'

She smiled and nodded, reluctant to show how hopeless she really felt. There wasn't the time or the money. She was going to fail and somehow that felt even worse now the others were all rooting for her to succeed.

'You need deep pockets, like the developers down in Kidbrooke,' Gavin continued. 'They've hired me to set up their community hub. They've got this amazing space, but they don't know what to do with it. They're aware the estate used to have a real sense of community, and they want to recreate that, so I'm looking at what people down there want and how to make it happen.'

'Nice gig,' said Riley.

'Yeah. I'm thinking about everything from art sessions to writing workshops, and all kinds of music stuff. It's pretty exciting and it's a rare and beautiful thing to be handed a project with a proper budget.' He turned to Riley. 'I'm going to set up some spoken word gigs as soon as the place is up and running. Why don't you come and take a look around one day.'

'We'd love to, wouldn't we?' Riley said. 'Erin used to be an events coordinator, didn't you?'

'It's true,' she said. 'About a million years ago.'

'What about after you close up here tonight?' Gavin said, with fresh enthusiasm. 'Any input would be massively appreciated. Between you and me, it's the biggest job I've had, and I'm feeling a bit out of my depth.'

He gave them the address and when he made his way out of the café, Erin felt grateful for the distraction. It would be nice to help someone else solve a problem, because she sure as hell couldn't solve her own.

***

The venue consisted of the whole ground floor of a newly built apartment block a stone's throw from Kidbrooke station. Gavin was waiting for them inside, and they followed him through to a collection of large, interconnecting rooms.

'We want it to be a day-to-night venue,' he said. 'I'm thinking this would be a café lounge kinda thing.'

Erin could easily envisage how the room could be made cosy with the right seating and lighting. 'Would you have book groups, things like that?' she said.

'Yeah, that's what I'm thinking. I'm already talking to this group who run a silent book club. You've probably heard of them, they're massive. They do that Desert Island Reads thing on YouTube.'

'The one with that woman from Parker who runs the bookshop in Chislehurst?' said Riley. 'She's so fucking cool.'

'That's right,' said Gavin. He turned to Erin. 'I love the vibe of your place, actually. Don't hate me, but I was thinking of copying your wall of books.'

'Great,' said Erin, with mock annoyance. 'You'll be nicking all my customers, next.'

'That's the good thing about this place,' Gavin said. 'It's got a built-in customer base. Five thousand new homes have been built around here. As long as we get it right, there's potentially thousands of customers within walking distance.'

'Nice.' Erin could only imagine the potential revenue of this place when it was up and running. 'Will there be a restaurant?'

'Yeah,' said Gavin. 'It's going to be pretty casual, though, just upmarket café stuff. Like your place.'

'It sounds like you're totally ripping off The Bookmark,' said Riley. 'You should be paying Erin commission.'

'I prefer to think of it as being inspired by Erin,' Gavin said, imperiously, as he walked through to a bigger space.

'Careful what you're inspired by,' said Erin, envious of all the potential. Gavin was young and hopeful and at the start of something, instead of the end, like her. 'You want to make a profit, don't you?'

'Yeah, but it's not the vibe of your place that's the problem, is it? It's rising costs, and not enough space to diversify. You've got plenty of good ideas between you, but not enough space to realize them.'

Erin couldn't help but be flattered by what he said. Maybe the demise of The Bookmark wasn't entirely her fault after all.

'And this would be a bar, with a raised area there for performances.' He pointed at the far end. 'Not a stage, exactly, but big enough for bands.' He swept his hand towards the centre of the room. 'We'd have tables and chairs, but they could be moved to make a dance floor.'

He carried on to a smaller room. 'I'm thinking this would be a workshop area for drawing, painting, writing, that kind of thing. We'd get local creatives to run the sessions, so that it's a proper community venture.'

'I love it,' said Erin. She could visualise everything he

mentioned so clearly. 'It's a great space and I think it will work really well.'

'Do you?' Gavin's eyes were imploring, and Erin saw that he really did feel out of his depth.

'I honestly do. And if there's anything I can do to help, just let me know. It might be ten years since I last coordinated any big events, but I still remember how to make a to-do list and manage.'

'I appreciate that,' said Gavin. 'I talked my way into this job, and I think they like the fact I used to live here, but I've been worried I might have over stretched myself. I'm more used to booking bands for gigs at The Amersham in New Cross than I am putting together a plan for an entire venue.' He lowered his voice. 'Between me and you, I'd love to manage the place myself, but I don't think I've got the experience they're looking for.'

'You've got it this far,' said Erin. 'And you seem to know what you're talking about to me.'

He smiled shyly. 'Thanks. Maybe I should put myself forwards for the job.'

'Reach for the stars,' said Riley. 'I have faith in you.' She punched him on the arm.

'And if there's anything I can do to help, you know where I am,' said Erin. 'I still know my way around a budget, a contacts list and a calendar. You can shadow us at the café any time you like, if that'd be useful.'

Gavin grinned. 'Appreciate it.' His smile dropped. 'I wish I'd been able to help with The Bookmark. It's a great place. It's a shame it's not working for you.'

Erin sighed. 'I'm beginning to feel like it's a lost cause.' She put her arm around Riley's shoulders. 'If I can't save it, maybe you could get a job here,' she said. She turned to Gavin. 'If you're in charge of hiring, then this one comes very highly recommended.'

Riley pulled away. 'Don't give up yet. We might be able to turn it around.'

Erin was moved by the hope in her friend's voice, but after viewing the bright modern space before her, she was fighting the opposing feelings of being inspired by all the potential, and fear that she'd left it too late to make the changes The Bookmark needed to survive.

Chapter Thirty-Four

Joe's house was on her way back home, so Erin parked outside and pressed the bell, hoping to catch him in. His grin, when he opened the door, was like sunshine. 'Well, if it isn't my favourite person in the whole world.'

'I bet you say that to all the girls.' She gave him a hug and closed the door behind them.

'I refute that accusation,' Joe said. 'And I'm glad you're here, I need your help with something.'

'What's that?' She followed him into the through-room, where three shirts were laid out on the cushions of the cream leather sofa, a jumble of ties next to them.

'I'm picking out an outfit for my first date.'

Erin had to stop her eyes going to the photograph of Nuala on the mantlepiece. Joe had never hidden his plans from her, and she'd been supportive of his hopes of finding love again, but now that he was putting the idea into practice, she felt suddenly protective of Nuala's memory.

'I'm meeting a lady called Pat at Montpeliers,' he said, seemingly oblivious to Erin's floundering emotions. 'Sorry we didn't pick The Bookmark; it just seemed a bit . . .' He stopped speaking, his fingers curling and moving in writhing fists. 'Close to home.'

'Don't be daft. You don't want an audience the first time you meet someone. I get that.' She clearly wasn't the only one who felt strange about this date. It must've taken a lot for Joe to make the arrangement, and the fact he didn't want to meet at the place that had meant so much to him and Nuala showed how much thought he'd given it. 'Come on, then, tell me about Pat.' She picked up a yellow and black striped tie and held it against a white shirt, then tried a pale blue one with narrow navy stripes.

'She's a widow.' Joe stood close, assessing the options alongside her. 'She worked for a literary agency in administration, but she's been retired for almost a decade.'

'Oo, a literary agency. So, she likes to read?' Erin picked up a tie with multi-coloured books floating on a yellow background. 'This could work.'

'Is it too much? I don't want to come across as whacky, or, I don't know, too keen to impress.'

'You really are nervous, aren't you?' Erin turned to see Joe's brow deeply creased. 'I don't think you need to worry. She's bound to love you, if she's sane, anyway.'

'What if she's not?' he said, lifting his wiry eyebrows. 'What if she's as bonkers as a box of spoons? What do I do then? Or what if we have nothing to say to each other and we're just sitting there, staring into our coffees?'

'Then you go to the loo and message me, and I'll call

you five minutes later with some kind of emergency that I need immediate help with.'

'Like what? It would have to be something urgent, like . . .' His fingers danced as he thought.

She put a hand on his arm. 'You really don't need to overthink this. It's going to be fine.' She looked deep into his eyes. 'It will be more than fine. It will be lovely. You're meeting a new friend, that's all. She doesn't have to be the next big love of your life. This is just date number one, so don't put too much pressure on yourself.' She turned back to the shirts and ties and breathed in through her teeth. 'Don't hate me, but isn't this a bit much for Montpeliers?'

'Is it?' Joe put his hands on his hips. 'What should I wear, then? I haven't been on a date since the seventies.'

Erin pointed to the maroon sweater he was wearing over an open-necked checked shirt. 'This works.'

He touched his collar. 'Not too casual? I don't want her to think I haven't made an effort.'

'You just need to be yourself,' she soothed, recalling having given Adam exactly the same advice. It was true, though. She might not have had a partner for an age, but she still believed being entirely yourself was the only way to enter into any meaningful relationship. 'These clothes are what you'd usually wear, and that's what someone meeting you for the first time will want, you being authentically you.'

Joe nodded. 'Thank you. Right, I'll do that then. What would I do without you? Now that's sorted, let's put the kettle on.' As they went through to the kitchen he said, 'How's things with you?'

'Oh, you know.'

'That good, eh?' Joe filled the kettle as Erin leaned against the kitchen units.

'I've been looking at a space down the road that's being turned into a community venue kind of thing with a café and bar and workshops, and it's made me see what can be achieved if you have the time and the money. The trouble is, I don't have enough of either.'

'Maybe I can—'

Erin froze. 'No, please don't think I'm asking for a handout.' Joe opened his mouth to speak, but she held up a hand to stop him. 'No. I would never have said anything if I thought you felt like you have to offer me money.'

'But—'

'Please,' she said, more firmly. 'It's up to me to solve this.' She wasn't even slightly convinced that she could pull the café back from the brink, and there was no way on earth that she would risk her friend's money being lost. He and Nuala had worked hard all their lives. Erin was already at risk of losing her mother's legacy, nothing could compel her to take Joe's hard-earned money down with her too.

Joe sighed and nodded. 'As you wish. So, do you have a plan?' He plucked two teabags from a glass jar and dropped them into mugs stained on the insides from decades of strong brews.

'Not yet. I'm not going down without a fight, though.

I can't. It means too much.' Her voice trembled, and when Joe turned his doleful eyes to her, she couldn't stop tears from falling.

'Oh, lamb,' he said. 'Come here.' He wrapped her in a hug, and she wept into his shoulder.

'It's not just the potential loss of the business that's upsetting me. I feel like, if I can't make it work, I'll be letting Mum down as well,' she said, straightening a minute later. 'That place meant everything to her.'

'Not everything,' said Joe. 'Not as much as you meant. She wouldn't want you to kill yourself trying to make it work because of a sense of loyalty to her. She loved you too much for that.'

'I wish I was more like her,' said Erin. 'She wouldn't have got herself into this position, or if she did, she would've known how to fix it.'

'Ha! Is that what you think, that the business never had problems until recently?'

'It didn't,' she said, taking the milk from the fridge and handing it to Joe.

'So, why did your parents sell next door?'

Erin frowned. 'They wanted to downsize after I moved out.'

'Sure, that was one reason, but the other was to release some equity to keep the business afloat during the recession. Did Mary never tell you that?'

'No, she didn't.' Erin searched her brain, but she couldn't recall any mention of The Bookmark in the discussions about her parents' move.

Joe took his drink over to the small table by the patio doors at the end of the kitchen and Erin followed. 'I suppose you had your hands full at the time, what with Jack, and your man bailing.' He rolled his eyes. He hated Andrew for what he'd done to Erin and never made a secret of it. 'I suppose she didn't want to add to your worries.'

The enormity of her childhood home being sold to keep The Bookmark afloat was still sinking in. 'I feel even worse now. They made a massive sacrifice to keep the business going.'

'Yes, but it shows that it's not just you who's found it hard. I think they should have told you, but I suppose they had their reasons, so there's no point getting into that. You're not letting anyone down by not having a house to sell to keep it going.'

'It wasn't a cash injection that kept the place alive. It was her.' She pictured her mother, beaming and dancing her way around the tables, stopping to chat to customers, and pet dogs. She made the place what it was. 'She was so full of ideas, so full of energy. If I was more like her . . .'

'If you were more like her, the place wouldn't have survived this long.' He put his hand over Erin's. 'Now, you know how much I loved your mother, but she could be impulsive and a tiny bit reckless. Henrik used to tear his hair out sometimes. And don't forget, they were both working. The Bookmark didn't have to sustain the whole family. Your dad's wages kept everything ticking when times weren't good at the café.'

This was all news to Erin. She'd always presumed the business had been a roaring success under her mother's lively management.

'And she loved that you were different to her. That's why she was so pleased you took over the café. You've always been a safe pair of hands.'

'Boring, you mean.' Erin leaned on her elbows and rested her chin on her hands.

Joe closed his eyes and shook his head. 'That's not at all what I mean.'

'I just wish I had her strength. She didn't let things get to her the way I do.'

'You are strong, Erin. Yes, your mother was a force of nature, but there are different ways to be strong. You have a quiet strength. You're the first person people come to with a worry. They know they'll get unwavering support from you. You couldn't carry the weight of other people's problems as well as your own if you didn't have a core of steel.'

'It's easier to share other people's burdens than carry your own, though. I've been such a coward, hiding from the reality of what's happening in my own life.'

'Have you been hiding, or have you been trying to do the right thing for everyone?'

Erin thought about that. At first, she'd been concerned about making Jack feel like he had to rush into a job he didn't want, and since then, she'd been trying to think of a solution before burdening anyone else. She'd been an emotional mess the whole time, though. Surely someone with a core of steel wouldn't spend half their time trying not to blub.

Joe fixed her with an intense gaze. 'Your mum said you reminded her of Ralph.'

'Ralph?'

'You know, from *Lord of the Flies*.'

Erin recalled the book and thought hard about the character. 'The leader? I don't think I'm much of a leader. She was the one who everyone followed. I'm dull in comparison.'

'You're not dull, Erin. You're reliable, and you're loyal. Ralph is strong, organised, and principled. He's good, like you're inherently good. He always tries to do the right thing, and that's an admirable quality. A rare one too. Your mum saw that in you.'

Erin let out a gasp. Her bottom lip wobbled. 'Mum said that?'

'She did. She admired you so much. She often said she wished she was more like you.'

The words speared directly into Erin's heart. 'I always wanted to be more like her.'

'Isn't that often the case with people we love? They shine in our eyes, and they see the brightness in us. That's what love does, it adds a sheen of light to this dark world.'

Erin gripped his hand. Maybe she wasn't a coward. Maybe what Joe said was true. 'Thank you.'

'I want you to understand that if you do have to walk away from the business, you're not letting anyone down.'

'It's her legacy, though. It only exists because of her, and if it closes, then it's like I'm allowing her to be forgotten. I'm desperate not to let that happen.'

'If you're talking about your mother's long-lasting impact on the world, then I'm pretty sure she'd see you as her legacy, not a café. You're the only legacy either of your parents truly cared about, and if Mary thought keeping the place going made you unhappy, or stressed, then she'd be the first to tell you to let it go. She wasn't afraid of change, was she? She was innovative and . . . as I said, she was sometimes impulsive. She always had one eye on the future.'

'True,' agreed Erin, because now she thought about it, it was. Her parents always put her happiness first, just as she would always do with Jack. 'But the thing is, running the café does make me happy. I only realized how much I loved it when it was too late.'

'Is it too late?' said Joe. 'I believe in my heart that things will turn out okay for you, my girl. You're made of sturdy stuff. You've proved that time and time again. And if it gets tough, I will be there to support you. We all will. If you want to fight for what makes you happy, you won't be on your own.'

Chapter Thirty-Five

Jack wasn't working that evening, and Erin was delighted to smell frying onions when she entered the flat.

'What are you making?' she shouted as she hung her coat on the hook in the hall.

'Fajitas,' he yelled back, over the sound of a rock ballad she didn't recognize pulsing from the small speaker they carried around the apartment when they wanted music. 'Ready in ten. Sit yourself down.'

She went through to the sitting room and saw the small table laid with plates and cutlery. Tubs of guacamole, salsa, and soured cream sat unopened in the middle. He'd gone to a big effort. 'What's all this in aid of?' she said, when he brought through a bottle of red wine and two glasses.

'Can't I make a nice dinner for my dear old mother?'

'You can . . .' She watched him pour the wine, her eyes narrowed. Something was going on. 'But I have a feeling there's a little bit more to this, so come on, what's going on?'

'Wait till I've brought everything through, then I'll tell you.'

She sat, unease growing in her core, as he deposited a steaming bowl of chicken, onion and peppers next to a plate of tortilla. 'Dig in,' he said.

She took a tortilla and dolloped the spicy chicken mix in the centre, then lay down the spoon. 'I can't eat until you tell me what this is about. You know I've got a sensitive stomach.'

He sat back in his chair. 'Okay.' He dug his fingers into his hair.

'Is it bad?' she said. 'You're not poorly, are you?' Her brain sped out of control, imagining him hooked up to a drip, chemotherapy drugs seeping into his blood.

'God, no. No, it's not bad. It's good, actually.' He took a spoon and spread soured cream in careful circles, watching the slop reach the perimeter of the tortilla. 'I've got an interview for a job.'

Her stomach flipped. Phew. 'That is good. Well done.' He was still staring down at his plate. 'What's the job?'

'Junior accounts executive for a small media firm.'

'That's fantastic. Executive sounds fancy. Get you.' This was excellent news. One gigantic thing off the worry list. She thought she'd like to have a junior executive as a son. She imagined telling people his job title with her chest puffed out with pride and a smile crept onto her face.

'Yeah, they call loads of jobs that. I think it's supposed to make up for the crap pay.'

'Well, I suppose everyone has to work their way up. Do you know how many rounds of interviews there are?' She dipped her head, trying to catch his eye. If this was such good news, why was he avoiding looking at her?

'I've got through the online stuff, so it's just the face-to-face interview to go.'

'Well done. You didn't mention it.' He usually chatted things through with her, or at least, she thought he did. Maybe they weren't as close as she'd imagined. The thought made her skin prickle.

Jack placed the spoon down carefully. 'No, I didn't expect to get this far, to be honest and . . . I'm not really sure I want it.'

'Oh?' This was exactly what she'd tried to avoid. If he was just applying for any old job because he knew they needed a full-time salary, she would never forgive herself.

'It's local, in Canary Wharf, so at least I'd be able to stay here if it comes off.'

'Oh,' she said again. There it was, the reason he couldn't meet her eyes. There were two reasons he was considering this job, money and proximity to home. She swallowed. 'You're not only applying for local jobs because of me, are you?'

'Nah, course not.'

She didn't believe him. Her wonderful boy was trying to fix everything for her. How had she let this happen? She pushed her knees tightly together to stabilise herself. She remembered what Joe said about her being strong and tried to galvanise that core of steel. 'I don't want you to take something you don't feel one hundred per cent about. You spend too much of your life at work to not be fulfilled in what you do.' How lucky she'd always been to enjoy her work. She desperately wanted that for Jack too. 'What would be your ideal job?'

'One I could get,' he said flatly.

'Seriously. Humour me. If you could have your dream job, what would it be?'

He scratched his nose and kept his eyes on his plate. 'It's not exactly the dream job, but it would be the dream start.' He glanced up then straight back down. 'A girl who was in the year above me at uni, she's a runner on BBC *Breakfast*. I've been talking to her a bit on Insta, and she's loving it. Every day's different, and she gets to meet all these interesting people. And it's got it all, you know, serious journalism, and entertainment. If I got the chance to start there, then I feel like I could work my way up. I daydream about being a producer one day. I reckon it would be a bit like being an events coordinator, but for TV.'

'Following in my footsteps, eh? You calling me an inspiration? Seriously, that sounds brilliant. You should go for it.' Erin grinned across the table and her lovely boy. 'What's stopping you?'

'It's filmed at Media City.'

'Where's that? West London? It would mean early starts, but you're used to that after working at The Bookmark.'

'It's in Salford, Mum.'

She worked hard to keep her expression impassive. 'Near Manchester?'

'Yeah, up north. A long way from here. That's why I'm going to see if I can get something local.' He spoke gently and Erin hated that he thought he had to couch things to manage her emotions.

She bit the inside of her mouth. She'd made her lovely boy believe she wouldn't be happy if he was anywhere but at home with her. 'Don't do that, love. You've got to go for what you want, not what you think I want. What's right for you is right for me,' she said, with urgency. 'I was talking about exactly this with Joe earlier. At first, I wanted to keep The Bookmark open because it's what I thought Grandma would want, but he made me see that she would want whatever was best for me.'

Jack's lips twitched. 'Yeah, I think she would.'

'And I want what's best for you and I definitely don't want you to worry about me, or how I'll react to the choices you make.' She waved a hand over the food on the table. 'You shouldn't have to go to these lengths to have a conversation with me.' She stifled a sigh. 'I'm sorry you thought you should put your dreams to one side because of me. I should never have made you feel that way.' She raised her glass. 'Here's to following your dreams.'

'I haven't even applied yet,' he said. 'And if I'm offered this other job, I should probably take it. It's brutal out there.'

'Getting an interview is worth celebrating.' She tipped

her glass towards him, and he lifted his and clinked it against hers. 'But it doesn't mean you have to take a job just because it's offered to you. I mean that.' She kept her eyes on his, trying to make him understand that she truly meant everything she said. It turned out that Joe was right, she wasn't a coward. Her love for her son made her strong.

'Thanks Mum.' They built their fajitas, and Jack filled her in on the company and the application process. When he'd finished, he paused with his rolled tortilla close to his mouth. 'How's the plan to keep The Bookmark open going?'

'I've been having some thoughts about that,' she said. 'And this evening puts it into perspective a bit more too. There's a lot of change around and about at the moment, and I've been kicking against it. I'm beginning to realize that maybe change isn't the problem after all.'

'Oh, yeah? What is?'

'Me,' she said. He opened his mouth, so she carried on before he could protest. 'Okay, maybe not me exactly, but the way I feel. The fear I've got of change. It's the fear that's the issue, the anxiety that makes me resistant to change.'

'Interesting,' said Jack, taking a bite and chewing thoughtfully.

'And I've always thought I was a bit of a wimp, and that my fear of change was all part of that.'

'A wimp? You? You're the strongest woman I know.'

Erin bit down on her bottom lip to stop the tears

coming. She realized then that she'd always seen her propensity for tears as a sign of weakness, but maybe that wasn't true either. It just meant she felt things deeply, and sometimes those feelings spilled out onto her cheeks. 'Thank you,' she said. 'When I realized that this resistance to change isn't serving me, I had an idea. It's a bold idea, and I've got less than three weeks to pull it off, so it might already be too late . . . but even if it is, instead of being terrified about it, I've got butterflies, and they're excited ones with fluttery wings, not the nest of hornets I usually get when I have to make hard decisions.'

'I like the sound of this,' said Jack, his eyes bright and interested. 'Tell me everything.'

And so, she did.

Chapter Thirty-Six

The fluttery butterfly's wings were still there when Erin woke up the next morning, and they intensified when a text from Adam appeared on her phone as she made herself breakfast. He was checking if she was in work that morning. She replied that she wasn't on shift until after lunch, and watched as the grey speech bubble appeared, followed by a message asking if he could pop over that morning. She replied, saying he could come at ten-thirty, since that would give her time to shower, wash her hair, and make sure the flat was in a decent state. She then sent another message, the one she'd drafted with Jack the previous evening.

Despite the fact she'd been watching the clock, the buzz from the intercom still made her jump, and when the knock on the door came, she seemed to have forgotten how to breathe.

'Hiya. Come in.' She noted he was wearing one of his smarter tops again, this one was a pale blue knit with buttons all down the front. His stubble was trimmed and shaped and he smelled of lemons and limes.

'Thanks for letting me come around. I've been dying

to tell someone about meeting Oliver.' He paused. 'Dying to tell you, actually.'

'It went well, then?' She turned and headed for the kitchen before he detected the blush creeping up her neck. He said what was on his mind. He wasn't playing any games, and it made her like him even more.

'It was amazing.'

'It's instant coffee, or tea, I'm afraid. All the good stuff is at the café.'

'Instant is fine,' he said. 'Thanks.'

'Tell me everything,' she said, busying herself with making the drinks, glad to have something to occupy her hands. No one had had this effect on her for decades. 'What was it like seeing him for the first time?'

He let out the air from his lungs. 'Weird. Good, but really, really strange. Sometimes it's easy to remember we're just animals with instincts, do you know what I mean?'

'Nope.' She laughed.

'Like, I felt he was . . . my young. I know it sounds stupid because I didn't even know he existed until a few weeks ago, but I recognized him in here.' He held his hand to his stomach. 'In my guts. In a visceral way, somehow.'

She understood because that's how she'd always felt about Jack. 'Sounds intense.'

'Yeah, it was, but it was easy too, if that doesn't sound too weird. He was funny, and he's got his head screwed on. Thank God for that, imagine if he voted . . .' He blew out his lips. 'No, let's not go there. It's all good. His mum's done a great job, I can't deny that.'

Erin suspected he said that for her benefit. 'I hope you told him that.'

'I did, kind of. I think I did anyway, without sounding patronising, I hope.' There was more uncertainty in his voice than she'd ever heard. 'And I tried to make it clear I understood his mum had her reasons for not telling me about him.'

'How does he feel about that?'

'He seemed more concerned I would hold it against her. He was keen to defend her, which I totally get. It's not ideal, is it, not telling someone you're having their kid?'

She could see how this would be tricky ground for all of them. 'Not ideal, no.'

'But I've got a choice, haven't I? I either hold it against her and regret all the things I've missed, that we've both missed, or I embrace the future and look forward to having a relationship with him from now on.'

'Very wise, Mr Darling.' She handed him his mug of tea.

'Thank you.' He lifted the mug. 'I was expecting a quaint little cup.'

'Nah, no such niceties here. Soz.' She took him through to the sitting room, wondering what he thought of her small space, then deciding not to give it another thought. She didn't need to worry about that. He liked her, that much was clear, and that was also what mattered, because she liked him too. Very much.

'Right, next thing on the agenda,' he said, taking a notebook from the bag he'd deposited by the side of the sofa.

'There's an agenda?'

'Yeah, I've got my journalist hat on now. You know I said I'd look into the people planning to take over next door?'

Erin's stomach clenched. She nodded.

'I started by asking around about the rents in Blackheath. Thanks for sending me a picture of the comparables Galmouth sent, by the way. That was very useful.' He flicked the pages of the notebook until he came to a list of businesses with figures scribbled next to them. 'People were reluctant to talk to me at first, but when I told them about how much Galmouth are trying to put your rent up, the colour drained from their faces and they started to open up.' He pointed at the first line. 'Let's start with the florists on Lawn Terrace. The document you were sent says their annual rent is one hundred and thirty pounds per square foot.'

'Is it more than that?' Fear that her plan was even more unattainable than she thought made her go cold.

'No.' He moved his finger to the next line. 'They pay seventy-five pounds, and their lease has years to run with no review period on the horizon.' He ran his finger down the page. 'The story was the same every time.'

The truth started to dawn on Erin. 'Galmouth lied?'

'Through their teeth.'

'Is that legal?'

'Not one iota.'

'The absolute shits.' Heat rushed up Erin's neck. 'How dare they try to destroy my business?' She balled her fists. 'I'm going to the police. They can't be allowed to get away with it.'

Adam put a hand on her arm. 'Hold on. There's more to this than just the lies about the local rents. If it's okay with you, I'd like to do a bit more digging into who's behind Galmouth, and what their connections are.'

'Okay. Let me know when I can approach Galmouth to address this, though. I'm running out of time.'

'Will do,' he said. He closed the notebook and reached inside the bag for an iPad. 'Next on the agenda – I've been looking on Rightmove,' he said in a rush. 'For somewhere to buy.' He tapped on the screen and opened an app, squinting as he scrolled down. He turned it towards her. 'What do you think about this place?'

'Kidbrooke Village?'

'Yeah. Too new? Is it a bit faceless? I'm useless. I don't know anything about buying a place.'

'It's in a great location, and you'd be able to do loads with it. It would be a plain canvas.'

He scanned the room, and as he did so, Erin checked the message that had pinged onto her phone. 'I like places like this with period features and all that,' he said, 'but I've never decorated anywhere before so I thought I'd be better off with somewhere new and uncomplicated. Does that make me a philistine?'

'Nah, just a bloke.' She winked so he knew she was joking. 'I've heard a lot of good things about Kidbrooke Village,' she said, setting her phone down beside her. 'And I might have a bit of business down there myself.'

'What?'

She tapped the side of her nose. 'Do you think you

could arrange to see that flat tomorrow afternoon? We could combine the two, if you like?'

His face brightened. 'You'll come with me to view it?'

'If you'd like me to.'

'I'll call the agent now.' He took out his phone, tapped on the screen and held the phone to his ear, and Erin picked up her phone and made plans of her own.

A reply to her message came a minute later, and Erin flushed with excitement. She was tempted to tell Adam, but she held off, because Jack should be the first to hear what was afoot. Buttoning her lips tight, she watched Adam bring his iPad back to life. 'I've written my last pages,' he said. 'I was too excited to sleep after seeing Oliver, so I decided to get my thoughts down on paper.'

'Well done,' she said. 'I've been putting mine off, but I think I'm ready to start now.' Only when it came out of her mouth did she realize it was true. She could see a future she wanted to commit to paper, and the thought was exhilarating.

'That's good.' He held her gaze. 'How do you feel about reading mine?'

'Erm, yes, I'd like to.'

'Now?'

'Now?'

'If you don't mind. Don't worry if you'd rather wait until book group.'

'No, no, now is good.' She held her hands flat, and he passed her the iPad. She glanced down and saw a document was already open.

'If it's okay with you, I'll go and hang around in the

kitchen while you read it,' he said, picking up his cup and getting to his feet. 'Doesn't matter how long you make your living from writing; it's still excruciating watching someone read your work.' He pointed at the screen. 'It's not too long, don't worry.'

'Why don't you make us another cuppa while you're in there?' Erin smiled up at him, moved by his nerves and the fact he wanted her to read it despite them. When he left the room, she turned to the screen.

***

I've never put down roots. I told myself I was the kind of plant that could grow in any conditions. Lift me out of the ground, shake off whatever native soil clings to me, and transport me somewhere new. I thought I could thrive with a little sunshine, a little food and water, and not much else. But recently, I've learned there is a difference between growing and thriving, a difference between a seed scattered carelessly by the wind, that beds in wherever it lands, and one that has been lovingly sown in fertile ground, and nurtured to grow to its full potential.

If you'll excuse me labouring the metaphor, I've realized I want to be a flower with roots that stretch deep into the earth to support me from the buffeting of the wind. I want to enjoy the sustenance from rich, familiar soil, and get stronger and brighter in my one perfect place in the world.

And I want to be the kind of flower found in a lovingly tended bed, alongside blooms of all different varieties, with bright, vibrant colours and roots which may have started somewhere else but are now planted firmly in the same soil as mine.

I used to think it was what showed above the earth that mattered. Now I can see I was running away from anything deeper. That was a mistake, because the best nutrients are found deep in the ground, and I suspect I have been unwittingly hungry for them my whole adult life. Now, I hope to reach down and eat my fill, with the help of the people who have always been much wiser than me, those who already have firm roots, and continue to blossom in the most beautiful way.

My days of uprooting myself are over. I want a place to call home, a relationship with my son and his new family, friends who have known me for longer than the time it takes me to file copy, and maybe more than that. Who knows?

What I do know, is my last pages are going to be different to the ones before. Oliver and his partner are having a baby. A new life is coming into this world, and I want to be part of the rich soil that child grows in. This marks a new beginning for me, and it feels like the start of something good. At the risk of sounding soppy, I feel like you and I could be at the start of something good too. I'd like to find out, would you?

***

Moved and flustered, Erin took a minute to compose herself before calling. 'Come back, I've finished.'

Adam appeared in the doorway. 'You can see why I didn't end up writing that novel, can't you? Ask me to write anything except the facts, and I turn into Mr Purple Prose.' He performed a flourish with both hands, so out of character they both laughed.

'I think it's lovely,' said Erin, searching her brain for something more accurate to say and failing. Her emotions were too big. 'Really lovely.'

Adam sat and took the iPad from her hands. 'Not too much?'

'Not too much at all.'

'Good.' They sat in silence. She became aware of the heat of his body next to hers. 'That last bit . . . I won't be reading that out at book group.' He turned to face her, and she thought her heart might leap out of her mouth if she opened it. Instead, she gazed into his eyes, hoping he could tell how deeply touched she was. 'That was for you, in case you hadn't worked it out.'

She willed her mind to find the right words to express how much she wanted that too. 'Thank you.'

He glanced away. 'Okay, well, I . . .' He turned the iPad off, clearly getting ready to leave.

Erin's heart pumped quicker. 'I'm scared,' she said. Where had that come from?

'Scared? Of me?' Adam moved to the corner of the sofa, further away, but angled towards her.

‘No.’ She tried to swallow, but her throat was tight. ‘Of . . . of feelings, I suppose.’

‘All of them?’ An amused smile lifted his lips.

‘Most, to be fair.’ She laughed then. ‘I suppose I’m most scared about getting hurt again.’

‘I understand that,’ he said. ‘Would it help if I told you I was scared too? This is the most vulnerable I’ve ever allowed myself to be – first with Oliver, now with you. What you said about being my authentic self really hit home. I’ve been avoiding intimacy my whole life, but I’ve decided to make a change.’

‘To put down roots,’ she said.

‘To bloom alongside other people.’ He arched his brow. ‘In a carefully tended flowerbed.’ He groaned and covered his face. ‘God, that’s awful, isn’t it? They should take back every award for writing I’ve ever been given.’

‘It’s not awful. It’s lovely.’ She prised his hands away from his face. ‘It’s perfect.’ His eyes met hers. ‘And I would really like to be a part of your new beginning, if you’ll be part of mine?’

He gave a tiny nod. ‘I’d like that.’ He took her hands.

‘Let’s be brave together.’ Her thumping heart told her she had the courage, she was strong enough at last to take a chance on whatever this turned out to be. She leaned forwards and felt his warm breath on her face, then the touch of his soft lips on hers.

Chapter Thirty-Seven

Erin, Jack, and Adam met Gavin outside the apartment block in Kidbrooke the following afternoon.

'Are you sure you've got time to look around here?' Erin asked Adam. She'd been flying high since they kissed yesterday, and her nerves about seeing him again today completely dissipated when he acted just as he always did. 'Don't miss your appointment for me.'

'Don't worry. I've been told to go to the marketing suite whenever I'm ready,' he said. 'Apparently there'll be someone there to show us around as long as we're there before six.'

He turned to Gavin. 'Let's have a look at this community space, shall we?'

Entering the first room, Erin started to tingle. It was just as she remembered it, but now it was fully furnished and the bar seemed well stocked. She marvelled at what could be done in a short time with a decent budget and willing staff. 'I'm so thrilled you got the job,' she said to Gavin. 'I think managing a community space like this will be good fun for someone with as many ideas as you. And I meant what I said, you can call on me any time you need help.'

'Thanks,' said Gavin. 'I'm going to take you up on that.'

Erin scanned the room like she used to when she was assessing a venue for an event, which was exactly what she was doing now. Her plan could work, she was almost sure of it. 'How much is the hire charge?' She tensed, preparing herself for disappointment. If the figure was too high, then there would be no point going ahead.

'Gratis,' said Gavin, beaming. 'Nada.'

Erin gaped at him, unable to believe what he said. 'Seriously?'

'Totally. I spoke to Miranda, the CEO, and she was bang up for all of it. Your idea of having a big opening night for the venue, and splitting the fundraising proceeds between community projects here and saving the café made her clap her hands like a kid at a circus, no word of a lie. She lives in Blackheath and goes into your place now and again, apparently. She said that The Bookmark was the only café she felt comfortable going to when her kids were small. You were proper welcoming, apparently, and didn't tut or complain when they made a mess. She says you make the best bacon sarnie in the south east too.'

Jack flung an arm around her shoulder. 'What goes around, comes around.'

Erin was moved beyond words. When she regained her composure, she said, 'Please tell her that the bacon sandwiches are on me for the foreseeable.' She looked around the group, biting her bottom lip. 'Do you think we can pull it together in time?'

'Only one way to find out,' said Gavin.

Erin's pulse pounded in her ears. It was a risk, but she was ready to take it for the sake of her mother's legacy and her own future. 'Are you sure it's okay, for half of the money raised to go towards helping the café get back on its feet? It's a business, not a charity. Are you sure it's not taking money away from—'

'Stop that right now,' said Jack. 'The Bookmark is part of the community, and it's not as if you plan to spend the money on a fancy car or a holiday. You just want to be able to afford to advertise, promote the café, and invest in its future. You're making sure it's still around for people to benefit from long term.'

'And we'll be completely open about where the money's going,' said Gavin. 'No one's going to be hoodwinked. And if half the people we've talked to actually perform on the night, people will be getting good value for money.'

He took a breath, looking suddenly awkward. 'Miranda was sorry she couldn't come to meet you this afternoon, but she said that if you're happy to work alongside me to arrange the event, then the whole project will be beneficial for both sides.' He looked at Erin as if willing her to agree, despite the fact she was sure she was the one getting the better deal.

If this lovely young man, and the CEO of the company he worked for, trusted her, it was time she started to really trust herself. 'Of course,' she said. 'Absolutely.' She gazed around the space, making a mental list of what needed to be done. Excitement built in her core. The potential of what she envisaged was dizzying. There was a chance it could change everything, and the thrill that made her feel light on her feet told her she was ready to fully embrace it. 'Right,' she said, rubbing her hands together. 'This event isn't going to plan itself. Let's get started.'

* * *

Erin's head felt like it was full of static on the day of the fundraiser two weeks later. The stakes were high. She'd calculated that if she could raise ten thousand pounds, then the rent rise would be covered for the first three months, and she'd have two thousand left to advertise and promote the business. It was a lot of money, hopefully enough to entice new repeat customers, and if she worked harder at cutting costs and increasing profit, then maybe, just maybe, the business would survive.

She'd never tried anything as audacious as pulling an entire event together in a fortnight before. Audacious wasn't a word that she'd ever associated with herself, but she had felt incrementally stronger with every new day recently, and the way Gavin and the others seemed to believe in her made her begin to believe in herself. Despite that, when Adam came to pick her up at 5 p.m., she was frazzled, and not just because of the niggling fear that she'd forgotten something crucial, like a PA system, or hiring bar staff.

She opened her emails on her phone and turned the screen to show him. 'Look what came through today.' He read the email from Galmouth Estates requesting the signed lease agreeing to the rent rise immediately, or confirmation she'd vacate the property on the day the lease ended. 'I knew I should have got in touch straight away to negotiate the rent rise down. Surely they can't still insist on it when I can prove they lied about those comparisons, can they?'

Adam scratched under his chin. 'No, I really don't think they can. And I've just found out some very interesting stuff about Galmouth Estates—'

'Ready?' Jack bounded into the room, his expression as bright and excited as it had been before his childhood birthday parties. He hadn't been offered the accounts executive job, but wasn't visibly disappointed. Erin had tried not to be either. Now she knew his dreams lay elsewhere, she let her hopes of keeping him close go, and because it was tied up with his future happiness, it had been easier than she thought

'Let's talk about Galmouth later. We've got enough to do tonight,' said Adam, dropping a quick kiss on her lips.

Erin glanced at Jack to see if he found the brief PDA uncomfortable, but her lovely boy was grinning from ear to ear. Of course he was. He wanted her to be happy, just as much as she wanted the same for him. That's what love was. 'Off we go, then,' she said, excitement almost lifting her off her feet. 'Let's get this show on the road.'

Chapter Thirty-Eight

Gavin was just inside the door, bouncing from foot to foot, when they arrived at the venue. 'I'm scared we've forgotten something,' he said, his gaze jumping from Erin to Adam, then Jack.

His nerves seemed to calm Erin. She took a steadying breath and put a hand on his arm. 'We've got this. If something goes wrong, we'll improvise. It's all good.'

'What if no one turns up? Maybe we priced it wrong. Will people pay twenty-five quid?'

Erin had been fighting the same thoughts herself. They'd promoted the evening as much as they could in the time they had, putting flyers on all the tables in the café, and lots of other local businesses had agreed to have posters in their windows and spread the word. Gavin had placed large adverts in the local press and had done his best to engage the people living on the estate, selling it as the opening event of the community space as well as a fundraiser for The Bookmark. But there was no guarantee their efforts would come to anything.

'The offer's good,' she said. 'Where else are people going to see a jazz band made up of some of the greats, two spoken word performers, a comedy drag act, and finish the night with tunes from a top London DJ? Thanks for arranging that, by the way.' Between her, Gavin, Joe, and Riley, they'd put together an impressive line-up of artists, all working for free. Mercy was even bringing along Jakub from the library, in his guise as comedy poet and drag queen, Bridget Bard-Oh. If this came off, Erin would owe a debt of gratitude to so many wonderful people.

Gavin's shoulders dropped. 'Yeah, you're right, it's gonna be good.' He nodded a little manically. 'It'll be fine, won't it?'

'It will be magnificent,' said Adam, striding ahead of them into the centre of the room.

Erin followed, her breath catching when she saw the enormous banner strung above the bar to the left with 'Save The Bookmark' in bright red letters. She made herself pause for a moment to take it all in. Even if tonight didn't raise enough to save the café, she had tried. She'd been brave and proactive in a way that she didn't know she was capable of, and the new knowledge that she could find strength when she needed it made her feel like she could face whatever was coming her way. A vision of her mother smiling and nodding appeared in her mind's eye. 'This one's for you, Mum,' she said, silently.

'No, this one's for you,' whispered the voice of her mother, before her smiling image melted away.

Choked with emotion, Erin crossed to the raised performance area, where a drum kit and an enormous speaker were already *in situ*. Joe and a few of his musician friends were seated to the right. Erin blinked at the sight of Lulu, dressed in a sky-blue sequined gown, offering the contents of a flask around to the assembled group. Her cheeks were fuller, and her skin brighter than it was at Joe's birthday. She looked ten years younger. 'So good to see you, Lulu,' Erin said, overjoyed to see this transformation. 'You look amazing.'

Lulu stood and twirled, like a child in a ballet class. 'Thank you. Thought I was on my last legs, but turns out it was just a bit of gastric bother. All sorted now. I'm a convert to healthy living. Better late than never.' She chuckled, raising a glass of sludgy green liquid and taking a slug.

Joe took a sip of the green liquid in his glass and grimaced. 'Jesus, if it means having to drink this concoction for the rest of my life, I think I'd rather be six feet under.'

A woman with close cropped white hair and bright eyes, who looked to be about Joe's age tapped him on the knee. 'Don't say that. We've got too much to look forward to, you and me. It's good for you, drink up.' She winked at Joe, who grinned like a schoolboy, knocked back the contents of the glass, then wiped his mouth with the back of his hand.

He turned to where Erin was watching with interest. 'Erin, meet Julia.' He gestured towards Erin. 'Julia, this is the daughter I never had. She's my family, and I have an inkling you two will get along famously.'

Julia stood and took Erin into a warm embrace. Erin was astonished to discover that being hugged by this stranger immediately felt right. She had a comforting floral scent and a hold that was both soft and firm. Julia pulled back and stared into Erin's eyes, holding her gently by the hands. 'It's a pleasure to meet you. I've heard so much about you.' She looked around the space. 'I can't believe you've made all this happen in two weeks. You're an impressive woman.'

'I don't know about that,' said Erin, following her gaze. People buzzed around the room, stacking glasses behind the bar, arranging red velvet-backed chairs around tables. She imagined seeing the thronging space through someone else's eyes, and had to admit, it did appear to be pretty impressive. 'And I certainly didn't do it all on my own.'

'You have a lot of willing helpers,' said Julia. 'For good reason, from what I can gather. I've been sitting here observing what's going on for a while now, and I can see how much everyone is rooting for this fundraiser to work. I get the impression that people want to pay you back for all the lovely things you've done for your friends and the community over the years.'

Erin blushed. 'That's a lovely thing to say, thank you.'

Julia squeezed her hands gently before letting go. 'I'd better let you get on. I get the feeling it's going to be quite a night.'

She wasn't wrong. By the time people began to arrive at seven, everything was set up and ready to go. Erin felt every thump of the double bass at the base of her throat when the jazz band struck up 'Fly Me to the Moon'. Soon they upped the beat with 'The Girl From Ipanema', and Erin watched in nervous delight as the queue at the bar grew, and the chairs around the tables filled with people, toes tapping, eyes trained on the musicians. Before long a couple of people got up to dance, and they were soon joined by others, until the floor was filled with swirling colour and a mass of moving limbs and smiling faces.

When the band took a break, Bridget Bard-Oh took over, making the audience roar at her risqué poetry set. Riley was on next. A sizeable crowd had collected behind the tables and chairs. Erin stood with Adam by a table at the back where Susan, her husband, and Bella and Sophia sat. Next to them were Hafsa and Amir, along with Mercy, Joe, Lulu, and Julia. Erin was too jittery with adrenaline to sit down herself. Gavin sidled up beside her, whispering, 'We're nearly at capacity.' He did a little shimmy. 'So we've reached our target before we even look at bar takings or the JustGiving page I set up. Can't believe it. It couldn't be going better, could it?'

Erin's head felt light. They'd done it. They'd raised the money. The café could stay open. She could hardly contain the elation building inside her, and was just about to answer him, when she heard her name called through the speakers. She looked up at Riley, who was opening and closing her hand, gesturing her to join her at the front. She shook her head, suddenly shy as heads turned to look at her.

'Come on, Erin,' said Riley. Erin felt a gentle push from behind and turned to see Jack mouthing for her to get up there. She swallowed hard, then made her way to the stage.

Riley took her hand as Erin squinted against the lights trained on the performance area, sweat trickling down her back. 'I'd like to introduce the brains behind tonight's event, before you lot are all too hammered to remember your own names, never mind anybody else's,' said Riley. The audience laughed. 'This is the one, the only, Erin McRae, owner of The Bookmark Café in Blackheath, friend to everyone, best boss ever, and the only woman who's ever really been like a mum to me.' She raised Erin's hand, and as the joy of Riley's words soaked into her, Erin felt a brightness start at her core and radiate through her, until she was sure her skin was visibly glowing. She squinted past the lights at the beaming faces of her friends, let her eyes find Adam, then Jack, and in that moment, her love-swollen heart told her that, with these people by her side, she could make it through anything.

'One of the reasons we're all here, as well as wetting the head of this amazing space, is to raise enough money to keep The Bookmark open for all the people who benefit from it,' said Riley, still holding onto Erin's hand. 'Because it's not just a business, or a café. It's so much more than that. It's a library for people who want to lose themselves in a book, it's a safe haven for anyone who needs peace and quiet. It's a warm and welcoming space for anyone who's lonely or just fancies a bit of company. It's whatever you need it to be, and that's because of this woman here.'

She turned to Erin, tears welling in her blue-green eyes. 'There's no judgement at The Bookmark. No one cares about your gender, the colour of your skin, where you were born, if you're rich or poor, old or young.' She scrunched up her face and turned to the crowd. 'Unless you're a dick. Then we'll judge you very harshly indeed. So don't be a dick, people.' She waited for the laughter to die down. 'Seriously, though, The Bookmark's always been a special place, right from when Erin's mum started it almost four decades ago.' She viewed the room, her expression turning serious. 'And we need places like that more than ever, don't we? Out in the big wide world people are forgetting that it's our shared humanity that connects us. Far too many people have lost sight of the fact that we can learn from our differences and become better and stronger in one diverse and glorious community.'

Erin listened, rapt like the silent crowd. She thought of Adam's last pages and his description of the flowerbed, filled with blooms of all different varieties. She felt a new appreciation of those words, and a bursting pride in the wonderful young woman standing beside her now.

Riley continued, as the audience hung onto every word. 'But since so many people seem to have forgotten that love is stronger and more powerful than hate, it's down to us to demonstrate that we still hold that truth in our hearts. We need to keep that knowledge alive in places like The Bookmark, where everyone is safe and accepted. In this mad, mad world it's crucial that there's always somewhere to go where a smile is guaranteed and the coffee is good.' She leaned forwards, 'And believe me, the coffee is very good, and I'm not just saying that because I'm the one making it.'

As if waking from a spell, the audience laughed. 'So I'll finish this little rant by saying thank you for coming out tonight in aid of these two brilliant causes, but please, please don't let this be where your support ends. After this evening, I hope we'll have secured the future of The Bookmark for a little while longer at least.' She pointed a stern finger at the crowd. 'If you all become our regulars, then we can keep it going long-term, so you know what to do, right?' She wagged her finger and the audience grinned and nodded along. 'That's agreed, then. Good. I'll see you all on Brigade Street soon. Tell me you were here tonight and I might just shake a little extra chocolate on the top of your cappuccino.'

As rapturous applause rang out, Riley turned to Erin. She dropped the microphone to her side and said quietly, 'Thank you for all you've done for me. I meant what I said, you've been more of a mum to me than my own ever was. I love you.'

Erin took her in her arms and gripped her close. 'I love you too, you brilliant, brilliant woman. Thank you. Thank you so much.'

They released each other, and Erin waved at the

still-applauding crowd as she left the stage to the sound of Riley announcing her first performance piece, 'Pants Up, Camera Down' to delighted whoops from the audience.

***

At the end of the night, Erin's cheeks ached from grinning. Everyone from book group offered to help with the last of the clearing up, but Erin insisted she, Riley, Gavin, Adam, and Jack could manage the rest. Susan and her family finally left the venue, Mercy trailing behind, after innumerable hugs and congratulations. It was now past midnight and everyone was ready for bed although, with the adrenaline still coursing through Erin's entire body, she was sure she wouldn't sleep a wink.

When Riley, Gavin, and Jack went off to dismantle the PA system, Adam led Erin to a chair. 'That was spectacular,' he said. 'What a night.' He paused. 'I didn't know what I was missing before I found your book group.'

She clapped her hands gleefully. 'You're a convert to the last page strategy at last! I knew I'd get you in the end.'

'Absolutely not,' he said laughing and taking her hands in his. 'You'll never convince me of that one. I mean all this.' He gestured out to the room. 'The way everyone came together to make it happen. I've never been involved in anything like it before. I didn't know how good it felt to be part of a group, a community where everyone wants the best for each other. It's . . . it's pretty bloody special.' He looked into her eyes. 'You're pretty bloody special.'

Her heart swooped so high she thought it might leap right out of her mouth. 'Back at'cha, Mr.' She squeezed his hand, hoping to convey just how much his words meant to her through her touch. After a moment of gazing at each other with daft grins on their faces, she said, 'Now I know how much the café means to everyone, not just me, I really, really hope we've made enough to give me the time to make the business work again.'

'About that,' he said. 'What I started to tell you earlier was that I've found out who owns the building.'

'Galmouth Estates own it, don't they?'

'Yes, but only one man is behind that company. He's called Julian Fengrove.'

The name meant nothing to Erin. 'Who's he?'

'The husband of Pam Bothick.'

'Now, I've heard that name before.' Erin tried to work out where, but couldn't pin it down. The speakers squealed as the leads were unplugged.

'She's a council bigwig and it turns out she's on the planning committee that would decide on the change of use for the old gift shop from retail to restaurant.'

'Oh,' said Erin, sitting up straighter.

'And guess whose name is on the application for opening a restaurant there?' He raised his eyebrows. 'Luke Fengrove, son of Pam and Julian. They must've hoped that, just because he doesn't have his mum's surname, and the building is owned by a company, no one would work out they're trying to play the system.'

'They didn't factor in your journalistic spidery senses, did they?'

'They did not. And I'm pretty sure that increasing your rent by eight grand a quarter to try to force you out, and lying about the comparables, would be seen as pretty shady by the members of the committee who don't happen to be related to the applicants. So, what do you want to do about it?'

Erin made a humming sound as she thought. She looked around the venue, the seed of an idea burrowing into her mind as she took in the space. 'I think it's time I spoke candidly to Mr Fengrove. If I arrange a meeting, want to come along?'

'Hell, yes,' said Adam. 'Happy to be your wingman.'

'Good,' said Erin. The seed of the idea was already growing roots and green shoots at an astonishing pace. 'And, now I know what's really going on, I've had another idea, but it might be completely bonkers.'

'Sounds like fun,' said Adam, an excited spark in his eyes. 'Go on.' The spark got brighter and brighter as she outlined her brand new plan.

Chapter Thirty-Nine

At the next book group, everyone was still buzzing with the success of the event. Tybalt seemed to sense the excitement in the air, winding around everyone's ankles, instead of settling in his usual spot on Joe's lap. Unable to keep her elation inside any longer, Erin said, 'I can still hardly believe it but, with ticket money, bar receipts and donations on the JustGiving page Gavin set up, we've raised twenty-seven thousand pounds.'

Riley whooped and Adam clapped so hard she was sure his palms must sting.

'That's enough to keep going, right?' said Hafsa, her fingers curling and uncurling on her thighs.

'And some,' said Erin, 'But let's talk about that later. We agreed that tonight is about our last pages.' Erin was bursting to tell them the outcome of her and Adam's meeting with Julian Fengrove the day before, but she didn't want to detract from the work they'd all done on what their futures held. An air of gravitas fell over the room. It felt like an important day.

She regarded her friends in turn, her heart full of love for each and every one. Hafsa was dressed in a hot-pink jacket with matching wide-legged trousers, and she looked as stylish as ever. Other than Susan, who'd already shared her last pages, she was the only one without a notebook on her lap. Mercy was scanning an open A4 pad, her lips moving as if practising the lines of a play.

'I've got an apology to make,' said Erin. 'I haven't quite finished my last pages yet. I'm working on them, though, and I promise they'll be ready soon.'

'Me neither,' said Hafsa. 'Sorry.'

'No need to apologise,' said Joe. 'You're busy people. Not like me, with all the time in the world to put pen to paper.'

'Why don't you start us off?' said Adam. His iPad sat on the table beside him, and Erin warmed at the memory of the words in his document.

Joe glanced around the group. 'I'm nervous. You'd think an old goat like me would be past that, especially when you think how many performances I've done over the years, but reading something out feels different.'

'You don't have to,' said Erin. 'You could just give us the gist, if you like?'

Joe took his reading glasses out of his shirt pocket, put them on and opened his notebook. 'No, we're all friends here,' he said. 'Here goes nothing.' He took a breath and started to read. 'I was wearing my wellies when I first met Nuala.' He glanced up with a glint in his eyes before focusing back on his pad. 'It was a Friday night in May, the date of the monthly dance in Killybegs, and I was running late after helping my dad gut the day's catch, so I probably smelled of fish too. Can you imagine a more alluring combination?' He paused as they laughed along with him. 'I decided no one would notice my footwear or my questionable aroma since I was in the band, sitting at the back with my double bass between my legs. But someone did notice. She noticed me, at least, just as I noticed her. You couldn't not, with hair the colour of flames and lips to match. She was a cousin of my friend, Archie, and she was visiting from a town a few miles away and from the minute I set eyes on her that was it for me.'

He sighed. 'She was only seventy-one when she passed. Back when we met, that would have sounded ancient. I would probably have said, "She had a good innings" and expected a man my age to be satisfied at having enjoyed a long and happy marriage. And I am. Truly, I know how blessed I was to have a woman like Nuala at my side for as long as I did. I said to Erin, a while ago—' he glanced up at Erin, his eyes full of gratitude '—that it's because of how lucky I was that I want to try my hand at the love game again. Because I'm not dead yet. In here—' he put his hand to his chest '—I'm still that boy in wellies stinking of fish. My hands might not be able to pluck the bass strings like they used to, but the music is still in my heart and my soul. And I want to share what is left of this joyful life with someone else who still dances, even if it is just in their mind.'

He coughed and lowered his voice. 'That person will

not be Pat.' He looked up and wiggled his grey eyebrows. 'Pat was my first foray into the mature person's dating scene, and I discovered over a coffee that seemed to last several lifetimes, that she does not have music in her soul. She does, however, have grumbling gallstones, a dicky hip and an irritable bowel. The delight she took in regaling me with the irregularity of her movements suggested this was her favourite topic of conversation. Possibly her only topic of conversation. I will not be repeating the experience to find out.' He lifted a finger and paused as Tybalt finally decided to take his usual spot on his knee. When the cat was settled, he continued, 'But, as you know, I was not deterred by Pat's unpredictable bowel movements, off-putting as they were. You've all met Julia now, and I think I'm right in saying she got the book group seal of approval?' He glanced up as they all agreed wholeheartedly. He smiled. 'That's good, because this exercise has reminded me that life is for living, and my last pages will be filled with me trying to make the best of every day with all that is left in me. The end.' He gave a firm nod with the final words, then smiled as the group gave him a delighted round of applause.

Chapter Forty

'That was wonderful,' said Susan. 'You're an inspiration, Joe. I hope I've got half your energy and positivity when I'm your age.'

'You'll be running your global perfume company from your super-yacht, by then,' said Riley.

Susan held up both hands to show crossed fingers. 'Who's next?'

'I'll go,' said Adam. He wiped sweat from his forehead and coughed a brief laugh. 'Is it warm in here?'

'You're not nervous, are you?' said Mercy. 'You're the only real writer here.'

'Ahem,' said Riley, giving her an exaggerated side-eye.

'Sorry.' Mercy lifted her palms. 'I think of you as a performer, more than a writer, but of course you write brilliantly too.'

'I'm only messing,' said Riley. She turned to Adam, who was looking more nervous by the second. 'Go for it, big fella.'

He cleared his throat, and it was all Erin could do not to reach out and take his hand. 'Don't expect too much,' he said. 'I'm definitely better at writing factual reports than stuff about . . .' He wobbled his head. 'Feelings, hopes, and dreams and all that.'

'Stop hedging and get the fuck on with it,' said Riley.

Adam blinked and started to read. Soon, his voice flowed less haltingly, and his beautiful words filled the room, making Erin's heart spill over, as it had when she read them to herself. This man was making himself vulnerable and he was doing it because he wanted to change the way he lived. She could hardly believe her luck that he wanted her to be a part of the new life he was forging for himself. She'd been a fool to resist him at first. Her feelings had been strong since the start and even just looking at him now, Erin was flooded with affection. When he finished speaking, having left off the final line which Erin knew was meant solely for her, he looked up through his dark lashes, a shy smile on his face. 'So that's me.'

'I very much like the idea of being in your flowerbed,' said Susan matter of factly. 'What a lovely metaphor.'

'Possibly a bit cheesy,' said Adam, putting the iPad down on the table and visibly relaxing. Erin wanted to take his face between her hands and kiss him, but even though she was sure they'd all guessed, she hadn't explicitly told anyone but Jack about their burgeoning relationship, and snogging his face off in the middle of book group might be an odd way to announce it.

'Not at all,' said Mercy. 'I think it's perfect.'

'This is a good place to put down roots, my man,' said Joe, stroking Tybalt and looking every inch a man who was happy with his place in life. 'I'll always be an Irishman at heart, but I've called this place home for as long as I can remember, and I wouldn't want to be anywhere else.'

Mercy put her hand to her chest. 'And you're going to be a grandfather. How precious.'

'Yeah, I've been invited to the baby shower,' said Adam. 'What exactly is that?'

'A dreadful American tradition,' said Susan dourly, 'where people buy presents for the baby before it's even born.' Her pinched-lipped smile was just about detectable. 'But I'll be changing my tune if Bella and Sophia ever get pregnant, I'm sure. I'll be the one hosting it, probably.'

'Unless you're off on your yacht,' said Erin.

'Well, yes, there is that.'

'I was hoping you might come to this shower thing with me,' said Adam, his eyes on Erin. 'Oliver said I could bring someone along.'

Erin's chest expanded with delight. She was tempted to glance around at the faces of her friends to see if they were taking note of this new turn of events, but she didn't. She said, 'Great. I'd love to.' To prevent anyone else commenting, she turned to Mercy. 'Are you ready to read your last pages?'

Mercy lay her hand flat on her pad. 'Do I have to go after Adam? I haven't got any pretty metaphors or similes to offer.'

'You don't have to go at all,' said Erin gently. 'Only read it out if you want to.'

'And I'm certain mine would be eviscerated in a writing group,' said Adam, 'because it was far too flowery. And it's not about the writing anyway, it's about the sentiment.'

'Okay, then. As long as you keep that in mind.' Mercy wagged a finger at each of them and waited for them to agree before lifting the pad and beginning. 'My parents were both born in Kenya, and that's where my troubles began. The stories I was told of wall-to-wall sunshine, of delicious food and auntie this, and auntie that, of cousins and friends, all much better than the people they knew here. English tea was drunk, compared with brews from home and found lacking. Always lacking. Nothing could compare with the colour, or smells, tastes, sights, and sounds of my parents' motherland.'

She breathed in. 'You might think this would make me desperate to see this magical place with my own two eyes, but no.' She lifted a finger. 'Where here, my mother saw grey skies, I saw autumn turn to winter, as reassuringly predictable as night follows day. I knew the grass on the heath would turn brown in the summer after two weeks without rain. I was comforted by the sound of the train rumbling past our house towards the city I grew up in. The green leaves turning red and gold were my colours. London's noise was the sound I knew, and the people I grew up with were my aunties and cousins, even if we didn't share blood.'

A sigh came from deep in her core. 'If you grow up in a house filled with sadness and regret, you will do what you can to take a different path. I chose to take no path at all. I decided to be content with what I knew. The risk of travel seemed great to me. It wasn't that I didn't want to see more of the world, it was more that I was frightened to feel the allure of distant lands. My parents had listened to the call, acted upon it, and never felt at home again. I belonged here, I felt at home, and I thought it was enough to read about all the places I would never see. But it isn't. Not anymore. I want to experience Kefalonia, not just read about it in *Captain Corelli's Mandolin*. I want to go to New York, not just through the pages of Colm Tóibín's *Brooklyn*. I want to see Times Square, I want to see Japan's cherry blossom, and then I want to come home again.' She turned to Riley. 'So I want to thank you—' she viewed the rest of the group '—and all of you, for making me think about what I want for the rest of my time on this earth. I have lived a cautious life, and it's time for me to grab whatever years I have left by the throat and shake it.' She made a twisting motion with her hands and mimed throttling, while she bared her teeth.

'Yes, queen!' said Riley.

'Good for you,' said Joe.

'Stop doing that now,' said Susan, patting Mercy's hands. 'But, yes, that's an excellent sentiment. Are you looking forward to Kenya in September?'

'I am,' said Mercy. 'But that's a long way off, so I've booked a weekend in Paris and four days in Venice between now and then.'

'Wow,' said Erin. 'That's impressive.'

'Now I've started, I can't stop. I'm like a child again.' She closed her pad with a slap. 'Now, who's up next?'

Before anyone could answer, they all turned at the sound of the door opening.

Chapter Forty-One

'What are you doing here?' said Riley, scowling at Chegs.

He remained in the doorway, swaying, before putting his hand out to steady himself. 'I knew you'd be at book group tonight. I've come to win you back.'

'I'm not a maiden at a fucking jousting match,' she said, crossing her arms.

'I'm not sure it's the right time for this, young man,' said Joe. 'Why don't you go home and sober up?'

'I want to talk to Riley,' Chegs slurred. 'I want to tell her how sorry I am.'

'Too little, too late. You made your choice,' said Riley, 'and since then, I've made a few of my own.'

'Off you go, Chegs,' said Erin. 'We're in the middle of something here.'

'Hold on. Maybe you should stay.' Riley stood. 'Take a seat.' Chegs stumbled into the room and Riley directed him into a chair at the other side while the others watched on, confused. Riley turned back to the group. 'If it's all right with you, I'll do my last pages now, and then Chegs can hear what I've got to say.'

'Righto,' said Susan, and Erin and the others sat back and waited for the scene to unfold.

Riley took her phone from her pocket and handed it to Adam who was in his usual upright chair at the edge of the group. 'Can you film this for me, please?' She adjusted the settings to make sure the shot was what she wanted, before moving closer to Chegs, who was slumped in a chair, breathing heavily. 'You happy to be in this if I post it?' she asked. He nodded mutely.

'My next chapters,' announced Riley. She dropped her gaze to the floor, then up again, her eyes bright and defiant. 'In the story of your life, plot and character matter most,' she began. 'And you need a structure, so I'll start with my inciting incident, the thing that changes the status quo.' She walked to the left, then returned to the same spot, a thoughtful expression on her face. 'Mine was my mum's first overdose.' She paused. 'Or was it? You see, it was *her* body limp, drooling onto the threadbare carpet, a needle sticking out of *her* arm, not mine. My body was still growing – too fast for my clothes to keep up, two inches of skinny ankles showing below last year's skinny jeans.'

The image of Riley standing over her mother, a scared, neglected child, appeared in Erin's mind and she wanted to scoop her up and hold her to her chest.

'And it's my story I'm telling, so let's focus on that scrawny kid.' She tapped her cheek. 'In terms of genre, my youth would be a work of worthy literary fiction, the kind where well-written tales of poverty and addiction win prizes.' She made her eyes wide. 'The only prize I won was for having the best cheekbones in our class. It was made up by the popular girls in Year 9, and they gave me a tatty piece of paper with a star drawn on it. I've still got it somewhere at the bottom of a drawer. You see, I was thrilled to be noticed by anyone beyond the kids on our estate.' She lowered her voice. 'They only spoke to me when they wanted me to deliver packages. I took those packages because that's how I got the money for the beans and bread we lived off – the diet that gained me the desirably gaunt face and award-winning cheekbones.' She vogued. 'Win, fucking win.'

She dropped her hands.'It's a bit bleak, so I'll spare you the rising action.' She addressed the camera and narrowed her eyes conspiratorially. 'But we all love a midpoint reversal, right? I went further than that. I changed genres. I left the award-worthy misery and embarked on a love story.' She put her hand to her chest. 'I won't lie; I thought it was a fairytale.' She gestured to Chegs. 'Cue Prince Charming.' He peered at the camera and smiled. Erin cringed as she anticipated what was on its way.

'Prince Charming invited me into his black-tie world. She shall go to the ball!' Riley did a twirl. 'For a while I stopped dreaming of the needle sticking out of my mother's arm every night, and maybe I should be grateful for that.' Her tone turned dark. 'But I'm not, because this love story ends with the cute, rich boy shaving my head because he wanted to see what it looked like.' She touched her fingers to her scalp where the hair was still only an inch long. 'And in the next chapter he moved The Wicked Witch of the West into his flat and shagged her.' She wrinkled her nose and turned her back on Chegs. 'So that's when I stopped reading.' She mimes closing a book and throwing it over her shoulder.

'And now the pages ahead of me are clean and bare and I'm excited about that. I'm going to choose the words I write in the coming chapters so very carefully and be very discerning about the characters I allow onto the page. Between you and me, I've already learned who my true supporting cast are.' She blew a kiss to her assembled friends, before focusing back on the camera. 'And I'm going to write and perform, to share my next pages with anyone who'd like to follow what comes next for me. My name is Riley Moore, and this is the start of my brand new story. You can find me on my social media channels and at the gigs I'll be doing, if you'd like to see where future chapters lead.'

Riley grinned and bowed as applause rang out.

'You are brilliant,' said Erin, getting to her feet and taking Riley in her arms. She tried to convey how sorry she was for all that her friend had experienced in her young life, and how much she loved her in the intensity of that hug, before letting her go because the others were queuing up to do the same.

A cough from behind reminded them Chegs was still there. Riley turned. 'You can go now,' she said.

He scowled. 'But I haven't said what I wanted to yet.'

'I'm really not interested. I'm the one doing the talking these days.'

Adam stepped forwards but before he had a chance to speak, Susan addressed Chegs, 'On your way, you silly little man.'

He peered up at her, as if not quite able to believe she was talking to him.

'You heard the lady,' said Joe.

'Want me to escort you to the door?' asked Adam, pulling himself up to his full height and looming over Chegs.

Chegs stood unsteadily and, with a practised expression of indignance, he left the café, wobbled down Brigade Street and out of sight.

Chapter Forty-Two

'I'm so proud of you,' Erin said to Riley, as they all took their seats again. 'Are you going to share that on TikTok?'

'Yep,' said Riley. 'And Insta.'

'What about Chegs, though? Won't he have something to say about it?' Erin didn't want Riley getting in trouble.

'I got his permission.' Riley moved her finger across the screen of her phone, then turned it to them, playing the part where she asks if Chegs is happy to be in the film.

'You're a clever one,' said Susan. 'Shrewd. I like it.'

'It's no more than he deserves,' said Mercy, 'treating you like that. He didn't know when he was well off, that boy.'

'Hate to be the voice of doom, but I think there might be an argument for him not being in a fit state to consent,' said Adam. 'He was absolutely hammered.'

'I can always take it down if he threatens legal action,' said Riley. She tapped the screen with a flourish. 'But it will have been shared a fair few times before he sobers up and thinks about checking. He always made noises about helping me with my career, he just never did anything about it. Now's his chance.' She put her phone down. 'Only Erin and Hafsa left now. Who's going next?'

'I'm not sure I'll be writing anything, actually,' said Hafsa.

'I'm not surprised you haven't got time,' said Susan. 'You're a busy GP with three kids. I'm astonished you've got time to read, never mind write.'

'It's not that.' Hafsa watched her hand as she stroked the fabric of her trousers. 'It's because I feel like I'm letting you all down. You've all made such brave and significant changes to your lives, and I've decided I'm not going to do that after all.'

'What do you mean?' said Erin.

'When we started this, I was questioning whether I still wanted to be a GP. I knew I wanted to help Zahra and people who were going through similar things, but . . . I've had a rethink.'

'What changed your mind?' said Adam.

'A woman came into the surgery in a bit of a state,' said Hafsa. 'Her son had recently been given an ASD diagnosis, and she didn't know where to turn.'

'Aren't people offered support after a diagnosis?' said Susan.

'Some,' said Hafsa. 'But not as much as I'd like. It was talking to the mother that reminded me why I do the job. She was a single parent, and she didn't feel like anyone understood what she was going through. Her focus was on her son's needs, but it was taking a huge toll on her mental health, and she came to me full of guilt and shame about not being able to cope. I was her first port of call. That got me thinking.'

'That's so sad,' said Riley. 'I can see why that would make you want to stay. What you do is invaluable.'

'Thank you,' Hafsa remained serious. 'At the end of that day, I arranged a meeting with the practice manager. I told her I'd been thinking of a career change, but that I'd had another idea. I asked her whether there would be funding for an extra clinic to support neurodivergent people and their families.'

'That's a brilliant idea,' said Erin. 'What did they say?'

Hafsa held her hands together in her lap. 'It hasn't been fully signed off yet, but it looks like it's going to get the green light. If all goes to plan, I'll do my usual GP hours four days a week but have a full day to dedicate to my new project. I've already booked a couple of courses so I'm up to speed on all the latest research and treatment options.' Her eyes were bright. 'I'm pretty excited about it.'

'I thought you said you weren't making changes?' said Adam. 'That sounds like a hugely positive change to me, one that will have a far-reaching impact.'

'That's right,' said Erin. 'Your last pages sound downright amazing.'

'I thought I was letting the side down by not changing jobs like I thought I would.' Hafsa looked around, her expression hopeful. 'I usually make a point of doing what I say I'm going to do. I felt like I was being weak by not following through on my initial plan.'

'Absolutely not. Sometimes the bravest thing to do is to stay put,' said Adam. He focused on Erin and warmth flooded through her veins. Turning back to Hafsa, he said, 'And you're changing things from within the system, and that's not always an easy thing to do.'

'Thank you,' said Hafsa. 'This exercise has been really useful in making me look at what I want from my life. I was beginning to think I'd taken the path of least resistance, like other people were in control and I'd gone along with it like a puppet, but now I don't think that was the case. I was just feeling jaded. Now I'm learning again and have got all these new plans, the dissatisfaction I felt has been replaced by a new enthusiasm.'

'So, your change is keeping things the same, but different,' said Mercy. 'There's a lot to be said for that.'

Erin saw her moment. 'Speaking of the same, but different.' She held her breath for a second, then let it out in a rush. 'If all goes well with the meeting I've got with the bank tomorrow, The Bookmark will be closing down for a bit, but only so I can make a few changes.'

'Oh,' said Susan, her brow furrowed. 'I thought the plan was to keep The Bookmark going.'

'It is, kind of.' Erin searched for the right words. She'd practised what she wanted to say at home in her flat but now, with her friends' eyes all trained on her, her excitement turned to trepidation again and her brain felt fuzzy. 'What I mean is, seeing the potential of that space in Kidbrooke gave me an idea, and what Riley said on stage cemented it. I love the idea of the café being a part of the local community, and I think it could be more things to more people if it was bigger.'

The group looked around the café. Joe cleared his throat. 'So, are you moving it somewhere else?'

'Nope, at least not if I can finance the new plan.' She glanced nervously at Adam and he nodded his encouragement. 'I've done the maths, and a business plan, and with the extra money from the fundraiser, plus if I mortgage my flat, I should be able to raise enough of a deposit to buy this building from Galmouth Estates and convert it into one big unit.'

Susan's jaw fell open. 'Are they selling?'

'Let's just say that during our meeting yesterday, they realized that their plans were no longer . . . viable, so they were pretty keen to get shot of both this unit and the gift shop before anyone looked any more closely at their business dealings. If my calculations are right, the mortgage payments should be less than the current rent, so that would make things a lot easier, and I'll have twice the square footage, so I can put on events, do workshops, all kinds of things I can't do with the space I've got. I want to make it into a real community hub.'

When she finished, a moment of panic made her blurt out, 'You think it's a terrible idea, don't you?'

'Of course not,' said Joe. 'Although, that saying

springs to mind: who are you, and what have you done with Erin? This is a big change, my girl.'

'I know, and I'm terrified, but I'm excited too,' she said. She clasped her hands in front of her. 'But I'm also worried that by changing the café, I'm messing with Mum's legacy.'

Joe shook his head. 'Your future is what matters, Erin, not the past. And it sounds like you're continuing her legacy by carrying on the café, and forging your own by making it bigger and better. I think Mary would be incredibly proud of you. I know I am.' His watery eyes told her it was true.

'It sounds like a good plan to me,' said Mercy.

'Me too,' said Susan. 'I'm so proud of you for deciding to make a change. I know how hard this must've been for you.'

'I'm excited!' said Riley. She turned to Erin. 'I take it I'll still be working here, right?'

'Of course, if you aren't too in demand after the response down in Kidbrooke. How many gigs have you got lined up now?'

Riley wiggled in her seat. 'Seven so far.'

'So far?' said Hafsa. 'That's amazing.'

'And I want to be the first performer when this place reopens,' Riley said.

'Naturally,' said Erin.

'It's going to be amazing,' said Adam, the lines beside his eyes creasing as he grinned. 'You're going to make it into a huge success.'

'You think so?' She searched his face, finding absolute conviction there and taking strength from that.

'I know so.' He reached for her hand. She let him take it, and with him and all her friends by her side, she allowed herself to believe it too.

Joe stayed behind when the others said their goodbyes. 'Can I have a quick word about your plans?'

Erin's heart thumped in her chest. Was he about to offer words of caution? Did he think she was being too ambitious? 'Of course.' They both took a seat at the table by the door.

'I've been giving this a lot of thought, so hear me out before you jump in, okay? I don't like you having to mortgage your flat. That's your home, yours and Jack's.'

He did think she was being reckless. He didn't trust her to make a go of it. Stomach twisting, she began to try to justify her decision, 'If I can—'

He raised a hand to stop her. 'Let me finish. I've been thinking for a while that it's time I downsized. What does an old man like me need with a three-bedroom house? I had a nice fella around to value it a couple of weeks ago, and you wouldn't believe the price he put on it.' He shook his head as if truly flabbergasted. 'And I've seen a nice little one-bedroom place on the ground floor . . . guess where?'

'Where?' Erin crossed her fingers under the table, praying it wasn't somewhere like Bournemouth or Eastbourne. She'd understand completely if he wanted to spend his next chapters by the sea, but the thought of not seeing her old friend daily made tears collect behind her eyes.

'The same place as you.' His gentle eyes searched her face, as if he was nervous about her response.

She blinked. 'Dartmouth Grove?'

'The very one. Would that be all right? I'm not planning to be a burden, and you must say if you'd rather not have me so close by.'

Erin flung her arms around his neck. 'Of course I want you close by. It would be perfect.' She sat back, blowing out her cheeks. 'I thought you were going to say you were moving away.' They beamed at each other. 'Just wait until I tell Jack. He's going to be over the moon.'

'When I move,' said Joe, his face turning serious again, 'there will be a fair bit of cash spare.' He took her hand in his. 'So I'd prefer it if you let me help with the deposit for this place rather than you mortgaging your home.'

He didn't think it was a bad idea. He wanted to help. Erin's heart felt like it might burst. 'You don't have to—'

'Stop that. I know what you said before, but who do you think are beneficiaries in my will? You and Jack. My family. Nuala and I agreed on it years ago. You've always been like a daughter to us, and I don't see why I have to be dead before giving you what's coming your way anyway. I'd rather you didn't argue with me on this.'

'But what if I can't make it work? What if I lose the money you worked so hard for?'

'I don't believe you will, but it's a risk I'm willing to take, if you are?'

'I'm scared.'

'I know, love, and that's no bad thing. It shows how much it means to you. It can be a driving force to make things work if you harness it right.' He lay his hand over hers. 'You know what they say, the bravest people are the ones who are scared but do it anyway. You'll let me help you?'

Tybalt bashed his head against her shin, then looked up at her with beseeching eyes, as if adding to Joe's argument. 'Thank you,' was all Erin could manage, although it wasn't nearly enough.

'No need to thank me. It's a selfish act, in a way. I want to see the changes and watch you and this place flourish.'

'You don't have a selfish bone in your body,' said Erin, hugging him again. Tybalt jumped onto Joe's lap, mewling his agreement, as Erin let the laughter and tears come.

Chapter Forty-Three

Erin and Jack were the first to arrive at The Bookmark on the day that everything was due to change. She could hardly believe how quickly things had moved over the last three months. Fengrove was keen on a quick sale and the builders who'd done a brilliant job on Bella and Sophia's house renovation had a free slot, so Erin decided to take the plunge before she had a chance to change her mind. Joe's house had sold quickly, and his offer had been accepted on the flat in Dartmouth Grove, so everything was falling into place. Now, though, feelings of nostalgia made Erin's certainty waver. She put her hand on the lid of the old Panasonic record player. 'What do you think Grandma would make of all this?'

'I think she'd be excited for you.' Jack joined her and put an arm around her shoulder.

'You don't think she'd say I was taking too big a risk?'

'Grandma?'

Erin laughed 'Good point. She didn't mind a bit of risk, did she?'

'Nope. And I think she'd be so proud of how hard

you've worked. You didn't give up when things got tough, did you?' He squeezed her to him. 'You stuck it to the man, and came out on top. I'm proud of you.' A buzz came from his pocket and he let her go, pulled out his phone and tapped on the screen. His eyes widened.

'What is it?' said Erin. Jack glanced up, red dots appearing on his cheeks. He was either frightened or excited, and Erin urgently needed to know which. 'Is something wrong?'

'No.' He turned the screen to face her. 'I've been asked to go up to Salford for an interview at Media City.'

'No way?' Erin took the phone from him and read it for herself. 'Oh, Jack. This is the dream!' When she looked up, he was biting his bottom lip. 'It is the dream, isn't it?'

He nodded slowly. 'It is . . . but . . .' He looked around the room, then back at her. 'If I get it, will you be okay? You've got a lot going on here.'

'Oh, love.' She took his hand. 'I know I said before that I don't want you to factor me in when you're making decisions about your future, but now I really, really mean it.'

'Yeah, I got the impression you might have been putting on a brave face when you said it before.'

'I should never have made you feel like that. I'm so sorry. I did mean it, in my mind at least. It just took my heart a while to catch up. But everything that's happened in the last few months has shown me that I'm stronger than I thought. And even if I have a wobble, there's other people around to shore me up. That's not your job. Your job is to spread your wings and fly.'

Jack paused, then nodded again. 'You are strong enough, Mum. I'm in awe of you.' He glanced around the room. 'If I get the job, I'll miss out on all the cool stuff happening here.'

Erin shrugged. 'Your choice. Take your first step on the ladder to becoming a TV producer, or wipe up mashed banana in Kiddies Corner for the rest of your life.'

'When you put it like that.' Jack laughed. 'I know you're just trying to make me feel better, but this place is going to be incredible.'

She smiled. 'It is, isn't it? And it will be a lovely place for you to hang out when you're visiting home.'

She felt at peace when she imagined Jack, home for the weekend, sipping a coffee in the new space. At last, she was ready to accept her son needed to make a life for himself away from her nest. They were in each other's hearts, and that was the thing that mattered.

She lifted the lid of the turntable. Her mother was in her heart too, not in a building, or an old record player. She did want to hear something that reminded her of the times they'd spent together in The Bookmark, though, so she left Jack's arms and bent down to open the cupboard. She found Miles Davis' *Kind of Blue* and showed the cover to Jack, who stuck out his bottom lip and nodded. He knew what it meant. Of course he did. Soon the strains of 'So What' filled the air.

Susan was the first of the helpers to arrive. She wore a green and white handkerchief tied around her hair like a fifties housewife about to tackle the dusting. '*Très chic*,' said Erin. 'I've never seen you with anything other than a neat bob. I like this look.'

Susan patted the handkerchief in the same way she often patted her hair. 'I wear this when I'm working on my perfumes. You don't want hair getting in the potions.'

'How's all that coming along?' asked Jack.

Lifting her sleeve, Susan approached. 'I'm devising a more masculine scent. What do you think of this?'

Jack sniffed her wrist. 'Nice.' He breathed in again. 'Very nice. I wouldn't mind a splash of that myself.'

She offered her wrist to Erin, who breathed in with her eyes closed. 'That's gorgeous. I'm getting . . .' She waved her hands, trying to find the right words. 'Woody and spicy things.'

'Very good.' Susan grinned. 'It's pepper, cedarwood, and a touch of patchouli.' She rolled her sleeve back down and turned to view the room. 'You sure we need to dismantle everything?'

'That's what the builder said. It's going to get messy when they knock through, and since the bookshelves are going to be a massive feature, spanning the whole back wall, not just this room, we need to box them all up.' However sentimental she felt about the café as it stood, she was more excited about what was on its way. There were plans for a raised area for live music and spoken word performances, and a long table along the furthest wall for art and other workshops. She'd already ordered more highchairs for mother and baby groups to congregate and been in touch with the silent book group Gavin had told her about. Instead of feeling terrified by the changes, she tingled with the thrill of all the possibilities.

Adam arrived, his face beaming when he came through the door. They'd both agreed to take their relationship slowly and he'd stayed at her flat for the first time last night. They hadn't planned it, but after they had dinner at Côte, he'd walked her home, and she found herself inviting him in. Waking beside him this morning felt like the most natural thing in the world. He'd popped home for a shower before coming here to help, and her heart still gave a little bounce in her chest at the sight of him. 'Where do you want us to start?' he said, when the others had all arrived and caught up over coffee and tea.

'The books, I think,' said Erin. They all turned to face the wall of shelves. 'We'll have to do the high shelves as a tag team. Adam, you go up the ladder and pass them down. Joe, you stack them in the boxes at the bottom. Susan, Mercy, and Hafsa, you do the middle, Riley and I will do the lower ones.' She picked Tybalt up from the floor. 'Sorry pal, you'll have to sit this one out. We don't want to drop anything on you, and I know you'd make it your mission to trip us up.' When she shut the door with him on the other side, he looked up at her with disdain before flicking his tail and stalking away.

It took longer to pack the books than it should because they couldn't stop themselves from exclaiming when they found a novel they'd once loved and sharing it with the group.

'Take it,' said Erin, when Mercy found a dusty copy of Thomas Mann's novella, *Death in Venice*. 'It probably came from the library anyway.'

Mercy opened the cover and pointed to the label covered with stamps. 'Ha. You're right, it did.' She held it to her heart. 'Little did I know, when I brought this here, that the next time I would see it I would soon be on my way to see Venice for myself.'

'I love Venice,' said Adam. 'Of all the countries I've been to, Italy is my favourite.' He viewed Erin from where he was perched on the ladder. 'We should go.'

Erin grinned, hardly able to contain her delight. She didn't have the same trepidation she usually felt when someone suggested something daring or spontaneous. And, anyway, a trip to Venice with a man she cared for and trusted was neither of those things. 'We should. Maybe in the spring when things are settled here?'

'Cool. It's a plan.' Adam passed down books to Joe and Jack, as if what he'd said wasn't even a big deal. It was a big deal to Erin. It was all a very big deal and, despite a natural undercurrent of nerves, she couldn't be happier. She never went abroad. It wasn't only that she didn't have the money, or that her overthinking stopped her. In all the time she'd run The Bookmark, she'd needed to pay for cover for even a day off, so she rarely took one. Now, if the business plans she'd devised worked out, and with the cushion of the money from Joe, she'd be able to give Riley as many hours as she wanted, and maybe even employ another member of staff. She might even work five days a week herself instead of seven, and the thought of spending her time off with Adam in Italy made her dizzy with excitement.

***

She tried to keep all the positive emotions front and centre, but when the last of the boxes was stacked against the wall and covered in dust sheets, her heart contracted. They all stood, dusty and tired, gazing around the cleared room.

'I suppose that's it, then,' said Susan. 'The end of The Bookmark as we know it. Time for bigger and better things.'

Erin viewed the empty fireplace. It looked dull without the bright vase and the blue candlesticks. A pattern of pale rectangles remained where the prints had hung, like ghosts of decor past. She looked forward to filling the new space with beautiful things and building it into a home from home for anyone who needed it. 'Thank you all for your help. You've been amazing. I couldn't have done any of this without you.' Erin held her palms together in a prayer of thanks.

'It's the least we can do,' said Mercy. 'If I added up all your kindnesses over the years, I would still find myself in deficit.' The others added their voices, all agreeing it was a small thing in comparison to what Erin had always given them, and Erin found it hard not to let their kindness spill out of her in tears.

Joe hugged her. 'Anything else need doing?' He let go and smiled. 'I'll need to give my knees a day to recover, but after that I'm sure I'll be ready to offer a helping hand.'

'You've done quite enough for now,' Erin said. 'But no doubt I'll be calling on you all to help put things back together when the building work's done.'

'Can't wait,' said Riley. 'I'm loving this for you. For all of us. It's going to be fucking mint.' She squeezed Erin tightly. 'Right, I've got to fly. Need to make myself beautiful for the good people of Greenwich.'

'I'll see you down there,' said Jack.

'Cheers, mate,' said Riley, slapping his hand on the way out. Erin marvelled at the lovely friendship that had formed between the two of them. The sleepover, as Erin euphemistically called it, hadn't been repeated and Riley had started a tentative relationship with a comedian she'd met at one of her gigs at Up the Creek in Greenwich, who Jack reported was a decent bloke. He'd better be. Erin wouldn't keep her mouth shut again if anyone treated Riley badly. That girl deserved the world, and somehow, Erin thought that with her new status as an up-and-coming spoken word performer, she might well get it.

The others said their goodbyes, all taking one last look around the place before they left. Finally, it was just Erin, Jack, and Adam in the empty room. 'It seems much bigger without any furniture, doesn't it?' said Jack. 'I can't wait to see it when it's twice the size.'

'I wonder how Mum and Dad felt when they first stepped in here?' said Erin, sensing the ghosts of her parents in the still air.

'Excited,' said Jack. 'And probably a bit scared about making things work.'

'Just like you now,' said Adam. 'But they weren't alone. They had Joe and Nuala to support them, and you've got us lot.'

'Thank you.' She smiled up at him with tears in her eyes.

'I'll see you two outside,' said Jack, as if sensing they needed a moment.

When the door closed behind him, Adam took a book with a dark blue cover from his bag. 'I bought this for you.' He handed it over and Erin read the cover, *The Midnight Library.* 'Have you read it?' Erin shook her head. 'It's about a woman who's given a chance to try out different versions of her life, the ones she might have lived if she'd made different choices. Nora, the main character gets to explore different endings.'

'Does she finally get a happy ending?'

'You'll have to read it and see for yourself, but it's more about what she learns along the way. She's trying to work out the best way to live. What I took away from it is that no one really knows. We're all just doing the best we can with the information we have.' He opened the cover. 'Hope it's not too cheesy. I wrote an inscription for you.'

Erin read the words, *To Erin, our story is to be continued . . .* She swallowed hard and lifted onto her toes to kiss him. 'Thank you.'

'Will you be reading the last page first?' He raised an eyebrow.

Erin pondered the question. When Adam first walked into book group she'd been riddled with anxiety and self-doubt. Now, she was starting a new, exciting chapter, and it was full of love and hope. On top of that, she had the confidence to believe she could make these new chapters the best of her life. She didn't need to know the ending, because she had faith in her own story. 'You know what, I don't think I will.'

Adam tried and failed to keep in his laughter. 'So, you're admitting I was right all along. Reading the last page first is ridiculous.'

She shook her head. 'I'm not admitting that at all. I'm just saying I might give your way a go since you bought me the book.'

He was still grinning when they reached the door. When they got there, he paused, then kissed her and went out to join Jack at the top of Brigade Street.

Erin let the door close and stood, gazing around at the room that had been such a huge part of her life. She was sure she heard her mother's laughter, and paused, her heart keening for more, but when she turned to look out onto the street, a pair of girls were passing, one with her head thrown back in delight. Her gaze landed on Adam and Jack, who were chatting together and smiling.

Her mother's voice wasn't in this room. It was inside her and she would carry it with her wherever she went. The Bookmark was special because of the people who filled the space, and the furniture they left their marks on, a reminder that they had once sat there and enjoyed a coffee with a friend or read a book that had spoken to their soul.

'Au revoir, old friend,' Erin whispered into the empty room. 'Thank you for the stories we made together. I can't wait to start my next chapter with you. I have a feeling it's going to be the best one yet.' She opened the door and stepped outside.

Epilogue

'Everyone gather around,' shouted Erin to her friends, who were wandering around the new space, marvelling at how well it had all come together. The bookcases that spanned the whole of the back wall were magnificent. The shelves were lit from above and Erin had interspersed the books with bright objects she'd found in Greenwich Market and at charity shops. The multi-coloured glass vase sparkled in pride of place at the centre.

The polished wood floor shone, and the coffee-themed prints were supplemented by original pieces of art by local artists, all of which were for sale. The leather armchairs had been returned to their original spot, and other, smaller armchairs sat around tables, replacing the upright chairs that had been there before. Kiddies Corner had its own larger area, next to a sensory wall with things to push, pull, twist and hold built into a cushioned surface.

Erin was overjoyed with the raised performance area constructed at the far end of what had been the gift shop. She stood on it now, surveying the scene with her hands clasped tight in front of her. It was time to make her announcement. She'd agonised about whether to call her new venture The Bookmark, but after much discussion with Jack and Adam, had decided that, since she was embracing change, and creating her own legacy, a brand new name for the café wouldn't be disloyal to her mother. It would signify a bright new future, and she was sure that Mary would approve of the name she'd chosen.

A dust sheet shielding the bottom of the long unit in front of the entrance to the extended kitchen was held tight by Gavin and Adam, who both wore enormous grins. The top of the unit was already piled high with cakes and pastries under glass domes, ready for the customers who would soon arrive. Jack, who was visiting home from his new flat in Salford, where he now worked as a runner on BBC *Breakfast*, put his open laptop carefully down on a table. Mercy's face beamed from the screen. She was sitting on a low terrace next to a Venetian canal, wearing sunglasses and an enormous sun hat, and they all whooped as a gondola passed by on the water behind her. The gondolier started at the noise, then laughed and waved as Mercy moved her phone so they could all get a better view.

'Glad you could join us, Mercy,' said Erin, as the boat disappeared from sight.

'Wouldn't miss it for the world,' she said, her voice tinny but excited through the speakers. 'I'm so proud of you.'

'I'm proud of all of us,' said Erin, taking in the

assembled group, her insides swooping again as she allowed her eyes to rest on each lovely face in turn. She gave Julia a warm smile. She'd slotted into the group seamlessly and it made Erin's heart sing to see Joe regain some of the energy he'd lost after losing his beloved wife. Erin was confident Nuala would have liked Julia just as much as she did. 'So much has happened since we started to think about our next chapters,' continued Erin. She held her finger up. 'Correction: we've made so much happen.' Jack, Adam and Joe had all told her that she was strong, and at last, she was beginning to believe it herself. In the end, she hadn't rolled over and allowed change to happen to her. She'd taken charge and made it work for her instead. She'd been courageous, and here they were, about to reap the rewards.

She unfolded a piece of paper which had wilted a little in the sweat of her palm, glancing down as Tybalt's soft fur brushed her ankle as he appeared by her feet. 'And with that in mind, please indulge me as I read out my long overdue last pages before the big reveal.'

'About time,' said Susan.

'Better late than never,' said Joe, chuckling.

'It's not too long, don't worry.' Erin's hand trembled at first, along with her voice. 'I am so glad you are all here to celebrate the opening of my new venture with me.' She swallowed, trying to encourage moisture into her dry mouth. 'I've always been a bit of an anxious soul, and I came to see my reluctance to try new things as a lack of courage. I thought I was weak, a bit of a scaredy-cat, but recently a very wise man reminded me that being frightened and doing it anyway is maybe the bravest thing of all.' She looked up to see Joe's eyes glitter with tears. Julia put an arm around his shoulder, as Erin put her hand to her heart.

'I didn't truly believe that for a long time. As you all know, the word *new* used to fill me with dread. I believed everything either had to stay the same, or have a quantifiable, predictable outcome, otherwise it automatically signalled danger. I had my reasons, but I know now that those reasons are part of my past, and I want to harness my newfound courage, to live in the present and look towards the future.' She scanned the group in front of her and gratitude swelled in her chest. 'Over the last few months, you have all taught me that change doesn't have to be synonymous with loss. Quite the opposite. It can signify endless possibilities. It can mean hope and the promise of better things to come.'

She glanced up and basked in the love reflected back at her. Her hands and her voice calmed. 'And you've shown me change, like courage, can come in many guises. It can be a tweak to the norm.' She caught Hafsa's eye and smiled. 'It can be the addition, or extension of something positive to your life.' She looked first at Susan, then Riley and Joe. 'It can be moving into unknown territory.' She waved at Mercy's image on the screen, and she waved back, then Erin blew a kiss to Jack. 'And it can even be staying in one place.' Adam grinned at her, saturating her heart with love.

'With your encouragement, love and support, I am heading into this new chapter of my life with confidence and positivity. I feel brave and hopeful and I couldn't have made this leap of faith without you by my side.' Tybalt chose that moment to mewl loudly. Erin laughed and bent to stroke his head. 'Yes, that includes you,' she said, before straightening and turning back to the glowing faces in front of her.

'We started out as a book group and ended up as family.' She took a breath. 'In that book group, you all indulged me by always reading the last page first. That's what led us to writing our own last pages, and that is what eventually led us here, to this wonderful space, and this bright, new, hopeful beginning.' She turned and gave the nod to Gavin and Adam. They let the sheet fall to reveal three words painted in forest green against a rich cream background.

'And in tribute to the chapters we wrote and shared, and the brave changes we've supported each other to make, it is my greatest pleasure,' said Erin, her heart full to bursting, 'to welcome you, my friends, my family, to The Last Page Café.'

Acknowledgements

I've worked with four brilliant editors since I began to write under the pen name Kate Storey, and I owe each of them a huge debt of gratitude. Talented powerhouse, Elisha Lundin, first commissioned *The Memory Library*, and neither of us could have foreseen how readers would take my first book about books to their hearts. I then worked with the wonderful Rachel Hart on *The Forgotten Book Club,* and the first stages of *The Last Page Café*, when wonderful Anna Nightingale picked up the baton, working alongside Jess Zahra to get it into the shape it's in now. I am very fortune to have had all of these incredible women at my back.

This book had the biggest rewrite of any I've worked on so far, and I'd like to thank Anna in particular for her insight, patience and enthusiasm throughout the editing process. Thank you to all the team at Avon for their support, hard work, and for feeling like a true publishing family.

Thanks also to my fantastic agent, Laura Williams. From contract negotiations, to early editorial, right through to celebrating the finished work, she's always by my side, and I am so very grateful to be in her stable.

To my invaluable early reader, Suzy Oldfield, thank you for your time and your honesty. I don't know what I'd do without you. Thanks also to Alan and Jean for introducing me to Michael, who has the best stories about running a café in Blackheath.

My thanks also go to the fabulous online reading community, especially bloggers Nicola @nothing.beats.a.good.book, Emily @aquintillionwords, Rachel @rachel_loves_to_read, Angela @ang.all.about.books, Kim @krbooks13, Charlie @x_charlieeexbooks_x and Lauren @teasandthankyou. Their support has blown me away.

The following Facebook book groups are wonderful, and also instrumental in helping new readers find my books: The Bookload, Fiction Addicts Book Club, The Fiction Café Book Club and The *Good Housekeeping* Book Room. Huge thanks to their brilliant administration teams (especially Kate Rutherford, Sarah Buckingham, Teresa Nikolic, Trina Dixon, Wendy Clarke and Emma-Louise Bunting) who give their time for free to spread the bookish-love. If you are looking for a place to share your love of books, I recommend these groups wholeheartedly.

The writing community is the most positive and supportive bunch of people you could hope to find. Both online and IRL, I've found my tribe, my strength and inspiration in the friends I have made since I began my writing life. There are too many to name individually, and I would hate to leave someone out, but if I've met you through writing, I'm talking about you.

I'd like to give fellow Avon author, G. D. Wright, a special mention for his boundless energy and inclusivity, despite a traumatic year. I'm so glad you're still alive, Gaz!

Finally, my thanks go to my family. I am incredibly fortunate to live with people who make me laugh every day, ensure my feet are always firmly on the ground, and fill my life with love.

If you enjoyed *The Last Page Café*, I would be very grateful if you could leave a brief review wherever you buy your books. Even a few words can make an author's day, and help new readers discover our books. Thank you! xx

Some stories stay with us forever . . .

The must-read novel of family, friendship and the power of storytelling.

This next chapter of life could just be the beginning of her story . . .

A charming and uplifting novel about family, community and the power of books, perfect to leave you feeling hopeful for the future.